A Homecoming For Murder

Also by John Armistead

A Legacy of Vengeance

A HOMECOMING FOR MURDER

John Armistead

Carroll & Graf Publishers, Inc.
New York

First edition 1995

Carroll & Graf Publishers, Inc.
260 Fifth Avenue
New York, NY 10001

Library of Congress Cataloging-in-Publication Data
Armistead, John.
    A homecoming for murder / John Armistead.—1st ed.
      p. cm.
    ISBN 0-7867-0197-8
    I. Title.
  PS3551.R4662H65 1995
813'.54—dc20   95-6849
                                          CIP

For
Mother and Ken, Thom and Mike

With special appreciation to Sergeant Tim Rutledge, Mississippi bureau of narcotics, Johnny Finney, private investigator and former chief of detectives, Tupelo Police Department, Denvil Crowe, assistant district attorney for the first judicial district of Mississippi.

Also, many thanks to my literary agent, Evelyn Singer, without whose insightful suggestions and efforts this work would be much impoverished, and to Sandi, David, William, and Audra for love and encouragement along the way.

A Homecoming For Murder

1

JESSE BONDREAUX EASED HIS AUTOMOBILE to a stop only a few feet from the edge of the cliff. Below the cliff a kudzu-choked hillside slid down to the railroad tracks. Beyond the tracks rose a smaller hill, likewise kudzu-choked, and beyond the hill sprawled cotton fields across a wide bottom. A pale-gray mist clung to the earth.

Jesse smiled and reached to his shirt pocket for the pack of Marlboros. Arranging to meet here in the cemetery was wonderful. This place helped to keep them off balance, unsettled them, so he could push harder.

Jesse liked to push hard enough to keep them rocking back on their heels. They were easier to control like that. The cemetery was perfect.

He glanced at his watch and frowned as he shook a cigarette out of the package. Quarter past five already. Five was the agreed upon time, and he had purposely arrived late. Keeping people waiting also helped.

But this party had not yet come. He didn't like arriving first. Nor did he like to wait. He reached into his trouser pocket for his silver lighter.

He looked up at the rearview mirror. He'd heard a vehicle coming. Yes. It was his party.

The car stopped directly behind his. He weighed the heft of the lighter in his hand. He would wait on lighting the cigarette. Better for effect.

The first raindrops splattered on the windshield. Through the mirror he watched the vehicle's door open, saw his party rise up out of the car, close the door and step toward his car.

Jesse rolled down the window. He spoke without looking up. "You're late. I don't like to be kept waiting." He placed the cigarette between his lips, flicked the lighter, and leaned his cigarette into the flame.

He took a deep draw, held it for a moment, then let the smoke slowly exhale. The smoke curled through the steering wheel and rolled against the inside of the windshield. He knew he ought to quit smoking.

In a lot of ways it didn't make much sense. He worked out with weights four days a week, tried to keep himself on a low-fat diet, played two hours of racquetball and jogged at least twenty miles each week—and smoked.

But what the hell. Smoking gave him pleasure. But nothing like the pleasure of jerking around a party like this one.

He waited, wanting to hear the quiver in the voice, the sound of a person off-balance, afraid, desperate. He especially enjoyed the desperation.

But his party didn't say a word, just stood there. Jesse scowled and turned his face to look up. He looked up right into the dark barrel of a handgun. There was a bright flash. A roar sounded with the flash. Jesse, however, only saw the flash. He was dead before his brain could register the sound.

GILLY BITZER DID HEAR THE SOUND. His eyes popped open. At once the air above him exploded with the frightened flight of blackbirds, thousands of them, accelerating from the juniper trees at the top of the opposite embankment, stampeding over the tracks and filling the sky above Gilly's head. Firecracker? Car backfiring? Gunshot?

Gilly was relishing the warmth of his blood rising, moving up from his stomach and soaking through his chest and shoulders, into his neck and flowing across his face. He breathed evenly, slowly, and smelled the thick scent of the coming rain. The coolness of the fall air touched his face, and his body was completely relaxed, float-ing, drifting on the soft sea of kudzu in which he lay, a browning green tide flowing down the west side of the railroad track's embankment.

Floating was wonderful. It was the best way to forget. Sure, lots of guys get divorced. Lots of guys lose their children. But most of those guys probably didn't care for their wives and families anyways. Not Gilly. He loved too much, too hard. That's why now he had to float up above the pain.

He squeezed the fingers of his right hand again on the smooth neck of the labelless, reused whiskey bottle and felt the solid comfort the touch of cool glass gave him—a comfort of warmth and strength, a womb of security, insulation from everything threatening. For a second, he remembered that as a child he and his brother used to collect empty whiskey bottles along the side of dirt roads in the country and sell them to Amos's father.

Amos Putt was a saint. Some said his stuff wasn't as good as his daddy used to make, but if ever Amos needed a testimony he could depend on Gilly Bitzer, that was for sure.

A full, heavy drop of rain splattered on his forehead, and Gilly smiled. He didn't mind the rain, not when the blood was warm and flowing.

He arched his neck. The birds were still streaming from the trees like a long black veil. The stragglers. Always in everything there were stragglers. Like Gilly. Always one of the last ones in or out. Always too late in life. And then the birds were gone.

Somewhere a car engine cranked, and Gilly, with effort, slowly propped himself on one elbow. Moments later the front grille of a pale-blue automobile nosed its way between a large dark-green juni-per and red-leafed pin oak on the opposite bank and stopped with its front tires almost over the edge. Strange place to park.

Someone got out of the car on the driver's side and moved out of sight. Another car cranked. Then, *bump*. The pale-blue car jerked forward slightly, then *thud-thud-thud*, and the front tires of the pale-blue car rolled off the edge and the frame slid on the grass, tearing sod and dirt as it jerked forward.

For a second or two the car teeter-tottered on the edge, the front end slowly sinking. A sharp scrunching sound followed and the car lurched forward, the rear tires jolting over the bank.

Gilly watched the vehicle plunge down the steep embankment, twisting as it fell, ripping through saplings and kudzu vines. It thudded to a stop only a few feet beyond the tracks. Gilly looked back to the top of the embankment. The front of another car, a small dark-blue car, was now between the juniper and the pin oak.

Someone was standing beside the car. Gilly squinted his eyes at this figure who now stepped to the edge of the bluff and was looking down at the pale-blue car. Gilly opened his mouth as if to speak but then froze.

Somehow things weren't right. It was a very familiar face. But something wasn't right. Wrong hat and raincoat. Something not right. But it was definitely someone he knew and knew fairly well.

He looked back at the car on its side, the bottom of the frame facing him, vines stretched taut from one rear wheel to the side of the bank. Then he looked at the face he knew . . . but the face was gone now. The dark-blue car at the top of the bank was backing away from the edge. He heard the engine whine as the vehicle sped away.

It was raining harder now. Gilly pushed himself to his feet, still holding the bottle by the neck. He swayed slightly and held up the bottle, staring at it. Almost gone. Time to go back to Amos. Bless his heart.

He lifted the bottle to his mouth and drained the last of the clear liquid into his throat, felt the fire slide down his throat into his stomach, then dropped the bottle. It was at once gobbled up by the kudzu.

Gilly stumbled down the bank and stepped over the tracks, the gravel crunching beneath his shoes. He reached out his hand to the upturned front end of the car to steady himself for a moment, then moved around so he could see inside.

He flinched and sucked a sharp breath. A face was staring at him. A face pressed against the windshield, wedged between the windshield and the dashboard. A man. His mouth sagged open and his eyes bulged like a squirrel that's just been headshot. The lips and nose flattened against the glass, and blood smeared the inside of the glass where the man's forehead touched it.

4

Gilly flinched again at the blast of the train whistle. He looked up just as the Burlington Northern locomotive thundered past him, and momentarily his eyes and the scowling eyes of the engineer leaning against the windowframe met. And then dust swirled about Gilly, and he shut his eyes tightly and held on to the top of the car. Suddenly he felt sick to his stomach and dizzy. The freight cars galloped past sucking at him, and he turned away from the train and plunged headfirst down into the kudzu.

MARCELLUS COLLIER, twelve years old, was stalking a squirrel when he heard the crack of the gunshot. He had already wandered over two small hillsides of marble grave markers since walking away from his mother.

He left her sitting in the grass in front of the grave of her good friend Cillie Thompson who had died of cancer the month before. Cillie Thompson had been thirty-three, the same age as his mother.

His mother placed a jar of daisies beside the mound of red dirt. Cillie's husband, his mother said, had ordered the marble marker for the head of the grave, but it hadn't arrived yet. There was a small metal-framed temporary marker which gave Cillie's full name and date of death. And that was all.

On the trip down from Memphis his mother had talked a lot about Cillie. They grew up together in Sheffield. They entered kindergarten together, graduated from high school together, roomed together in college, were in each other's weddings, and now she was dead and buried. "My best friend," his mother kept mumbling over and over.

Marcellus wasn't sure he actually had one best friend. He had three best friends. He and Chucky and John and Alex all four went to the same school and lived in the same neighborhood in Memphis.

They played on the same baseball, football, soccer, and basketball teams. Marcellus was a better athlete than any of the others. He was, to be sure, taller and heavier than they were. That was because his mother held him back in the fifth grade.

Holding him back was supposed to enable him to "catch up." She said she'd started him too early, that he wasn't as mature as the others in his class.

5

Nevertheless, Marcellus still didn't read too well. He wished he was smarter. Smart like Chucky. Chucky could read anything. Alex and John weren't much smarter than Marcellus. They only made B's. Chucky made all A's. Marcellus had made a B in the fourth grade. Other than that, all he ever got were C's. He wished grades were given for PE. He'd get an A in PE.

All the way down from Memphis his mother talked about how she couldn't believe someone as young and full of life as Cillie could be dead. Why did this happen? Marcellus didn't try to answer his mother's questions. He just let her talk while he looked out the window at the thick Mississippi woods speeding past.

His sister April had fallen asleep before they passed Holly Springs. She was still asleep on the backseat when they got out of the car at the cemetery. April would be ten next month.

The rain had just begun to fall. Marcellus held a stick in his hand as he followed the squirrel scooting in the grass between the large trees. Wind gusts spun yellow leaves from some of the trees and red leaves from others.

Tomorrow Marcellus would have a real gun in his hand, not a stick, and he would be in real woods with his grandfather. His grandfather was a sheriff and wore a Smith & Wesson pistol on his belt.

Marcellus had hardly slept the night before thinking about going hunting with his grandfather. His mother picked him up as soon as school was out. April was already in the car. On the ride down as his mother talked about Cillie, Marcellus thought about going hunting.

He jumped when he heard the gunshot. It sounded so close. He heard his mother scream his name. He didn't answer. Instead he walked in the direction of the gunshot. His mother continued to shout his name.

He heard a strange thudding sound like metal crashing into metal and then the blast of the train whistle. He walked on in the middle of the narrow cemetery drive.

The rumble of the train grew louder, and then he saw a car, speeding, bearing down on him. His legs were locked—he couldn't move—and he heard his mother shriek.

Then the car was by him. It had swerved at the last moment, ripping past him and missing him by inches. If his hand had been raised to his side, the car would have torn it off. He watched the car slide around the curve and disappear over a hill.

His mother was clutching him, grasping at him. *"Fool! Fool driver!"* she screamed in the direction the car had gone.

Marcellus didn't think he knew the driver, wasn't sure. Maybe he'd seen him before. He wasn't sure. It all happened so fast. Over and done with. But he did see the eyes—wide and frightened or fierce eyes, like those of an animal—staring at him from behind the windshield as one quick swipe of the wiper blade cleaned the rain-splashed glass.

The car was gone and his mother crushed him against her chest, but he could still see those eyes—and he knew there was a particular look in those eyes, a look which held him, took him in, fixed him.

His mother was now holding him by the shoulders at arm's length, her eyes wide and wild also, lips quivering. "Are you all right?" she said.

He nodded. She snatched him against her chest again and convulsed with loud, agonized sobs. She was shaking, squeezing him and he was aware of the rain now soaking though his shirt and running down his back. He struggled to breathe, and turned his head against her chest. At the same time, he wondered if the rain would affect their hunting tomorrow.

2

GROVER BRAMLETT, sheriff of Chakchiuma County, Mississippi, stood looking out his office window. The clouds to the northwest hung heavy and dark. Rain was beginning to blow against the windowpanes.

Bramlett sighed and clamped his jaw tighter. "Rain, rain, go away. Come again some other day," he mumbled through his teeth. Tomorrow was the first day of squirrel season, and he was taking his grandson Marcellus hunting. Both of them had been looking forward to this day for months.

This afternoon, Bramlett's eldest daughter, Margaret, was driving down from Memphis with the kids. Next week was fall break at the school Marcellus and April attended. Marcellus was going to spend the week with Bramlett and Valeria while April stayed with a friend in Birmingham.

Margaret and John, her husband, were flying to Cancun for the week. John had won the trip by selling a ton of insurance. Today he was in Mobile on business and would drive up to Birmingham tomorrow to meet Margaret.

A whole week! Bramlett could hardly believe it. He and Marcellus could hunt three or four times, maybe get in a couple of mornings of fishing, watch wrestling together on TV, and tonight was the high school football game, then tomorrow at dawn—

"Excuse me, Sheriff."

Bramlett turned around. Robert Whitehead, administrator for the sheriff's department, stood at the doorway of the office. Whitehead was a retired Army colonel who liked a place for everything and everything in its place. He was tall, lean, and ramrod straight in his bearing and in his interpretation of office procedures.

"Yes?" Bramlett said. Irritation showed in his tone.

"That Corvette patrol car will be delivered next week and—"

"I haven't decided yet," Bramlett said. The words spat out. And immediately he regretted the sharpness of his tone.

Whitehead stiffened, swallowed hard, and said, "Yes, sir." He retreated from the door quickly.

Bramlett turned back to the window. He sighed again. He shouldn't have spoken to his administrator like that, but he just couldn't think about that fool Corvette right now.

It was a forfeiture vehicle, seized from a dealer trying to sell several rocks of crack cocaine to one of his undercover deputies. Bramlett wondered again whether he should have simply auctioned off that Corvette like any other car seized from a dope pusher.

But Deputies H. C. Curry and Johnny Baillie kept telling him it was too nice to auction off and why didn't he convert it into a patrol car like the highway patrol was now doing with confiscated vehicles. "People kill for machines like that," Curry had said with a strange look in his eye.

People kill for many reasons, Bramlett mused, still looking at the ominous clouds. A cold shudder suddenly rippled through his shoulders. He gave a quick shake of his head as if to shake away the dark foreboding passing through him. Such an intuition of something awful about to happen often came at the precise moment some long-anticipated pleasure was about to occur. He couldn't explain it.

Ella Mae, his secretary, stepped into the doorway. She smiled sympathetically, and said, "Anything I can do?" She was tall and trim, mid-fifties, and was the only secretary Bramlett had ever had.

He scratched the back of his head. "It's the rain, Ella Mae," he said.

"And Marcellus and you are supposed to go hunting in the morning," she said, her face showing a teasing pout.

He looked at her sharply. "*Supposed* to? We *are* going hunting."

She smiled and nodded. "Have a good weekend, Sheriff. It's past five-thirty. Time to go." She stepped out of the doorway and returned to her desk.

Bramlett took his hat from the halltree in the corner of his office and hurried out the door. Ella Mae was pulling on her raincoat. Always prepared, thought Bramlett. He walked toward the door to the parking lot.

"Sheriff," Deputy Harrelson called. Harrelson was new. Seemed like he'd make a good officer. Comes from good people. Bramlett paused and looked at him.

"We've just had a call from the railroad depot. An engineer on the Burlington Northern radioed as he passed through heading for Birmingham that a wrecked car was beside the track on the northwest edge of town."

"Send Drumwright to check it out," Bramlett said.

He pushed open the door and half trotted toward his car in the gusty rain. He hurried not so much to get out of the rain as to get home to see his grandchildren.

SHERIFF BRAMLETT PARKED HIS CAR in the carport. The two-bedroom white frame house was the same one a thirty-year-old Bramlett had purchased just over three decades ago for his family.

He opened the car door and pushed himself up. The effort caused him to grunt, and for a moment he wondered if he should have signed up for that weight-loss course they were having down at the church.

Then he remembered his wife Valeria was in the house working on a feast, and he rejected the idea. God made Grover Bramlett big. He was born big. Who was he to mess with God?

He'd hoped to see his daughter Margaret's Buick LeSabra in the driveway when he arrived. She was going to stay for supper, then leave Marcellus while she and April continued on to Birmingham.

He glanced at the garbage dumpster in the corner of the carport, and the strange dry tingling in his mouth sharpened. Last night, he'd opened the lid of the dumpster and dropped his package of Red Man chewing tobacco onto the coffee grinds and plastic bags of kitchen garbage.

Now, almost twenty-four hours without nicotine, his hands were constantly in motion and his mouth felt like it was turned wrong side out. All because when his daughter Margaret phoned the other night she said Marcellus insisted she purchase a type of bubble gum that was made to look like chewing tobacco and came in a foil pouch just like the real thing.

"He wants to be like you, Daddy," she said. "He declares when he's fourteen he's going to start chewing because you started at fourteen."

He shook his head as he opened the door from the carport and entered the kitchen. Valeria was washing something at the sink.

"Thought they would be here by now," he said, loosening his tie.

"They'll be along directly," she answered, not looking up.

He walked up behind her and leaned down and kissed her on the back of the neck. At six foot two and better than two hundred fifty pounds, Bramlett towered mountainlike over his wife, who at a petite five foot even, was shorter than any of their three daughters.

"Cut it out." She twisted her shoulders. "I've still got fifteen things to do before supper."

He unbuckled his belt and pulled it out enough to free the holster. "Thought they were leaving right after lunch," he said, placing the holstered pistol on top of the refrigerator.

"After school. I told you that. You never listen to me." She glanced toward the refrigerator. "You unload that thing?"

He grunted uh-huh, then said, "Only takes two hours to drive from Memphis."

"Relax, Grover. They'll be along before long."

"But it's raining . . ."

"Raining?" Her tone told him she hadn't noticed. "Oh, dear. Not tonight . . ." She turned off the tap and dried her hands on her yellow-checkered apron.

Bramlett chuckled and walked into the den. "Makes for an interesting game," he said over his shoulder. He liked football when the conditions were hard on running backs. He himself had played on the line two years in the hard-nosed, teeth-jarring Mississippi junior college league. Those two seasons left him with bad knees and a boxer's nose.

She followed him into the den. "But not rain at homecoming.

All those girls in their pretty dresses . . ." There was apprehension in her voice.

He sank into a large tan recliner chair. "Not raining hard yet." He pulled the lever on the side, and the footrest sprang out. He picked up the remote control for the television, pushed a button and settled deeper into his chair as the weather channel came into view.

Valeria said something about having saved a newspaper clipping for Deputy H. C. Curry. Then she went back into the kitchen.

Bramlett remembered seeing the article with the photo in the morning paper. The photo was of the Sheffield High School's homecoming court. Curry's niece was this year's black queen.

More rain was predicted. He held up the remote control and pressed the Off button. He wished Margaret, Marcellus, and April were here already. He'd always been nervous about his children driving in the rain. He'd worked too many accidents as a deputy in years gone by.

Bramlett pushed himself up out of the chair and crossed the room to one of the windows. He looked out. "Rain quitting already," he said. But he wasn't really looking at the rain. He was looking for his daughter's car.

He stepped into the dining room and flipped on the wall switch for the small chandelier suspended over the long oak table. On the table were neatly placed ten unframed watercolor paintings.

His painting class at the Etowah Community College was having a show in mid-November and each student was to submit three paintings. He had selected these ten and set them out for Margaret and the kids to look at so they could help him select the three for the show.

He looked up at the doorway. Valeria was standing there smiling at him. "I think Margaret will be surprised at how good you've gotten." She glanced at the table and frowned. "Put away that outhouse. Margaret won't like that."

He looked at the painting of the teetering privy half sunk in a rolling sea of vigorous bramble and chest-high ragweeds. It had a nice sky. Burnt umber and ultramarine blue.

"I think I hear their car," she said, turning from the doorway.

* * *

12

"I'M STILL TREMBLING," Margaret said as soon as they came into the den.

Bramlett hugged his daughter and grandson and lifted his granddaughter and sat in the recliner, snuggling her in his lap. "What took y'all so long?" he said.

"We stopped at Rosehill Cemetery. I had flowers for Cillie's grave. Some fool driver was speeding out of the cemetery and almost ran over Marcellus. Scared me to death."

"We still going squirrel hunting, Paw Paw?" Marcellus said, grinning.

Bramlett laughed. "You probably don't care anything about that now, do you?" He set April on the floor and stood up. "I got something to show you," he said to the boy.

"Grover, don't fool with that gun now," Valeria said. "Y'all can look at it after supper. You remember Margaret and April have to eat and leave right away for Birmingham." She turned toward the kitchen. "And maybe you'd best talk with your daughter about all this hunting business."

Margaret followed her mother. "I don't mind. But he isn't *eating* any squirrels."

Valeria stopped and whirled around, giving Bramlett a hard look. "*Nobody* is eating any squirrels. Don't you bring those things home, Grover. I mean it."

Bramlett winked at Marcellus. He'd talk with him later. Right now he wanted to give him the twenty-gauge Harrington & Richardson single shot. It was the very gun Bramlett's father had given him when he was a boy. Later on, maybe when Marcellus finished high school, Bramlett could give him the Winchester Model 12.

"Supper's ready," Valeria said. "Everybody wash up."

THE TELEPHONE RANG just as they were sitting down to the kitchen table. "That's for you," Valeria said to him.

"Y'all go ahead," Bramlett said, walking toward the wall phone.

It was Deputy Falkner, the night dispatcher. "Sheriff, Drumwright just radioed in about that car beside the railroad tracks. There's a body in it. Victim of a gunshot to the head, looks like."

Bramlett gave a low grunt. "Call in Baillie and Curry and Robert-son. Tell them to meet me there. Exactly where is it?"

"It's at Rosehill Cemetery. Right at the very back where the tracks cut through."

"Cemetery?" he said, gnawing at his lower lip and looking back to the table where Margaret was helping April's plate to turnip greens and Valeria was laughing at something Marcellus had just said. "I'm on my way." He hung up the phone. Immediately there was a sharp tightness in the middle of his chest.

3

ROSEHILL CEMETERY WAS AT THE EDGE of the city limits on the northwest side of town. Sheriff Grover Bramlett hoped to make a quick check to be sure everything was in place—and with Deputy Johnny Baillie in charge he had no doubt it would be—and then get back to the house in time to leave early for the game.

He drove between the two massive brick pillars at the entrance of the cemetery and followed the narrow asphalt lane which wound through small hillocks of tombstones and well-cared-for lawn. Oaks and sweetgums spread leaf-thick boughs forming a canopy over the road.

Bramlett headed toward the rear of the cemetery where a grove of junipers stood sentinel on a bluff overlooking the single railroad track coming from Memphis seventy miles to the northwest headed onward toward Birmingham, one hundred sixty miles to the southeast. The line cut across the northeast corner of Mississippi. As he rounded a curve, he could see the flashing blue-and-white warning lights of several patrol cars in front of the juniper grove.

Johnny Baillie met him as he got out of his car. Bramlett felt more comfortable with Baillie supervising a crime scene than any other deputy he had. Baillie brought to his work a dynamic of youthful energy (he was not yet thirty) and the same sure-handed no-effort-wasted efficiency the sheriff admired so much a decade earlier when the young man played guard on Sheffield High School's state championship team. In spite of the fact that Johnny Baillie's father had once been a member of the Klan, the young man had proved his loyalty to Bramlett again and again.

"It's a white male," Deputy Baillie said. "His driver's license says he's Jesse Bondreaux. Curry recognizes him as a teacher at the high school. We're trying to locate the principal and checking for any family."

H. C. Curry was the other guard on that team. Like Baillie, he was quick as a cat. They were the first two deputies Bramlett hired after winning his first election. Curry was, in fact, the first black deputy the department had ever had.

Bramlett followed Deputy Baillie a few yards alongside the juniper grove to a place where the descent down the embankment was easier. He nodded at the two paramedics standing beside the ambulance, waiting.

Bramlett knew the paramedics would have checked the victim as soon as they arrived. It was the department's standing policy that, if the paramedics thought there was even a faint flicker of life, they would take the person immediately. Otherwise, they left the body until the medical examiner-investigator arrived.

"Watch the kudzu," Baillie said to the sheriff. "It's tricky."

Following the deputy, Bramlett picked his way down the vine-infested hillside with the beam of his large flashlight. Then he walked to the vehicle-turned-on-its-side, around which were clustered several deputies.

Jacob Robertson held the beam of his flashlight on the face mashed against the inside of the windshield. Robertson was also a member of that state championship basketball team and the third deputy Bramlett had hired. In spite of being six six and two hundred ten pounds as a high school senior, Robertson was never a starter. Yet, whenever he went into the game he displayed a fierce determination that Bramlett loved.

Robertson was a born and bred country boy, and came from very religious, hard-working people. He, like H. C. Curry, was still unmarried. Johnny Baillie, on the other hand, married his high school sweetheart and already had two kids.

"Can't tell yet if it's a contact wound or not," Robertson said.

16

"If it is, the weapon will be in the car, won't it?" Bramlett said.

He didn't say it with much conviction. A contact wound usually indicated suicide. A suicide would be nice. Nice and neat, and he wouldn't have to fret about whoever was driving the car that almost ran down his grandson.

"We haven't searched inside yet," Robertson said in answer to the sheriff's comment about the weapon.

"Not yet," Deputy Adam Martin said. Martin's voice was high enough to be a woman's. His face was behind a video camera. He had the camera aimed at the vehicle and was working his way around the back bumper.

"How much more?" Bramlett asked.

"Almost done," Martin said. He was walking around the front of the car. Another deputy was taking flash pictures with a still camera.

H. C. Curry stood in the middle of the railroad tracks. He was making a sketch of the scene. "Run your tape from this rail," he said, pointing at the track, "to the top of the front bumper." A deputy with a fifty-foot steel tape measure pegged the tape in front of the rail.

"Dr. Thompson is on his way," Baillie said before Bramlett could ask. Dr. Greg Thompson was the medical examiner-investigator of Chakchiuma County.

They couldn't move the body out of the car until Dr. Thompson arrived, pronounced him dead, and examined the immediate scene. Bramlett stepped back and reached to his rear trouser pocket for his tobacco pouch. He gave a faint moan as he felt the empty pocket. "No witnesses, I suppose?"

"Nothing but that report from the engineer," Baillie replied. "The call came in from the depot at five thirty-seven. The train didn't stop here. Went straight on through to Alabama."

"That does it." Adam Martin said, lowering the video camera from his shoulder.

Deputy Steve Drumwright came down the hillside and walked up to Baillie. "I just phoned the principal at the high school," he informed the other deputy. "He said he doesn't know of any family locally. Said it's probably on the victim's file at the school office, that everybody has to list a next of kin."

Bramlett glanced at his watch. He needed to leave. And he knew

H. C. Curry was even more eager than he was to get away to the game. His niece, the black queen, would be chauffeured into the stadium in a convertible in just a little while.

The sheriff turned and looked to the other side of the vehicle where Curry stood. The deputy was still working on the crime scene sketch. "H. C., you 'bout done with that?" Bramlett asked.

Curry nodded, "Yes, sir. This will do it." He made another notation, then closed his notebook.

"How am I supposed to get down there?" a graveled voice said.

The beams of several flashlights swept to the top of the bluff. Dr. Greg Thompson, the medical examiner-investigator of Chakchiuma County, stood at the edge. He shielded his eyes from the light now suddenly focused on his face. Thompson was tall and thin, gray-headed and distinguished-looking, and seemed, to Bramlett, to enjoy his work with the sheriff's department more than a physician should.

The sheriff nodded at a young deputy standing a few feet away. "Help the doctor down, son," he directed. The deputy immediately turned to climb the hillside.

Bramlett walked to the rear of the vehicle and shined his beam across the bumper. "You saw this?" he said to Johnny Baillie. He now held the beam steady on a scuffed and dented part of the bumper. "For sure he didn't drive over that bluff himself. Looks like somebody in another vehicle helped him out a bit." He lifted his gaze to the dark mass of junipers at the top of the bluff. "Might rain again," he continued. "Check for any tire tracks or footprints you can make casts of, Johnny. Then seal this place off and post a watch for the night. There's not much else we can do here now. But I want you and H. C. and Jacob here at first light in the morning to go over this whole area."

Dr. Thompson moved forward and leaned over to peer closely at the face pressed against the windshield. " 'Evening, Grover," he said, not looking at the sheriff. Two deputies held their flashlight beams on the face.

"We could lower you down into the car if you wanted a closer look, Greg." Bramlett enjoyed teasing the good doctor when he could. He knew Dr. Thompson wasn't going to crawl up onto the side of the car and lower himself down to the body.

"Humph," the doctor grunted. "I don't need to crawl in there

18

to see he's dead. Y'all pull him out so I can get a better look at him."

H. C. Curry and Jacob Robertson climbed on top of the car and pulled the body up through the window. Three other deputies lowered it to the ground and stretched the man out in the tall shag grass.

His blond hair was a bit on the long side, and he was wearing faded blue jeans and a lightweight sea-green jacket. To Bramlett he appeared to be about thirty-five or -six. There was a single small bullet hole about an inch above the left eye.

Dr. Thompson knelt down and felt under the man's jaw for a pulse. He turned the head a couple of times, moved the front of the jacket aside to expose the front of the shirted torso, then ran his flashlight beam all over the victim's clothing.

"Just this one wound to the head as far as I can see now," he said, pushing himself up. "Looks like a near discharge wound. Definitely homicide." He smiled pleasantly and said, "Y'all can bag him now."

Sheriff Bramlett spoke to Johnny Baillie. "Contact the crime lab folks in Jackson right away. They should be able to be up here by noon tomorrow. It'll be noon 'fore I can get here myself."

"This is Friday night, Grover," Dr. Thompson said with a soft chuckle. "That means lots of shootings all over the state. Those Jackson people may not be here till middle of the week." He chuckled again and took a microcassette recorder out of his inside coat pocket.

Don't worry," Deputy Baillie assured the sheriff. "Everything's under control." He almost smiled. Bramlett wasn't sure he'd ever seen Johnny Baillie smile. "You and that grandson of yours just shoot a bunch of squirrels."

Bramlett grunted and moved to the other side of the doctor.

"I'll have the post mortem finished sometime tomorrow afternoon," Dr. Thompson said. He shined his flashlight on his watch. "Got to run along now. Told the wife we'd be there in time to see the convertibles drive into the stadium with the court."

H. C. Curry grinned at the doctor. "You know my niece is the queen?"

"Oh, really?" Dr. Thompson said. "Which one?"

Curry blinked hard and his grin sank into a flat expression of

confusion. He didn't answer. Bramlett thought the deputy was trying to figure out if the doctor really couldn't tell black from white
or was jerking him around or what. To Bramlett, Thompson's style
of humor was obnoxious.

Bramlett put his hand on the back of Curry's arm. The muscles
were rigid. "Go on," Bramlett instructed the deputy. "Help the
doctor up the hillside and then you run along. We won't be here
much longer."

"Jacob is supposed to go with me," Curry said.

Bramlett remembered that Curry's girlfriend Lizzie had lined up
the tall, girl-shy Jacob Robertson with a date. He'd never known
him to be interested in anything but fishing and hunting. It was an
amazing thing. Could this be the young man's first date?

"Okay," Bramlett said with a soft laugh. "Go on."

The two deputies started toward the newly trod pathway through
the kudzu leading up the hillside.

"Wait. I'm coming." Dr. Thompson hurried after them. The two
deputies did not slow up.

Bramlett chuckled and turned to look again at the automobile.
"Nice car," he said.

"Toyota Celica," Johnny Baillie said. "New."

"Schoolteachers make a lot more than they used to." The sheriff
arched his back, then continued. "Well, Johnny. Mrs. Bramlett's
gonna skin me if I don't get back to the house."

The deputy nodded. "Go on. I'll take care of everything."

Bramlett nodded, too. He had no doubts that the deputy would
do just that. He turned for the path up through the vines.

VALERIA OPENED HER PURSE and double-checked to be sure she had
her set of keys. Marcellus had already gone out to the car. Just as
she started to close the back door, the telephone rang.

She glanced at her watch. She should have left ten minutes ago.
Maybe it was Grover calling to say he was tied up. Maybe one of
the girls.

She hurried back into the kitchen and lifted the receiver off the
wall phone. "Hello?"

There was a slight static on the line as if the call was coming from a car phone. "Is the boy there?" The voice was muffled and nasal, quite unfamiliar yet strangely familiar at the same time.

"Boy? You mean Marcellus . . . ?" Valeria said. Then, "Who is this?"

There was silence. Then the line buzzed dead.

Valeria replaced the receiver on the hook and stood staring at the phone. What in the world . . . ? Then she gave her head a quick shake and hurried out the back door.

4

JACOB ROBERTSON WAS UNCOMFORTABLE. He hoped his necktie wasn't crooked or had moved enough to show the edge of the white plastic clip behind the knot. He wanted to lift his hand to check it, but, at the same time, didn't want to call attention to it if it *was* crooked.

How long had it been since he'd worn a tie? He couldn't remember. And this tie, a brown clip-on, was the only one he had.

He wished somewhere along the way someone had taught him how to tie a tie. Only the old men at Shiloh Baptist where he went to church wore ties—and all of them were clip-ons.

Jacob stood on the front porch of the cottage with H. C. Curry and H. C.'s girlfriend, Lizzie Clouse. Lizzie had lined up Jacob with a blind date. The date was one of Lizzie's fellow teachers, Nena Carmack.

Having to work the crime scene at the cemetery made both H. C. and Jacob a bit rushed in picking up Nena and Lizzie for the game. Still, they were only fifteen minutes late.

Nena opened the door and smiled at him. Jacob's lungs froze. She was the most beautiful woman he'd ever seen. He stammered as he tried to speak when Lizzie introduced them.

When they were all in the car going to the game—Curry and Lizzie in front, Jacob and Nena in the backseat—Curry said they were running late because they had to stop by the cemetery. "It was Jesse Bondreaux," he said. "Shot dead."

Lizzie's head gave a slight jerk. She made a motion as if she were going to turn around and look at Nena, but stopped. She said, "Why?"

Curry shrugged. "Who knows?"

Nena said nothing. Her head was turned, looking out the window, and Jacob couldn't see her face. He did notice her hand tightening into a fist against the fabric of the seat between them. The fist began shaking violently.

BY THE TIME SHERIFF GROVER BRAMLETT got back to the house, the others were gone. Margaret and April were on their way to Birmingham, and Valeria and Marcellus had gone to the game.

Damn, he thought. Margaret didn't get to see the paintings.

Valeria had left his game ticket on the table in the kitchen along with a note: "We'll be sitting in our usual places." That meant the fifty-yard line, three rows from the top.

As soon as he entered the stadium, he went to the concession stand and bought three boxes of popcorn and three cups of Coke. Holding the cardboard tray in both hands, he weaved his way through the crowd milling around the track and then up the stadium steps.

When he reached the third row from the top, he lifted the tray chest-high and said "Excuse me" thirteen times as he squeezed his bulk down the row, trying not to step on any woman's feet or fall into anybody's lap or spill the Cokes on anyone's head.

"Why didn't you get diet drinks?" Valeria asked.

"It's a football game," he said, nudging his bottom down between Marcellus and a man on the other side of his seat. He could never understand why someone as trim as his wife would drink a diet drink. For all he knew, diet drinks caused cancer or something.

He felt a hand press on his shoulder. "Hello, Grover." It was a woman's voice. He half turned his head.

Katherine Topp's face was just beside his. She was close enough for him to smell her perfume.

23

" 'Evening," he said, lifting his Coke cup in lieu of touching his hat brim.

She laughed and sat back. She and her family usually sat directly behind him and Valeria.

He turned around and nodded at her husband Robert and the two younger daughters. He couldn't remember their names.

Katherine Topp leaned forward again. Her face once more was only inches from Bramlett's. She was in her late thirties, pretty, and had a teasing smile. Her dark hair brushed against his cheek, and he recalled that the last time he'd seen her, she was a blonde.

"There's something I need to talk with you about," she said, still smiling. "Maybe next week, okay?"

He nodded.

She patted his shoulder twice in a friendly manner, then leaned back again.

Bramlett took a sip of his Coke and looked toward the field. The visiting Brownsville High Warriors in black-and-red uniforms were already in front of their bench, jumping up and down, linemen butting heads, running backs stretching their thigh muscles, coaches pacing nervously back and forth along the sideline staring at their clipboards.

Bramlett leaned his head close to Marcellus's ear. "Tell me about the car that almost hit you in the cemetery."

Marcellus was cramming a handful of popcorn into his mouth. He shrugged and chewed, swallowed, then said through the popcorn still in his mouth, "Dark, small." He swallowed again and took a gulp of his Coke. "The driver was wearing a funny hat."

"Man, woman? White, black?"

He shrugged again and took another handful from his box. "White. Man, I guess."

The Sheffield High Tigers tore through a cheerleaders-held paper wall on which was lettered in white and blue poster paint "Whup Up On the Warriors" and charged screaming toward their bench. Bramlett almost lost his grip on his box of popcorn as Marcellus jumped to his feet when the home fans rose cheering.

As everyone settled back into the seats again, the sheriff saw H. C. Curry and Jacob Robertson, both now dressed in coats and ties, walking down the track with their dates. Curry was with Lizzie

24

Clouse, a vivacious yet serious high school teacher who had once phoned Bramlett asking what percentage of his deputies were "men of color."

There was a glow about her face, and her skin was the rich color, it seemed to Bramlett, of milk chocolate. Seeing her reminded him of the tragedy of her mother.

The woman was killed only a few years before. He'd worked the case hard—and still suspected the husband did it—but never did prove a thing, never got an indictment.

Bramlett couldn't remember ever seeing the young woman with Robertson. She was taller than Lizzie, long-legged and lean, with shoulder-length red hair and very fair skin.

Bramlett smiled. He was glad to see Jacob out with a woman.

He heard Valeria's voice, looked in her direction. She was grinning and pointing. "There's Rumi," she said. "Isn't she lovely? And would you look at that dress Vicki Ann is wearing? Doesn't she look just like a queen?" Vicki Ann, this year's white queen, was the daughter of Rumi and Howard Skelton, two of Bramlett's least favorite people.

For the first time Bramlett noticed the temporary stage near the east end zone upon which, in folding chairs decorated with blue and white crepe paper ribbons, sat the Homecoming Court—queens and maids in antebellum-style dresses with their male escorts in black tuxedos. Rumi's daughter Vicki Ann and H. C.'s niece perched in the middle chairs, flanked by their court.

Rumi Skelton and her husband Howard sat in a special section for parents of the court several rows below Bramlett. The worst thing about homecoming, as far as Bramlett was concerned, was the extra long half-time.

Marcellus dropped his empty popcorn box to the concrete floor, and Bramlett handed him his own half-eaten box. The announcer's voice blared on the PA system, echoing from one side of the stadium to the other, asking everyone to stand for the national anthem and please remain standing for the invocation.

After the high school band finished the anthem, the distinctive voice of the school's principal, Lynwood Wilson, sounded over the PA. "Before we have the invocation, I would ask you to bow your heads for a moment of silent prayer for the family of one of our teachers who died tragically this afternoon—"

Immediately, a shocked silence blanketed the two thousand-plus people jammed into the stands.

Bramlett almost dropped his cup. His eyes shot to the spot where he'd seen Curry and Robertson and their dates sit down earlier.

"Jesse Bondreaux," the principal continued, and a mixture of gasps and murmurs rippled along the rows of seats around Bramlett. The sheriff could see the side of Curry's face, could see the muscles tense and knew this unexpected action by Principal Wilson had taken the deputy as much off guard as it had himself.

"Let us pray," another voice said over the PA, a voice Bramlett didn't recognize, a twangy voice, no doubt one of the local preachers.

Before the preacher had invoked "Almighty God" there was a sharp screech toward Bramlett's right, over in the student body section. Bramlett looked and saw someone, a girl, running down the track toward the concession stand—followed immediately by two other girls. The preacher intoned his prayer, and most heads, but not all, Bramlett noticed, were bowed with eyes closed.

"Stupid principal," Bramlett mumbled as the prayer ended.

The kickoff followed, and Bramlett put an arm around Marcellus and squeezed and smiled. This was a football game! He didn't want to think about murder and mayhem. Not now. What could be finer? Of course, a good chew would be nice, but . . . whatever.

During the half, the queens with their court walked to the middle of the field, were each crowned, cheek-kissed, and presented a bouquet of roses by the principal, and then everyone stood to sing Sheffield High's alma mater. The ceremonies ended, and Valeria wanted to go.

Both Marcellus and Bramlett pleaded more time. They stayed until the middle of the third quarter. Sheffield trailed the Brownsville team by twenty-one points.

"CAN I SEE THE GUN NOW?" Marcellus said to Bramlett as soon as they walked into the house.

Bramlett put his arm around his grandson's shoulder. "Let's sit

26

down for a bit and let me ask you about something." He moved them into the den.

When they were seated, Bramlett massaged his forehead with his fingers and attempted a smile. "Tell me again about that car that almost hit you in the graveyard."

Marcellus shrugged. "It was dark. Maybe blue or black. Small. Like a Honda or Toyota."

"Two door, four door, what?"

"I don't remember."

Bramlett nodded, reminded himself not to look too concerned, then said, "And the driver? What did you say he looked like?"

Marcellus made a face. "He was wearing a funny hat. And he looked at me as he went by."

That was the part Bramlett didn't like to hear. He pressed his fingers into the knot in the middle of his chest, then asked, "Can you describe this hat?"

Marcellus squinched up his nose and gave a slight shake of his head. "I'd know it if I saw it again."

"Was he old or young?"

The boy rubbed his hands on his knees. "Old."

"How old? Real old?"

He shook his head. "Naw. Not real old. Old like Mommy."

Bramlett couldn't suppress a smile. He'd have to remember to tell that to his thirty-three-year-old daughter.

"You said a white man?"

Marcellus nodded.

"Fat, thin, what?"

He shrugged. "I dunno. Not fat. Maybe . . ." He shrugged again and shook his head. "I couldn't really see him good. There was rainwater all over the windshield. I remember the wiper and then I saw his face—looking at me. His eyes . . ."

"What about his eyes?"

Marcellus cocked his head. "They . . . they looked sorta wild or something. Maybe scared, too. You know what I mean?"

Bramlett involuntarily drew a deep breath, released it, nodded and said, "How many people were in the car?"

"Just one. I didn't see anybody else."

Valeria came into the family room carrying a tray with three glasses of lemonade. She stopped, her brow furrowed. She looked from Marcellus to her husband, immediately reading concern in his face. "What's going on?"

Bramlett drew another long breath and leaned back in his chair. He said, "A possible homicide victim was found at the back side of the cemetery not long after Margaret and the kids were there."

Valeria gasped. "That teacher?" Her lips parted slightly and her eyes widened. "And . . . and you think . . ."

Bramlett shook his head. "I'm not thinking anything specific."

"But you think there's a possibility . . ." Again Valeria didn't finish. Her lips pressed tightly together as if prohibiting her voice from uttering another sound, another question. She stood holding the tray.

Marcellus looked from his grandmother to his grandfather and then back to his grandmother again. There was confusion in his eyes. He didn't speak.

Valeria placed the tray of glasses down on the coffee table. "Let's all just sit down and think about this." She smoothed the front of her skirt and sank down onto the couch beside Marcellus. Her eyes were on Bramlett. "Speak plainly, Grover. You think there's a possibility the person who almost ran over Marcellus could have just killed somebody?"

Bramlett was looking toward the fireplace. He shrugged his shoulders. "There's no way whoever was in that car could have known who Marcellus was even if he got a good look at him—which I doubt. It was raining, the driver was speeding, and, if it was the one who was involved with this shooting, he was panicked out—probably not really focusing on anything."

Valeria closed her eyes and folded her arms around Marcellus.

Bramlett ran his tongue over his parched lips, then looked at Marcellus. "This is not something to talk about. You understand?"

The boy nodded.

Bramlett placed his hands on the arms of the recliner and pushed himself up. He walked across the room to the cool fireplace and turned his back to it as if it were blazing. He hadn't laid the first fire this fall, yet there he stood with his hands outstretched behind him as if expecting the fireplace to warm the deep chill he felt.

28

5

JACOB ROBERTSON CUT HIS EYES toward the woman sitting beside him in the booth at Shoney's. Nena Carmack had shoulder-length hair, red—almost golden—and smooth, pale skin. He noticed her fingers on the water glass. She had such long, slim fingers, and a tiny waist as well.

He'd been apprehensive about this evening ever since H. C. had told him Lizzie wanted to fix him up with Nena. The only thing H. C. told him about her was that she taught Spanish at the high school and was good-looking.

She was more than good-looking. To Jacob she was the most lovely woman he'd ever seen in his life. And, in spite of the fact that they had been together for almost three hours now, the two of them had hardly said two words to each other.

The silence between them had not been awkward, however, due to Lizzie's constant talking. Jacob remembered her from high school. She and H. C. had dated briefly. She'd been a cheerleader. He recalled she was quite popular and was friendly with everyone. But he'd never really known her well.

"What you going to get, Jacob?" H. C. Curry said to him, looking up from the menu.

"I want a hot fudge sundae," Lizzie said.

Jacob's stomach was queasy. He supposed he'd have to eat something. Maybe the fish sandwich. "I don't know . . ."

"What about you, Nena?" Curry said.

"I really can't eat anything," she said. She spoke quickly, almost snapped it out like she was angry.

"Hey," H. C. said. "Why don't we all go to the mall at Tupelo tomorrow?"

Jacob frowned. "We got to work tomorrow."

"We'll be through early. The sheriff will be back from hunting by noon, we'll all confer, then he'll let us go."

"That might be good," Lizzie said. Her eyes were hard on Nena as she spoke. "What do you think, Nena?"

Nena drew a breath and released it, opened her mouth as if she were going to speak, but said nothing. She gave a slight shrug of one shoulder.

"Jacob, we need to shop for some glad rags for you," H. C. said. "These ladies could help us."

"What?" Jacob said. He had no idea what H. C. was talking about.

H. C. laughed. "Nice clothes, man. When you bought something beside hunting and fishing apparel? Or something for your pickup?"

Lizzie punched H. C. with her elbow. "Leave Jacob alone. He's interested in more things than just hunting and fishing, aren't you, Jacob?" she said, looking at him. Before he could reply, she turned her eyes to Nena. "But that's a great idea. We could all go to the mall and then to a movie or something while we're there. What do you think, Nena?"

Nena didn't respond. She lifted her water glass slowly, sipped, and then set the glass down gently.

Lizzie looked back to Jacob. She was nodding and smiling. "It'll be fun. What kind of movies do you like, Jacob?"

He swallowed and said, "I don't go much." He had difficulty getting the words out. His mouth was very dry.

A waitress came to the table and held her notepad ready. "Can I take y'all's order?" she said.

"Give us another minute." Lizzie's eyes were on Nena again.

The waitress walked away.

Nena seemed to shudder slightly, then said, "Excuse me." She slid out of the booth. "I'll be right back. Just order me a Coke." Then she hurried away toward the rest rooms across the room.

30

Jacob shifted uncomfortably in his seat. He felt flushed. He should never have let H. C. talk him into this blind date. The woman obviously didn't care for him.

Lizzie reached her hand across the table and squeezed Jacob's hand. "Listen, Jacob," she said. "This has nothing to do with you. You understand? Nena . . . well, she used to date Jesse Bondreaux."

His head twisted slightly and his eyes widened. "What?" Immediately he felt a dislike for this dead man he'd never even known.

Lizzie nodded. "Yes, but, you see, she quit seeing him over a year ago. It's history. But . . . well, this is upsetting to all of us." She was talking fast. "We saw him every day at school. He was popular with the students." She paused and glanced in the direction of the rest rooms. Then she continued. "No telling how they are going to react. You saw some of that at the game. Most of them have never even known anyone who has died."

Jacob took a large gulp of the water from the glass and set it down carefully. He knew his face was burning. He should have never let Curry talk him into this. Never.

GILLY BITZER SWAYED UNSTEADILY as he walked along the curb. He had been singing "Amazing Grace" and couldn't remember the fourth stanza. He had no problems with the first, second, third, and fifth, but he was completely blank on the fourth. He was just starting at the beginning once more when his eyes fell on the telephone booth at the edge of the parking lot beside the Shell service station.

The station was closed and dark. There was a bright security light on a high pole directly behind the booth. The light illuminated the entire area.

Gilly lurched toward the booth. He had one more bottle back at the place, but it wouldn't last out tomorrow. He would have to go back to see Amos, and he needed more money.

He entered the booth and closed the door. The overhead light came on, Gilly dug his fingers into his trousers pocket and drew out the change. Forty-eight cents. A quarter, two dimes, and three pennies.

The Chakchiuma County telephone directory hanging by a chain under the pay phone was coverless and missing some of its fore and aft sections. He lifted the book and carefully turned pages until he placed his finger on a particular name.

He dropped the directory, deposited the quarter, awaited the dial tone, then punched the buttons.

The call rang twice and then was answered.

"It's me," Bitzer slurred with a chuckle. "Gilly."

"Who?"

"Gilly Bitzer."

"Why are you calling now? Are you drunk?"

"I need some money."

"Come around tomorrow. I might find something for you to do."

Bitzer chuckled. "I don't think you understand. I ain't talking about leaf-raking money. I saw something today."

"What are you talking about?"

Bitzer gave a low laugh. "I was down at the railroad tracks by the cemetery. The weirdest thing happened. This car sudden like comes falling off the bank and lands down by the tracks. And inside the car is a man that's been killed. Then I saw the person standing at the top of the bank who just shoved that car off." Bitzer laughed again.

There was silence on the other end of the line.

"You there?" Bitzer said, still chuckling. "Anyway, I'll be coming by tomorrow."

"No. Don't come here. Phone me tomorrow afternoon. We'll talk then." There was a click. The other party had hung up.

Bitzer held the receiver to his chest and fell back against one side of the booth. "Now how in the hell does that fourth stanza go?" he said out loud. He started from the beginning once again.

TWO HOURS LATER, H. C. Curry rolled over and looked at the digital radio clock on the lamp table beside his bed. He blinked his eyes several times, trying to focus. Eleven forty-nine. He'd been in bed for almost an hour and couldn't fall asleep. He couldn't get his mind off the new forfeited Corvette that was being transformed into a patrol car.

Who was Sheriff Bramlett going to assign it to? Would he just

leave the decision up to Whitehead? Whitehead was just an administrator. He didn't know squat about who should drive what anyway.

Just that morning Whitehead told Curry that the car would be in
sometime next week and, no, he didn't know who was going to get
it. "That decision has not been made yet." Whitehead said it as if
he were the one to decide.

Surely the sheriff wouldn't let Whitehead just pick out whoever
he wanted to give the Corvette to. Would he give it to Robertson?
No, that'd be stupid. Robertson would rather have a truck, if anything. What about Baillie? Had he talked to the sheriff about it?
Maybe . . .

The thought gnawed at Curry and he snapped the sheet off his
chest. His mother kept the house too warm.

The phone rang. He fumbled with the receiver for a second, but
lifted it before a second ring. His mother had given him the phone
last Christmas. "Maybe those calls you get all hours of the night
won't have to wake us up, too," she said.

It was Lizzie. "H. C., you need to come over here right away.
Jo Ann's all upset. It's got something to do with Jesse Bondreaux."
Jo Ann Scales, a white woman, was Lizzie's roommate. She, like
Lizzie and Nena, taught at the high school.

H. C. had never been very comfortable around Jo Ann. She didn't
laugh or tease like Lizzie and Nena did. Of course, tonight Nena
was not herself because of this Bondreaux thing.

Jo Ann was so serious all the time. Sometimes he thought maybe
she just didn't like him because he was black. But that didn't make
sense. She roomed with Lizzie, and Lizzie was black.

Jo Ann's whole world revolved around her students. There was
always a particular one that she was upset about. It could be a
problem at home, or with grades, or sickness. Whenever H. C. was
around her, that's all she talked about.

"She cares," Lizzie tried to explain to him. "She can't just leave
it at work like almost everybody else does."

IN LESS THAN FIFTEEN MINUTES he was sitting on the couch in Lizzie's apartment with Jo Ann Scales beside him. She was wearing a
pale-yellow terry-cloth bathrobe and had her knees drawn up against

33

her chest with her arms wrapped around her legs. Her long, narrow face seemed paler than H. C. had ever seen it, and her chestnut hair fell across her face.

Lizzie was sitting cross-legged on the floor beside the coffee table in front of the couch. Her dark, intense eyes were fastened hard on Jo Ann. Lizzie, who was rarely still for more than three seconds and always seemed to H. C. to be energy squeezed tight, was now perfectly motionless.

Jo Ann shook her head. "I . . . I just don't know . . ." she said. "I don't know if I should say anything."

"Tell him what you told me," Lizzie said.

Jo Ann sighed wearily before she spoke. "None of this may have anything to do with Mr. Bondreaux's death. I just don't know . . ."

Lizzie reached with her hand and squeezed the woman's arm in a reassuring manner. "It's all right. Just tell what you know."

Jo Ann opened her eyes and gazed across the room. "Sometime ago a student came to talk with me. She was very upset. She said . . ." She paused and gnawed at her lower lip, then continued. "She said she was in love with Mr. Bondreaux." She paused again, held her breath, then released it. "You have to understand it's not uncommon for girls to develop crushes on men teachers. And this girl was one of several who liked to drop by his house. He's always been like that . . . you know . . . welcoming students—maybe encouraged them—boys and girls, to come over to his place. I'd never heard anyone suggest anything *wrong* was happening there. But, well, this girl told me she and Mr. Bondreaux had been . . ." She paused again, breathed in and out quickly, then said, ". . . *intimate*, if you know what I mean."

Curry's jaw tightened. "How old was this guy?"

"Mid-thirties, probably," Lizzie said. There was a hardness in her voice.

Curry rubbed his forehead with his hand. Sheriff Bramlett was right. Good people seldom get murdered. If you scratch around long enough, you'll usually find some stink somewheres. Chicken crap on somebody's shoes, the sheriff was fond of saying.

"Anyway, she was upset," Jo Ann continued. "Confused. She thought she loved him . . . but she also loved her boyfriend. And she *told* her boyfriend about Mr. Bondreaux and herself. Of course, the boyfriend became enraged, as one can well understand. And she didn't know what he'd do."

"Who's this girl?" Curry said.

Jo Ann shook her head. "I hate to get her involved if it's not really necessary."

Curry rubbed his palm on his knees, then tightened his hands into fists. He wasn't sure how far or fast he could push her. "What else?" he said.

"I talked to Mr. Wilson about it. Lynwood Wilson was the principal of Sheffield High. Curry, like all black folks in Sheffield, was quite proud that one of their own was principal of a high school which was two-thirds white. At the same time, although he couldn't say exactly why, he wasn't very impressed with the man.

"What did he say?"

"Well, I told him I suspected there might be some indiscretion involved. I hated to say anything at all. But I didn't tell him the girl's name. You see, this isn't the first time something like this has happened."

Lizzie sat up straight, her eyes widening as she stared at Jo Ann. "What do you mean?"

"Last year . . . back when Nena was dating him . . . I'd had another girl come talk with me about him. She didn't come right out and say Mr. Bondreaux had been intimate with her, but I suspected it. I simply told Nena I thought he ought to be more careful, that he probably didn't realize how strongly some of the girls felt about him."

"What did Nena say?" Lizzie asked.

Jo Ann shook her head. "She blew up. Told me Jesse would never lay a hand on any student and for me to mind my own business."

"Was this before or after Nena stopped seeing him?"

"Before. In fact, I think she broke up with him shortly afterwards. That made me think I'd probably been right."

"You're going to have to give us the names of these kids," Curry said.

She shook her head again and closed her eyes. "I don't want anybody to get hurt . . ."

"A man is dead," Curry said.

Jo Ann, her eyes still closed, nodded slowly. "I understand that.

I understand that." She opened her eyes and looked beyond Curry. "Mostly kids went to his place. But some adults. Noel Hackott was a close friend of Jesse's."

"Tell me the names of the kids." Curry clamped his teeth together hard as he waited for her to respond.

She sighed again, then said in a faint voice, "Gail Topp, Rozelle Kample, Cora Hartley, Duvall Ellis, Vicki Ann Skelton, Lillie Fay Conlee . . ." She paused and her eyes focused on him. "But . . . these are all good kids . . ."

Curry had been writing hurriedly in his pocket notebook. "Listen to me, Jo Ann. We're dealing with murder here. I need to know which of these girls you suspect was sleeping with him."

She shook her head. "Not now," she said. "I can't say now."

Curry nodded. He knew there was no point in pushing her further. She was tired and upset. He could wait till the morning.

He stood, and turned toward Lizzie. Then he remembered the last time Lizzie had called him about a problem Jo Ann was having. He looked back at her. "What about the fellow who was stalking you. What was his name?"

She shrugged. "It was nothing."

"Edwin Charles," Lizzie said. "And it *was* something. He's still around, but he hasn't bothered her in a while. For a time, though, I thought he'd never quit. If she hadn't made me promise not to call you again, I would have."

Curry studied Jo Ann's face for a long moment, then said, "I'll talk to you tomorrow." She didn't reply.

Lizzie took his hand and walked him to the door. "I guess you'll have to talk to Nena, too."

He gave a quick nod. "We'll want to talk to anyone who knew him well."

"It ended bitterly for her. I think she almost grew to hate him. We talked about it while they were breaking up and for weeks afterwards. She found out he was also seeing a secretary in Tupelo. She refused to have anything else to do with him. She never mentioned him again." She paused and sucked gently on her upper lip, then said, "I tried to phone her after we got home tonight. Just to see how she was."

"And?"

36

Lizzie frowned. "She wasn't home. I can't imagine where she was."

Curry shrugged. "Maybe she just went driving around."

Lizzie shook her head. "Maybe."

He took her chin gently in his fingers and tilted up her face. "I love you, girl," he said.

"I love you, too," she replied, moving her lips toward his.

CURRY LEFT THE APARTMENT and returned to his car. As he put the key into the door, he heard a car engine rev. He looked up. The taillights of a small, dark car flicked on and the car wheeled into the middle of the street and sped away into the night.

6

SHORTLY BEFORE THREE O'CLOCK in the morning, Valeria Bramlett threw back the covers and sprang out of the bed. "This is ridiculous," she said. "I'm going to sleep on the couch."

Bramlett turned on the bedside lamp and propped himself up on one elbow. "What's wrong?"

"You, Grover," she said, shoving an arm through the sleeve of her robe. "You can't be still. Every time I'm just about asleep, you suddenly bounce around."

"Here," Bramlett said, swinging his feet to the floor. "Come back to bed. I'll take the couch. Besides, I'd planned to get up at four-thirty anyway."

"Four-thirty? You can't be serious. You're waking Marcellus up at four-thirty?"

He slid his feet into his slippers and stood. "Not until five-thirty. I'll have breakfast ready by then. We'll leave at six and by sunup be in the woods."

She folded her robe back onto the end of the bed and slid beneath the covers. "Grover, I know you're excited, but please try to be quiet. Don't go clanging around when you start breakfast. You'll wake him too early." She pulled the covers tightly about her neck and shut her eyes. "Be careful with those guns," she said with a yawn.

38

Bramlett cut off the lamp and closed the door as he left the bedroom. He went into the den and stretched out on the couch just as the clock on the wall bonged three times.

Since going to bed four hours ago, he might have dozed off, but he couldn't remember doing so. For weeks he had been looking forward to going hunting with his grandson on the opening day of squirrel season.

The coming dawn would bring that opening day. And now suddenly he was torn between wanting to go hunting with Marcellus and wanting to arrive at first light at the graveyard so he could personally supervise the crime scene investigation. At the same time, he knew Johnny Baillie would do as thorough a job as he himself.

Yet the thought that a fleeing killer had come face-to-face with his grandson gnawed and jerked at Bramlett's mind like a puppy playing with a rag. He wanted this man caught and caught quick. He wanted him locked up before the sun set. He wanted everybody in the department on it right now. It didn't matter that it was Saturday.

When the clock struck again, this time once, Bramlett knew it was three-thirty. He pulled himself up from the couch and turned on the end-table lamp. He took several deep breaths. His stomach felt like it was clawing its way up his chest like a cat claws its way up the side of a piece of furniture.

He went into the kitchen and put on a pot of coffee. Then he took the tackle box which contained his watercolor supplies and set it on the table. He had an hour before he ought to start the biscuits. He would paint. Perhaps a memory painting of a barn he'd done several times.

And then, at four-thirty, he would put away his painting gear and cook breakfast and wake up Marcellus to eat at five-thirty, and then the two of them would be in the woods a half hour before the sun came up, walking slowly through the sodden leaves. The air would be crisp and they would talk. Talk not about what happened yesterday, but other things, like basketball and soccer. Just the two of them.

The investigation would still be there later in the morning. Maybe by the time he got to the cemetery Johnny Baillie would already have the killer in custody. Anything was possible.

39

*　　*　　*

THE TELEPHONE HAD RUNG four times before Lizzie Clouse realized the sound was not merely a part of her dream. What time was it anyway? She reached for the lampswitch and put her feet on the floor.

She walked to the door. The phone had stopped ringing. Jo Ann had answered it. Lizzie shut her eyes tight and leaned against the doorjamb.

"What?" Jo Ann said, standing in the hallway beside the phone table. "Who is this?" Then, "Why now? It's not even six o'clock." A pause. "Of course you're upset. Where do you want to meet?" Another pause, then, "Why there? That's so far out . . ." She sighed. "Okay. Okay. I'll be right there." Then she hung up the receiver.

Lizzie opened her eyes. "What's wrong?"

Jo Ann shook her head hard and hurried back into her bedroom. "I have to go."

Lizzie followed her into the room. Jo Ann was jerking on a pair of jeans. "Why now? Who was that?"

Again, she shook her head. "I'd rather not say. I won't be gone long." She took a pullover sweater out of a drawer and looked at Lizzie. "This is a horrible thing. I wish I didn't know about it. I wish you didn't know anything about it, either."

"What are you talking about?"

Jo Ann shook her head and shoved one arm through a sleeve. "I can't say anything now. This is awful." Then she forced a smile. "Tell you what. I'll make pineapple pancakes when I get back, okay? We've still got some coconut syrup. Maybe we can talk then."

"Jo Ann, this is crazy. I'm going with you."

"*No,*" she said, pulling the sweater over her head. "I won't be gone an hour. Two at the most. Go back to bed."

And, grabbing her purse off the back of a chair, she ran out of the apartment, slamming the door behind her.

Lizzie stood staring at the closed door. Something was wrong. Something, she felt, was terribly wrong.

7

H. C. CURRY ARRIVED at the cemetery by dawn. The gray leaves of the pin oak at the edge of the embankment were turning red in the gathering light. Johnny Baillie and Jacob Robertson were already there.

Curry ducked under the yellow crime scene tape and walked to the edge of the bluff, giving a wide berth to the area where the car had gone over. Several deputies were hunched over, moving slowly through the kudzu, pulling aside the broad leaves and searching the ground. They wore clear plastic gloves.

Johnny Baillie stood at the top of the bank. He was, like Curry, of medium height. Both weighed the same 140 pounds that they had weighed when they played together on Sheffield High's basketball team ten years ago. Baillie wore his brown hair cut short, military fashion. He held himself very erect, almost as if he were standing at attention, or parade rest, at least.

Johnny Baillie and Jacob Robertson were the first white friends H. C. Curry ever had. Except for the sheriff and these two, Curry didn't feel particularly close to any white person.

Occasionally, his girlfriend Lizzie reminded him that perhaps he was using the term *friend* a bit generously to describe his relationship with his two fellow deputies. "After all," she said, "neither one has ever asked you home to supper, has he?"

And, more than once, she had reminded him, "Johnny Baillie's father was KKK. That's the way Johnny was brought up. You better never depend on him to protect your black backside."

Still, he felt they were his friends. He was especially close to Jacob. Jacob was one of those salt-of-the-earth kind of guys. One of Jacob's brothers worked with one of H. C.'s brothers at PeopLounger, a furniture outfit in Nettleton.

Curry surveyed the enclosed area of the crime scene.

Johnny Baillie held up a small cellophane bag. Curry noticed there was a certain twinkle in Baillie's pale-blue eyes. That twinkle was the only evidence Baillie gave that he was pleased about something.

"Twenty-five caliber casing," he said. "Found it up here." He nodded toward the edge of the bluff where the vehicles had been. "Got a decent tire track, but no footprints. Too many rocks and heavy vines on the ground."

One of the deputies near the tracks held up an empty whiskey bottle. "Want it?" he said.

"Yes," Baillie said. "What do I have to say? Every piece of litter, every beer can, cigarette butt, everything."

"Hey, I got a cigarette butt," another deputy said with a laugh. He held up a plastic bag. "Got lipstick on it."

Baillie grunted, then turned back to Curry. "We also found a set of keys over yonder." He nodded toward an area of thick weeds near the top of the bluff. "A couple of Toyota keys. Haven't tried them, but I'd bet next month's salary they fit."

Curry nodded and looked across the tracks where Robertson and three other deputies were wading in kudzu, hunched over the broad leaves. "Last night I talked with a woman who knew some things about him," he said. "It's not a pretty picture."

"I want to search his house," Baillie said. "Jacob can take care of this."

Curry nodded. He wasn't sure whether Baillie had heard him or not. Whenever the sheriff placed Baillie in charge of an operation, the young man was like a bulldog holding on to a bone. He was focused and single-minded and wouldn't let go. Curry knew from past experience that his friend would settle down in an hour or two. He would be able to hear then.

*   *   *

JESSE BONDREAUX'S RESIDENCE was an old shotgun house in east Sheffield, vintage 1920's. A large water oak shaded the narrow front porch. Unkempt azaleas crowded both sides of the house.

Johnny Baillie fumbled with the set of keys found at the crime scene, selected a likely one and started to insert it into the lock.

"What the hell . . . ?" he said. The door was ajar. He pushed, and it swung wide open. Plate-glass fragments lay on the floor of the doorway.

Curry grunted. "A new crime scene," he said.

The top half of the front door had four narrow windowpanes. The one closest to the lock had been shattered.

Baillie kneeled down for a closer look. There were four dark red spots on the hardwood. "Could be blood," he said, his tone leaving no room for doubt.

Both men stepped carefully over the glass fragments and moved into the front room. The cushions were carelessly thrown on the floor, the paintings on the walls were askew as if they had been looked behind, and the drawer of a small end table was hanging open.

They moved across the room to the doorway which led to the bedroom. "Damn," Curry said softly as he stepped into the room. "Looks like a tornado just left." Clothes were piled in the middle of the floor. The drawers of the chest of drawers were pulled out and empty of contents. The bed had been stripped, and the mattress pulled halfway off the box springs.

Baillie gave a low whistle. "You said you heard some things about this guy?"

"Not a very nice man," Curry said.

"Like how?"

"Like, how would you like it if you found out a thirty-year-old-plus man was messing around with your fifteen-year-old daughter?"

Baillie gave no reaction. His eyes surveyed the ransacked room again. Then he looked up.

"Beaded ceiling," he said. "You have any idea what that costs these days to put in a house?" Baillie was building a new home in west Sheffield.

43

The loud pop of a backfire caused both men to turn toward the doorway. There was the unmistakable rumble of a large motorcycle outside. Then, suddenly, silence.

"We need to report this break-in and get the area taped off," Baillie said, walking quickly toward the front door. Curry followed behind him, wondering if Baillie was trying to give him an order. The fact that Sheriff Bramlett had placed Baillie in charge of the cemetery crime scene didn't necessarily mean he'd been placed in charge of the whole investigation.

Curry sometimes wondered if Johnny Baillie was planning to run for sheriff when the old man retired. He was right behind Baillie as he stepped onto the front porch.

Standing in the driveway beside his Harley-Davidson low rider was Rabbit Murphey. He stood with his fingerless-gloved hands on his hips, his head tilted and his eyes squinted as he looked up at the two lawmen. Murphey's red hair twisted in thick, tight locks away from his skull in all directions.

"Where's your helmet, Rabbit?" H. C. Curry asked, stepping down off the porch.

Rabbit Murphey grinned. He was missing an eyetooth. "I keep telling y'all them things are dangerous," he said. "They obstruct vision."

Curry himself had stopped Murphey for not wearing a helmet too many times to count. He wasn't sure whether the city judge had ever levied a fine or not. In fact, he couldn't remember seeing Rabbit Murphey wearing a helmet on his motorcycle. Ever.

"What y'all doing here?" Rabbit asked.

"That's what I need to be asking you," Johnny Baillie said. He was still standing on the porch.

"What's going on? Where's Jesse?"

Curry and Baillie exchanged looks. Curry then said, "You haven't heard?"

Murphey's eyes grew wider. "What?"

"He died last night. We're treating it as a homicide."

Murphey let his hand fall from his sides. He whistled through his teeth, then said, "You serious?"

Curry nodded, his eyes studying Murphey's face, watching for evidence of lying or shock or both.

Murphey scowled. "In there? You mean, somebody killed him in there?" He nodded toward the house.

"No, not here," Baillie said. He stepped down to the ground quickly. His eyes were also glued to Murphey's face. "You a friend of his?"

Murphey threw one leg over his bike and sat back in the saddle. He shrugged. "Naw. Just had a few beers together. I gotta go to work."

Murphey thumbed the ignition switch, and the engine roared. He swept up the kickstand with his boot, and the motorcycle snapped forward. Rabbit Murphey and his machine were almost a block away before the noise of the Harley was faint enough for either deputy to be heard by the other.

Curry turned back to the house. "I know where to find him if we need him," he said. Rabbit lived with his mother in a small frame house near Martin's Crossing and worked at Wal-Mart.

Curry followed Baillie back into the house and into the bedroom. The room was long and narrow with plantation shutters covering the windows on one side. It was the only bedroom in the house.

Baillie kneeled down beside the bed and looked underneath. He reached and pulled out a gun case and two gun bags. "Can't believe our burglar missed these," he said, standing up. "Guns to be pawned are about as good as cash." He moved across the room.

On the floor in front of the rolltop desk were strewn papers, pens, and notebooks. Curry bent over and picked up a checkbook.

He turned the pages of the book, then said, "Gee damn!"

"What?" Baillie said. He was standing at the window holding back the curtain. The bright morning light flowed softly into the room.

"Sizable deposits. Not the kind of money schoolteachers make." He flipped a page of the bankbook. "Ten thousand dollars deposited on the fifteenth. Another ten thousand a week before that." He turned several more pages. "Five thousand. Seven. This guy had some big money rolling in from someplace."

Baillie frowned. "High school kids hanging around his house all the time . . ." He paused and nodded knowingly.

Curry shrugged and intoned I-don't-know. "But if he was into drugs, that could be what the break-in was all about."

Baillie made a face. "Maybe. But not an addict, I wouldn't think." He looked back at the guns.

Curry laid the checkbook on the desktop and walked to the lamp table beside the bed.

There was a cassette recorder beside the telephone. Attached to the receiver was an inexpensive recording unit. The unit's cord was plugged into the recorder.

The drawer of the lamp table was half open and inside was a jumbled pile of audio cassette tapes. He picked up one and looked at the label. "Nothing," he said. "No labels or dates or anything."

"Maybe he wasn't a neat guy," Baillie said.

"Our burglar wasn't interested in recordings of telephone conversations. Or, maybe he didn't know what this was." He shrugged and said, "Anyway, I'll take these and start eavesdropping." He lifted a handful of the tapes out of the drawer and stacked them neatly on the table.

Sticking out from the bottom of the table lamp was a Post-it note. Curry pulled it out and held it up. " 'Call Tidwell' and 'See Noel,' " he read out loud. He jotted down the names in his notebook. "Jo Ann Scales mentioned a Noel Hackott was a friend of Bondreaux's."

Baillie retrieved a torn photograph from the floor. The picture was taken in a restaurant. It was torn down the middle. The smiling face of Jesse Bondreaux looked up at Baillie. Bondreaux was Hollywood handsome. In the photograph his hand rested on the slim hand of a woman. The picture was torn away just above her wrist. He handed the photo to Curry.

Curry's brow knit, and he slowly shook his head.

"What is it?" Baillie said.

"Nothing. Just . . . just wondering . . ." He didn't want to say it, but what he was wondering was if the hand in the photo belonged to Lizzie's friend, Nena Carmack.

8

GROVER BRAMLETT AND MARCELLUS were back at the house by noon. They'd shot no squirrels. Marcellus had fired at a couple of rusty buckets they'd seen.

"Angie called just a few minutes ago," Valeria said as they walked into the house. Angie Burton was Valeria's second cousin. "She said Jimbo would be glad to take Marcellus down to the park after lunch to play basketball."

Bramlett nodded. Carius Park was a small city park with an outdoor basketball court, two tennis courts, and an assortment of slides and swings for small children. It was only a couple of blocks from the house.

"Jimbo's got his driver's license now," Valeria said. "I knew you were going to have to go back to work for a while."

"That'll be good," he said. He remembered seeing Jimbo playing for the high school junior varsity basketball team last season. He was a rangy kid, almost as tall as Bramlett. "I'll be back as soon as I can."

Oftentimes a case like this schoolteacher thing was wrapped up in a day or two. Sometimes only hours. Maybe this one would be one of those.

*   *   *

H. C. Curry and Johnny Baillie sat in the captains' chairs in front of the sheriff's desk. It was just after one o'clock. Bramlett leaned back in his swivel chair, propped both feet on a corner of the desk, one foot crossed over the other.

Curry related his late-night conversation with Jo Ann Scales. He read the names of the students that Jo Ann had given and then laid the list on the desk corner.

Bramlett dropped his feet to the floor. He ran his tongue around his gums. His face felt flushed, and he wondered if the two young men noticed. Sometimes his face did that quite unexpectedly, and he found it very annoying.

He picked up the list of names. "Check out Bondreaux with state narcotics. See if they got anything on him." He scanned the list, then looked at Baillie. "No word yet from the crime lab folks?"

"I just phoned," the deputy said. "They left Jackson around ten. Should be here any time now."

"What about the canvass of the neighbors?"

"Jacob is doing it right now. He's got three men on it."

The intercom on the desk buzzed. "Sheriff, the man from the railroad is here," Ella Mae said.

The two deputies followed Bramlett into the conference room. Will Vaughan, a rail-thin man with black shiny eyes and a nose that had obviously been broken more than once, half rose from one of the folding metal chairs at the table as the three lawmen shook his hand and introduced themselves. Vaughan was in his mid-forties, wore denim jeans and a khaki shirt, and was an engineer with Burlington Northern. The noon train returning from Birmingham had dropped him off in Sheffield at Sheriff Bramlett's request.

"Now," the sheriff said after all were seated, "tell us what you saw."

"It was just about five-thirty yesterday evening. We don't begin sounding the warning for the first Sheffield crossing till after we pass that section. But then I saw the car up by the tracks and a man by it, so I sat on my horn. I didn't know what had happened, whether it was wrecked or junked or what. It wasn't five or six feet off the tracks, looked like."

"Tell us about the man."

Vaughan shrugged. "He was old. Definitely sixty or seventy."

"White or black?"

"White."

"How was he dressed?"

Again Vaughan shrugged his shoulders. "Suit coat. No tie. More like a tramp, if you know what I mean."

"Did he have a weapon in his hand?"

Vaughan shook his head. "Naw. Not that I saw. He was just standing beside the car looking up at me."

"Could you identify the man if you saw him again?"

"Sure. I think so." His eyes suddenly widened. "Oh, yeah. He was wearing a baseball cap. Pittsburgh Pirates."

Bramlett chuckled, exchanged knowing looks with the two deputies, then said, "Gilly Bitzer. He's never without that cap."

He pushed himself up. "Thank you, Mr. Vaughan. I'll have someone drive you to Memphis." Both deputies stood quickly. Bramlett looked at Baillie and said, "Have Bitzer picked up."

Baillie nodded and hurried away. Bramlett walked toward his office with Curry following.

"Sheriff," Deputy Lawrence Gough called. At twenty-one Gough was the youngest of Bramlett's deputies. He looked like he was no more than fifteen. "Sheriff, the crime lab investigators are here."

Bramlett nodded. "I'll have Johnny Baillie take them out there," he said to Gough. Then he turned to Curry. "H. C., you and me are going to run down that principal. What's his name?"

"Lynwood Wilson."

LYNWOOD WILSON LIVED in one of the few newer homes on Martin Luther King Jr. Street in north Sheffield. On either side of Wilson's ranch-style brick house were small vinyl-sided cabins more typical of the neighborhood.

Before integration, Wilson had been a history teacher and assistant football coach at the black high school. After the merger of the two schools he was named assistant principal. Two years ago, the principal, a white man named Jud Longest, retired and the school board elevated Wilson to that position.

Wilson had a mustache which looked to Bramlett like a thin line drawn with an eyebrow pencil, and his graying hair had receded high above his forehead. His thick-lens glasses magnified his eyes, and he smiled continually if not sincerely.

He led Bramlett and Curry into the den and offered them seats on a caramel-colored sofa. Wilson himself sat down stiffly on a matching wing-back chair across from them. Bramlett noticed there were no pictures or paintings on the walls.

"Naturally, we're all in a state of shock," the principal said, still smiling. "Mr. Bondreaux was one of our finest teachers. He was selected Teacher of the Year two years." He said this without conviction, Bramlett noticed.

Wilson opened a file folder in his lap and thumbed through the pages. "I brought this home with me from the office last night after I went down to the school to look up his next of kin."

"How long had he been teaching at the high school?" Bramlett said.

"Four years. He came to us from New York."

Bramlett's eyebrows raised.

Wilson quickly continued. "But he's a native of Mississippi. From Iskitini. That's down South near Columbia."

"What about his family? Was he married?"

"The file says he was divorced. That would have been before he came here."

Bramlett nodded, thought on this for a moment, then said, "I understand he was quite well liked by the students. Some even used to hang out around his house."

Wilson blinked his eyes, looked at the wall somewhere behind and above Bramlett's head, then nodded. "Yes. Mr. Bondreaux was quite involved with students outside the classroom. He chaperoned dances, made out-of-town trips with the chorus and things like that."

"Do you know of anyone he may have been having a problem with? Anyone—maybe another teacher or a student—who Bondreaux had a conflict with?"

"No. Not that I know of."

Bramlett noticed the man's forehead was beginning to perspire. He was getting where the sheriff wanted him. "Do you think there's any possibility Bondreaux was involved with drugs?" Bramlett's eyes were fixed on the principal's face.

Wilson's eyes blinked more rapidly and he looked back at Bramlett. "Drugs?" His face revealed genuine surprise. "No . . . I would never have suspected that."

"Would you have suspected anything else about Mr. Bondreaux that would have been . . . *not good* for one of your teachers to be involved in?"

Wilson shook his head. "No . . . no, I wouldn't say anything like that." The principal's eyes were jerking all around the room.

Bramlett leaned back in his chair, folded his arms across his chest and looked hard at Wilson. Finally, he said, "With all these kids hanging around his place . . . there never was any suspicion about him and any of these teenage girls?"

Wilson's Adam's apple bobbed suddenly. He was perspiring heavily. "No. Anything like that which was substantiated would be here in the file." He held up the file folder. "Y'all can take this with you if you want."

Bramlett was silent for a long moment, letting the man sweat in the glare of his gaze. Finally, he said, "Thank you," and pushed himself up and nodded at Curry. "We'll give you a receipt."

The deputy stood also and reached for the folder.

"I'm sure we'll be talking with you again, Mr. Wilson," Bramlett said, putting on his hat and turning toward the front hallway.

THE AUTOMOBILE SLOWED to a quiet stop on the opposite side of the street from the basketball court at Carius Park. The driver's window slid down as the engine idled.

The driver watched the shorter of the two boys dribble quickly from the free throw line and make a lay-up against the backboard. The ball rolled around the rim without going through the net, then fell to one side, bouncing on the concrete. The taller boy grabbed the ball on the first bounce and passed it back to the younger boy.

He dribbled back to the free throw line, held the ball, and turned and glanced briefly in the direction of the car.

The window slid up, and the car began moving forward again and in moments was gone.

9

"NO EVIDENCE OF ANY NARCOTICS in the vehicle," Billy Astles said to Bramlett. Astles was the chief investigator with the state crime lab, a short, stocky man probably not yet forty. He was all-business, taciturn, and never smiled. He ignored any and all pleasantries, and went right to work at a crime scene. Bramlett wouldn't have cared much about spending an afternoon fishing with the man, but, as far as investigators went, there was none the sheriff respected more.

A wrecker had already lifted the automobile up onto the cemetery road. "The tire casts y'all made of the second auto look like a mid-size—could be domestic or import," Astles continued. "We'll let you know something right away."

Both of the vehicle's doors were wide open, and two investigators were inside taking fingerprints.

"I've sent an officer to the hospital to retrieve the victim's clothing," Astles continued. "You'll have a complete workup by the end of the week."

Bramlett grunted. "Trails get dead cold in a week. How about a couple of days?"

The chief investigator shrugged. "We'll see."

Bramlett knew he'd be lucky to get anything before Thursday.

Astles's men were probing through the kudzu as Bramlett's deputies had done that morning. They had found nothing new, a fact which pleased the sheriff.

Bramlett and Curry returned to headquarters. Johnny Baillie met them as they came in the door.

"Gilbert Armstrong is in the conference room," Baillie said. "He's the next of kin. Came up from Iskitini. I gave him a cup of coffee. He hasn't been here ten minutes."

"Found Gilly Bitzer yet?" said Bramlett.

"No, sir."

The two deputies followed Bramlett into the conference room where a lanky man with stringy blond hair stood staring out the window at the courthouse across the street. He turned as they entered the room and smiled shyly. His teeth were gray and his face severely acne scarred.

"I really didn't want the coffee," he said apologetically to Baillie, nodding toward the untouched Styrofoam cup on the table edge. "I never learned to like it."

"We appreciate you coming up, Mr. Armstrong," Bramlett said when they all were seated at the table. Curry placed a legal pad in front of himself.

Armstrong wiped his mouth with the back of his hand. "Hadn't seen Jesse in years. Didn't even know he was back from up North."

"You were listed in his file as next of kin," Bramlett said.

Armstrong nodded. His eyes were as pale as the faded denim shirt he was wearing. "We're first cousins. Our mamas were sisters. His mama, of course, is dead now going on ten years, I reckon. Actually, I guess my mama is as next of kin as I am. What comes first, a first cousin or an aunt?"

Bramlett gave a wry smile and said, "I guess it don't make no difference. You were the one he listed."

Armstrong shook his head. "Still can't believe it. Jesse dead. They tell me somebody shot him in the head."

Bramlett nodded. "I don't suppose you know if he was having a conflict with anybody or anything like that?"

"Hell, like I done told you, I ain't seen nothing of him hardly since he left Iskitini right after high school. Probably ain't seen him since he come back for his mama's funeral." He gave a snort. "After y'all called, the funeral parlor phoned to say that I needed to make the arrangements while I was here. Ain't ever done that before."

"He didn't have any brothers or sisters?"

"Naw. Just him. His daddy run off and left them when Jesse was real little. I don't remember him at all. I'm sure Jesse don't, either."

"I understand Jesse was married at one time."

"Yeah. Some girl he met up North. She come with him for his mama's funeral. Then I heard they got a divorce."

"You remember his wife's name?"

He shook his head. "No, sir. Maybe Mama does."

Bramlett nodded. "Do you know of anyone in your family who might have been in contact with him recently?"

"No, sir. Like I said, he never come home. At least, not after his first year in college, anyways. That first year he come home a lot. He was going to State, you see. And Tidwell was still in high school?"

"Who?" Bramlett said.

"Tidwell Dixon." Armstrong scratched behind one ear and smiled. "She was a honey. Miss Everything in high school. Most beautiful, homecoming queen, all that stuff. Anyways, after she graduated, she left Iskitini and never come back no more, either. Her folks are dead now, too, by the way. Rich as everything, they was. I sure thought Jesse ought to marry her. But . . ." He paused and shrugged his shoulders. "He didn't."

"What ever happened to this Tidwell Dixon?" Johnny Baillie asked.

Armstrong turned to look at the deputy. "She never come back, either, like I said. I ain't got no idea where she is now."

"Thank you, Mr. Armstrong." Bramlett, rose and extended his hand. "I know they're expecting you at the funeral home. We're deeply sorry about your cousin."

Johnny Baillie escorted Gilbert Armstrong out of the conference room. Curry said to Bramlett, "We found the name Tidwell at Bondreaux's house. It was on a note. Said, 'Call Tidwell.' "

Bramlett nodded and reached into his back pocket, then remembered, and patted its emptiness. He said, "Run a check on the name with DMV and the highway patrol and anything else you can think of. Also, see what you can find out about his former wife. Get a name from someplace. Armstrong's mother maybe."

Curry nodded and left.

Bramlett returned to his office, closed the venetian binds and sat down behind his desk. He opened the bottom right-hand drawer

54

and withdrew a sketch pad and a drawing pencil. There was a knock at his office door. Jacob Robertson stepped in. "We finished the neighborhood canvass," he said.

"And?" Bramlett said. He slipped the sketch book back into the drawer.

"We talked to everyone on his block on both sides of the street. The only one we haven't talked with is the next-door neighbor on the east side. Someone said they're out of town for the weekend." He looked down at his notes. "Clarence Rawls, who lives across the street, saw Bondreaux leave in his car about five o'clock. Hazeline Klein, who lives two doors down, saw a dark-blue compact-size auto parked in Bondreaux's driveway about three forty-five. She was driving home from work."

Bramlett caught his breath, then said, "Blue compact?"

Robertson looked momentarily surprised, not expecting the interruption. "Yes, sir," he said. "Anyway, Doris Webster—she lives across the street down a door—noticed a light on in the house about ten o'clock last night. She was walking her dog. There was a car in the driveway. She doesn't have any idea what kind it was. The light was off and the car was gone when she came back from a walk around the block." He paused and looked up at the sheriff.

Bramlett nodded and scratched his chin. "That helps put a time on the break-in."

Robertson closed his notebook. "Anything else?"

"I want you to go over that house of Bondreaux's. Curry and Baillie have been through it, but they don't know construction like you do. Take Baillie and check it out again."

"What am I looking for?"

"Someplace somebody could hide whatever whoever broke in was looking for."

"Any idea what that might be?"

"Something somebody would kill to get his hands on."

"Yes, sir."

Bramlett grunted and waved his hand, dismissing the deputy. Then he pulled open the drawer again.

H. C. CURRY DREW A BLANK in checking out the name Tidwell Dixon. He then left headquarters and drove the seven blocks to the red-brick twenty-unit apartment complex in which Lizzie lived. There were ten apartments on the first floor and ten on the second. The front door of each unit opened onto a long concrete gallery.

Curry had been dating Lizzie more than three years now. They had gone together for a few months in high school, then went their separate ways after Lizzie left for Ole Miss.

Like Curry, she'd grown up on a farm. Her mother, Naresse, was murdered three years ago. It was during the investigation of her death that Curry and Lizzie started seeing each other again.

They had talked at times about marriage, but then backed off. The problem was mainly on Lizzie's side. She said she still had a lot of things to work through concerning her mother's death. He told her he could wait a little while but not forever.

Last night he and Lizzie had talked about getting Jacob and Nena together again, and now he wanted to tell her he'd talked with Jacob about the four of them going out to eat fish tonight. Lizzie now needed to phone Nena.

Lizzie jerked the door open to his knock. "I was just going to call you," she said, backing up to give him room to enter.

He noticed the anxious look in her eyes. "What's wrong?" he asked, quickly closing the door behind him.

"It's Jo Ann. She left before dawn—there was a phone call—and she was upset. But she said she'd only be gone an hour or so. She should have been back by eight o'clock. It's already past three." Both of her hands were clinched into fists.

Curry put his arm around her shoulders and led her to the sofa. They sat down together. "Now, calm down. Maybe she went home or something." Jo Ann was from Fulton.

Lizzie shook her head and hit the top of her legs with her fists. "No," she said. "I just talked with her mother. She said Jo Ann wasn't coming home this weekend." Her eyes were intense, wide. "Something is wrong, H. C. I *know* it."

He pulled her firmly against his chest. "I'm sure she's all right," he said gently. "I'll check with the highway patrol. Maybe she just went to the mall at Tupelo or something. We'll find her."

Lizzie whimpered softly, and Curry wondered what all Jo Ann Scales knew about Jesse Bondreaux that she'd not told him last night.

10

SHERIFF BRAMLETT LEANED out of his office door and spoke to his secretary, Ella Mae Shackleford. "Where's Curry?" he asked.

Ella Mae looked up at him over her reading glasses. Her fingers paused for a moment on the keyboard of the computer. "Haven't seen him," she said, smiling. Ella Mae always smiled when she answered a question. She was a widow, in her mid-fifties, and had two grown sons. Bramlett often said he'd shoot anybody in town who hired Ella Mae away from him.

Bramlett grunted and returned to his desk. No sooner had he sat down than Ella Mae buzzed him on the intercom. "Sheriff, Mr. Noel Hackott would like to see you."

"SIT," SAID BRAMLETT to Noel Hackott with a wave of his hand. The man was in his mid-thirties, balding, with a pug nose and double chin. Bramlett had known his parents. His father had been a dentist. They all went to church together. Hackott still attended and sang in the choir. Just like Bondreaux had. Just like his wife Valeria did. And, he recalled, Hackott drove a red BMW.

"Sheriff, I was a close friend of Jesse Bondreaux. Naturally, I'm quite distressed at what has happened." He paused and wiped the sweat under his nose with an index finger. "I can't imagine who'd do such a thing."

"Neither can we, Noel. Is there anything you can tell us about all this?"

The man shook his head and shuddered in the same motion. He appeared to be very agitated. "No, no. I just wondered if you knew anything yet."

Bramlett pursed his lips, made no immediate response, then, in a moment, said, "And just what was your association with Jesse Bondreaux?"

"Just good friends. That's all." He put his hand to the side of his face. "I would be happy to help sort out his personal belongings at the house if you would like."

Bramlett raised one eyebrow. "Really? Well, that's very considerate of you. Are you related to Mr. Bondreaux?"

"Oh, no. Like I said. Just friends."

Bramlett nodded and smiled. "I'm sure the family would want to take care of his stuff. You understand."

Hackott cleared his throat. "Jesse . . . had some videos of mine. I would like them back."

"Videos? What kind of videos?"

Hackott shrugged. "Just old videos."

Bramlett smiled and said nothing for a long time. His gaze did not move away from the man's face. Finally, he stood and said, "All in due time, Noel. All in due time." He held his smile. "I do appreciate you coming in. Would you please leave your phone number with my secretary? Then I can contact you if I need to."

He took the man by the elbow and escorted him to the door. Hackott blinked his eyes rapidly and stood staring at the sheriff.

Bramlett backed quickly into his office and closed the door.

"I SENT BAILLIE AND ROBERTSON BACK to Bondreaux's house," Sheriff Bramlett told Curry when the deputy returned to headquarters. "Robertson used to do carpentry work during the summers when he was in high school. He knows houses. If there's dope or anything stashed away somewhere in there, he'll find it." He nodded thoughtfully, then added, "And you and me are going to follow up on some of the kids Jo Ann Scales mentioned to you."

THE HOME OF THE DR. ROBERT TOPP FAMILY was in the wealthiest neighborhood in Sheffield. The house was built with stone quarried in nearby Tishomingo County. The towers on the corners of the second floor reminded Bramlett of a castle. He'd known the Topp family for years.

Robert Topp was a surgeon. He and his wife Katherine had met while they were both students at the University of Mississippi. They married before he went to med school, and Katherine often laughingly referred to the fact that she put Robert through school waiting tables in Jackson.

Robert had grown up in Sheffield, where his father was a druggist. Bramlett vaguely remembered Robert as a stoop-shouldered high school student wearing thick, horn-rimmed eyeglasses who was planning to enter the ministry, but later, while in college, changed to premed.

Katherine was from Houston, and returned home frequently to visit her parents and go shopping. She was president of the hospital auxiliary, a leader in the Junior League, and heavily involved with several charitable organizations. She and Valeria often did church work together.

The Topps had three children—two younger daughters and Gail, a high school student mentioned by Jo Ann Scales as a frequent visitor at Jesse Bondreaux's house.

Robert Topp answered the front door. He was wearing a blue-and-red jogging suit and his eyes blinked rapidly as he looked at the two men. He was of medium height, a bit overweight, and wore an expression of confusion in his eyes.

After the sheriff introduced Curry, he said, "We've come to talk to Gail."

"What?" The confusion in the man's eyes deepened.

"May we come in?" Bramlett said, stepping forward.

Topp retreated, allowing the two lawmen to enter. "Yes . . . of course," he said. "Excuse me . . ." He turned and quickly walked down the hallway and turned through a cased door opening.

The walls of the hallway were painted off-white and hung with large abstract paintings.

Curry whistled softly. "You mean just one family lives here?"

Bramlett smiled. "The rich get richer . . ." His voice trailed off.

A moment later, Katherine Topp appeared with her husband trailing behind her. He was nervously patting his thinning hair.

"Why, Grover," Katherine said. "What a delightful surprise."

She was tall and thin and held a cigarette chest high in one hand. Her smile was as pretty as ever, but Bramlett could see the concern in her eyes.

He introduced Curry, then said, "We came to talk to Gail. We're investigating the murder of Jesse Bondreaux, and we're talking with several students. We were told she used to visit his house occasionally."

Katherine took a long draw on her cigarette, exhaled through her nose and mouth, then said, "I think you must have her confused with someone else."

"Is she home?"

"What's going on?" Robert asked.

Katherine smiled at him. "It's just a routine thing, isn't it, Grover?" She gave her husband's arm a squeeze of assurance. Then, without waiting for a reply from Bramlett, she continued. "Why don't you go ahead with your jogging, dear. Isn't Tom waiting for you at his house? Go on. I can handle this." She winked at Bramlett and gave Robert a gentle push on the shoulder.

"Grover, you and Mr. Curry go on into the den. I'll get Gail. She's upstairs in her room."

Robert hadn't moved. "I think she's gone back to sleep," he said to Katherine.

Katherine smiled at Bramlett. "You know how teenagers are. They can't get too much sleep. Out late and all that." Then she looked back at Robert. "Go on now," she said. Her smile was gone and her tone firm.

With a slight tilt of his head Bramlett indicated for Curry to come with him. They entered a wide room with a high ceiling. The walls were paneled with knotted pine.

There were several groupings of couches, easy chairs were positioned about the room, and clusters of family photographs were on each of the walls. The two men stood looking through the sliding-glass doors at the large swimming pool beyond the patio until Katherine Topp appeared a few minutes later with a bleary-eyed teenager in tow.

Gail Topp was a plain-looking young woman, several inches shorter than her mother, and wore faded jeans and a pale-yellow sweatshirt. She frowned and squinted her eyes as her mother said, "You know Sheriff Bramlett. And this is Deputy Corey."

"Curry," Bramlett corrected.

Katherine smiled. "Let's all sit down here, shall we?" She patted the back of a easy chair near the fireplace. The mantel of the fireplace was white marble, and arranged before it were two couches facing each other and the chair behind which stood Katherine.

Katherine and Gail sat down together on one couch and Curry sat on the other one. Bramlett took the chair in between. He leaned forward slightly, tried to look pleasant, and said, "Gail, your name was given to us as one of the students who used to visit Jesse Bondreaux's house." He paused, watching her expression. There was an immediate tenseness in her face. He continued. "Did you go there often?"

She shrugged. "I don't know why anyone would have given my name. I only went a couple of times with Vicki Ann Skelton."

"Did Vicki Ann go often?"

Gail shook her head. "I guess. Well, I don't know, really."

"What did y'all do there?"

She shrugged again. "Talked and listened to tapes."

"Tapes of what?"

"Music."

"What did you talk about?"

Again she shrugged, then yawned. "About who was dating who. Stuff like that." She made a face. "It wasn't very interesting."

Bramlett noticed Katherine's mouth was set tight as she watched her daughter. He looked again at the girl and asked, "Do you have any idea who would want to harm Mr. Bondreaux?"

"No, sir."

"Did he have a problem with anyone while you were around him?"

She shook her head. "No, sir. Like, I said, I really didn't go there but a couple of times."

"Who was there when you were there?"

"Just Vicki Ann and Cora Hartley. One time it was just me and Vicki Ann."

"Did you ever see any adults there?"

"No, sir."

"We have reason to believe some girls may have been very close to Mr. Bondreaux. Could you give me their names."

Katherine Topp frowned and looked hard at Bramlett. She opened her mouth as if to speak, but said nothing.

Gail cut her eyes to her mother, then looked back at Bramlett. No sooner did their eyes meet than she quickly looked away. "I'm not sure," she said, now looking at the wall.

"What about Vicki Ann?"

She swallowed hard and made another quick head shake. "Maybe. No. I don't know, really."

Bramlett's eyes focused on the girl's face. "Gail, we think Mr. Bondreaux may have been *very* friendly with some of the girls. Do you know anything about that?"

"What are you trying to say, Grover?" Katherine asked.

Bramlett ignored her, still watching the girl's face. He pressed, "Do you know anything about that?"

Gail Topp chewed on the side of her mouth. Her face began to pale. "I don't know anything about that," she said softly.

"Did you ever see him with his hands on a girl?"

Katherine put her fingers to her mouth. She was staring with concerned eyes at her daughter.

Gail was still looking at the wall. She shook her head slowly and spoke hardly above a whisper. "No."

"Did he ever try to put his hands on you?"

"No." Her face was very pale now.

"Really, Grover," Katherine said, looking back at him.

Bramlett grunted. "Okay," he said. "I think that will do for now, Gail. If something comes to mind, phone me. Okay?"

She nodded and looked down at her hands.

Katherine Topp slid closer to her daughter and put her arms around her and hugged firmly, then released her.

Curry and Bramlett rose to their feet. Katherine stood also and led them to the front door.

Bramlett paused in front of the door and turned back to her. "At the game you said you wanted to talk to me about something," he said.

She closed her eyes and slowly shook her head. "It can wait," she said. "It's nothing. Really."

As the two lawmen walked back to the patrol car, the sheriff asked, "Well? Was she telling the truth?"

Curry gave a low snort. "Maybe. At least in what she said. But I think she knows a lot more than she's saying."

"I think you're right," Bramlett said, reaching for the car door handle. "I do smell chicken crap."

THE HOME OF THE SKELTON FAMILY was only a block down the street from the Topps. As Curry drove, Bramlett thought of how the Skeltons had intertwined with his own family over the years. His wife Valeria and Rumi Skelton were close friends. When it was announced that Rumi's daughter Vicki Ann had been chosen homecoming queen, Valeria was as excited as if it had been her own daughter.

Bramlett remembered when Rumi moved to Sheffield. Vicki Ann was quite young, had not even started school yet.

"That poor child," Valeria had said, referring not to the child but to the mother. "Not even twenty-five years old and a widow already."

Valeria took the young widow under her wing. They became fast friends in spite of the age difference. Valeria helped her find child care for Vicki Ann, introduced her around to folks at the church, and talked to Howard Skelton, Sr., president of the Merchants' and Farmers' Bank in Sheffield about finding a place for Rumi.

Rumi did get a job at the bank, and two years later she married Howard Skelton, Jr., son of the bank president. The wedding, though small, was a very nice affair. Valeria had been in charge of the arrangements.

It had now been over fifteen years since Rumi and her daughter had moved to town. She and Valeria were perhaps not as close as they once were, yet they remained good friends. Only last month, Rumi had gone with Valeria and Katherine Topp over to the Delta to visit Valeria's sister Sissy in Cluster, a tiny town near Greenwood.

Howard Skelton, Rumi's husband, was not one of Bramlett's favorite people. The Good Book said men were to earn their bread by the sweat of the brow, and Bramlett didn't think Howard Skelton had ever broken a sweat in life at anything, except maybe tennis. He became president of the bank a few years ago after his father died.

Curry wheeled the patrol car along the curving, tree-shaded brick driveway and parked in front of the columned two-story house. Off to one side was a four-car garage. A Cadillac and a Mercedes were parked in front of the garage.

Howard Skelton opened the front door. He grinned and looked surprised at the same time. "Grover!" he said, extending his hand. "I didn't know you worked on Saturdays."

"Hello, Howard." Bramlett took the offered hand. "You know Deputy Curry?"

Howard Skelton shook Curry's hand strongly and invited the two lawmen inside. They followed him along the glossy hardwood-floored hallway to a large sitting room with two double French doors which opened onto a wide patio. A kidney bean-shaped pool was beyond.

"Sit. Sit," Skelton said. "Can I get you something to drink? Coke? Iced tea?"

Bramlett eased himself down into a leather armchair and shook his head. Curry sat in a matching chair while Skelton sank into the pink floral-patterned sofa. In front of the sofa was a cocktail table on which was a huge book of Andrew Wyeth's watercolors. Bramlett resisted the urge to open the book. He looked at Howard Skelton and told himself to smile.

"So," Skelton said. "What can I do for you?"

"We were mighty proud of Vicki Ann being homecoming queen," said Bramlett, crossing one leg over the other. "Curry's niece . . ." he paused and nodded at the deputy, then continued, "was the other queen."

"Is that so?" Skelton said, smiling stiffly. "She certainly is a beautiful young woman."

"Thank you," Curry said, beaming.

"We wanted to talk to Vicki Ann," said Bramlett.

Skelton's smile faded and his brow furrowed. "Why? What's wrong?"

"Is she here?"

"As a matter of fact, she's not. She and Rumi went to Memphis this morning to do some shopping. I don't expect them back till this evening. What's wrong?"

"It's about this teacher who was killed yesterday."

Skelton nodded slowly. "Horrible thing." His face showed concern.

"Vicki Ann's name was given to us as one of several students who used to visit his place occasionally and—"

"She hasn't been there in a long time. We put a stop to that."

Bramlett turned his good ear slightly toward Skelton. "Why?"

"Didn't think it looked right. I even talked to the principal about it. Teachers don't have any business having children over to their houses after school."

Bramlett shifted in his chair, keeping his eyes on the man's face. He noticed a slight tightening of the jaw, and the ears were turning white. "And what did Mr. Wilson say?"

"He said he'd talk with Bondreaux about it. I don't know if he did or not." The tightening of his jaw was more noticeable.

"I know this has been hard on all the students. How is Vicki Ann taking it?"

"She's fine," Skelton said. A flush of redness was rising up his neck, contrasting with his white ears.

Bramlett gave a smile. "Good."

"Of course, she's a very sensitive girl. The news was distressing to everyone. I don't think she's ever known anyone who was killed—murdered—before."

Bramlett nodded, his eyes still on Skelton's eyes. Then he asked, "And what time do you think Vicki Ann will be back?"

Skelton stood abruptly. "I can't imagine anything she could tell you about that man. I'm sure there are other students who knew him much better." His tone was agitated.

Bramlett rose to his feet. Curry immediately stood also. Bramlett's eyes were leveled at Skelton's eyes. "We'd just like a few words with her." He said it slowly and firmly.

Skelton walked toward the hallway, obviously expecting them to follow. They did. "I don't know what she could tell you," he said. There was a hardness to his voice. "I don't think there's any need upsetting her more than this thing already has."

"Appreciate your time, Howard," said Bramlett, putting on his hat at the doorway. Skelton shut the door quickly behind them as they stepped onto the porch.

ROZELLE KAMPLE WAS ALSO ONE OF THE NAMES Jo Ann Scales had mentioned. H. C. Curry and Sheriff Bramlett sat in the living room of her home in west Sheffield. It was a neighborhood of working-class families on the other side of town from that of the Topps and Skeltons.

Rozelle's mother, puffing on a cigarette and avoiding Bramlett's eyes, sat on the arm of a recliner. She was a thin, angular woman, with a look of hardness in her face.

Rozelle held her face in her hands, moaning softly, with her legs curled up under her on the couch. Her brown hair fell in tangles about her face.

"Is this necessary?" Mrs. Kample said. There was a sharpness to her voice. She still didn't look directly at Bramlett.

Bramlett tried to smile reassuringly, consciously attempting to imitate the warm, comforting smile he remembered seeing on his beloved grandfather's face fifty years before. He loved his grandfather's smile.

"Yes, ma'am," he said. "Like I said, we're talking with all the students at the high school who seemed to know Mr. Bondreaux well. I understand you . . ." He paused and turned his face with its grandfatherly smile toward the girl. "I understand you were a special friend of Mr. Bondreaux."

She lowered her hands, and her shoulders shivered. She certainly couldn't be described as pretty. She was, as some were prone to say, full figured. On a sixteen or seventeen-year-old that looked fine. Yet, Bramlett imagined, in ten years or so this girl would have a serious weight problem. He liked her at once.

"He . . . he was the *best* teacher I ever had," she said. "He cared . . . I can't believe he's gone!"

"We were told you were one of several students who used to visit his house after school," Bramlett said. "Could you tell us who else used to go there?"

Curry opened his notebook onto his knee.

The girl mentioned the same names Jo Ann had given. "These are the ones who still come ..." she said. "There've been others. But some don't come anymore."

Bramlett's brow knit. "And ... just what did y'all do at Mr. Bondreaux's?"

Rozelle looked up at him, confusion in her eyes. "Do? What do you mean?"

"Yes!" the mother said, now looking at him. "Just what *do* you mean?"

Bramlett tried to make his smile even more disarming and trust-evoking. "Well, when I was in high school the last thing any of us would ever have wanted to do was visit a teacher's house after school."

The girl stared at him uncomprehendingly. "We just ... just talked. You know ... listened to music and stuff like that."

"What did y'all talk about?"

"Mr. Bondreaux treated us like ... well, not like we were children, you know."

Bramlett nodded as if he understood. "You mean he treated you like you were an adult."

She nodded and looked down at her hands.

He continued. "How did he do that? I mean, treat you like adults?"

She looked up at him briefly, then back at her hands before answering. "I mean he wasn't always on our backs about this and that. You know. He would listen to you when you talked."

"You said some students stopped coming around. Could you give me their names?"

She wiped the sides of her face with her hands. "Bill Mosley for one. He and Mr. Bondreaux ... had a blowout one day. Mr. Bondreaux told him he wasn't welcome there anymore."

"What was it about?"

She shook her head, then said, "I think it had to do with a test Billy took in Mr. Bondreaux's class. He'd failed it."

"Who else used to go over to his house?"

She shook her head. "I don't remember."

Bramlett didn't speak for a while, studying the girl's face. Finally, he said, "I'm told some of the girls who were going to Bondreaux's house had been intimate with him."

The girl blinked her eyes and looked up at him. Her lips parted slightly.

"How dare you!" her mother said, popping up to her feet.

"I'm only asking—"

"Get out of here! I'm calling an attorney." She stepped directly in front of Bramlett.

He held up a hand as if expecting her to strike him, and, at the same time, rose to his feet.

He nodded at Curry. The deputy was at once out of his chair and following the sheriff out the door.

JACOB ROBERTSON SLID the wire coat hangers along the bar in the closet one by one. He meticulously went through the pockets of every coat. Johnny Baillie was taking all the books—hundreds of books, more books than either of them had ever seen anywhere except in the library—down from the shelves in the front room and piling them on the floor. "Maybe there's a secret pocket in one of these," he said before he started pulling the books down.

Bondreaux owned more dress suits than Robertson had any idea a person might have. There were at least ten in this closet—and several others, probably older ones, in the closet in the front room. And neckties. There must be thirty or forty neckties on this rack, he figured—and not a single one a clip-on.

What tie am I going to wear tonight? The same one I wore last night? Or should I stop by Wal-Mart and get a new one?

He thought about Jesse Bondreaux, the man who owned all these neckties. This man used to date Nena Carmack. *And I can't even tie a tie!*

He slid the last coat-hangered suit across the bar, then peered closely at the walls of the closet. Beaded board. In a closet! They don't build houses with this anymore.

On the rear wall of the closet was the electrical switch box. He opened the gray metal door. All twenty amp fuses. Wiring probably would be sub-code today.

He started to close the door. His hand suddenly froze. Switch box? Wasn't there one in the kitchen?

He hurried out of the bedroom and strode into the kitchen, his boots echoing on the hardwood floor.

"What is it?" Baillie called from the front room.

Robertson looked at the switch box located in the middle of the rear wall. He snatched open the back door and leaned out, looking down the side of the house. An electric meter was attached to the clapboard siding on the exact opposite side of the wall from the switch box. He pulled the door shut.

Baillie came into the kitchen. "Find something?" he said.

"Got a screwdriver?" Robertson asked, brushing past him and striding back to the bedroom.

"Screwdriver? What for?"

"Never mind." Robertson took his Swiss Army knife out of his pocket, folded out the stub-bladed Phillips screwdriver and began taking the holding screws out of the face of the switch box.

"Two switch boxes," he said. "The other one's got the meter." He dropped the last screw into his cupped hand and poured them onto the top of the chest of drawers next to the closet. "These screws weren't tight. Hardly holding."

He pulled the entire box from the wall and, grinning, turned around holding the back side toward Baillie. Baillie looked puzzled, uncomprehending.

"No wiring," Robertson said, setting the switch box on the floor.

He took his flashlight out of his back pocket and stepped into the closet. Baillie waited silently. In a moment, Robertson backed out of the closet, turned around and tilted his head toward the gaping opening where the box had been. He handed Baillie the flashlight. "Take a look," he said.

Baillie peered down into the opening. There was a shallow shelf. On the shelf were five small plastic bags.

70

12

IT WAS ALMOST SUPPERTIME. Sheriff Grover Bramlett hunched forward on his desk, one hand on each side of the blotter, staring down at the five small plastic bags of cocaine. Deputies Baillie, Robertson, and Curry sat in the chairs in front of the desk waiting for him to speak.

Bramlett leaned back in his swivel chair, pulled thoughtfully on one ear, then said, "Seems simple enough. Drugs, high school kids hanging around his place, money in the bank . . ."

He paused and shook his head. Several of the names Jo Ann Scales had given were children from families he knew. The Topps, Skeltons, and Conlees were members of his church.

He continued. "But things that seem simple seldom are. If the man was doing business with other people—outsiders—he could have gotten crossways with them on something. Could even be a professional hit."

Johnny Baillie frowned and shook his head. "Pushing Bondreaux's car off that cliff . . . ? Doesn't seem very professional."

Bramlett nodded his head slowly. "There's something else twisted in here. I don't have any idea what it is, but I just . . ." He paused and drew a deep breath, held it a second, then exhaled. "There's got to be more physical evidence that we don't have yet."

"We searched the house twice," Curry said.

Bramlett gave a low snort and looked hard at the deputy. "What about the crawl space under the house? Y'all been under there?"

None of the three answered.

"Then do it," Bramlett commanded. "Now."

Curry scowled. "It's almost dark," he said, jutting his jaw slightly. "Be easier to check it tomorrow during daylight."

The sheriff glared at the deputy for a moment before he spoke. "You got plans for tonight, I reckon."

Curry nodded.

"Okay. But I want that crawl space checked tomorrow."

He then spun his chair around and faced the window, waiting for them to leave. He heard the deputies rising out of their chairs and moving out the door. Things were never simple, he reflected. Especially rotten things.

AN HOUR LATER, Jacob Robertson parked his pickup in the red dirt front yard beside H. C. Curry's Toyota. Curry was sitting in a ladder-back chair on the front porch of the unpainted, tin-roofed house. Robertson noticed Curry wasn't wearing a tie at all.

"No young man calls on a young lady unless he's wearing a tie," his mother had told him at the house when he was getting dressed. He hadn't had time to stop at Wal-Mart and he hated to wear the same tie he'd worn last night, but he buttoned his collar and clipped the tie in place.

Now, seeing Curry tieless and wearing a denim jacket as he stepped off the porch and walked toward his truck, he yanked off the tie, stuffed it between the seat cushions and opened the cab door.

"We'll go in my car," Curry said. "Unbutton your collar."

SWANDLE'S CATFISH HOUSE was a short drive over a graveled road from the state highway just under five miles into Etowah County. Nena Carmack, Lizzie Clouse, Curry, and Robertson weaved single-file through the standing, waiting-for-tables customers when "Party of four, Curry" was called out by the orangish-haired plump woman in tight-fitting white jeans and a red-and-white checkered western shirt. Swandle's was always crowded on Saturday nights.

Waitresses with sizzling platters of fried catfish, hushpuppies, and French fries rushed from kitchen to tables, and perspiring busboys hurried to tables as soon as finished customers rose, clattered plates, large plastic iced tea glasses, and mangled fish skeletons into large carrying bins, and whisked damp sponges over the plastic red-and-white checkered tablecloths, and set out clean utensils and paper napkins.

A gaunt-cheeked waitress with what appeared to be a genuine smile came to their table and took their orders.

Curry squeezed Lizzie's hand hard, trying to reassure her. Jo Ann still wasn't home yet when he and Jacob went to get Lizzie.

He noticed the bandage on the back of Nena's hand. "What happened to your hand?" he asked.

"Oh, it's nothing," she said with a shake of her head. "I was cleaning under the bathroom sink this morning and cut it on some of the plumbing. It's fine. Really." She shook her head and smiled. "This has been a week when everything has gone wrong. My car is in the shop and I had to borrow my father's. And then . . ." She paused, then shook her head indicated she wasn't going to say more.

He nodded and looked over at Lizzie. Her eyes were shut tight, and she had her fingers pressed into her forehead. "You okay?" he asked.

"I'm sorry. I can't even think straight. I'm sick with worry about Jo Ann."

"Has she ever left without telling you?" Nena asked.

Lizzie shook her head. "This thing with Jesse Bondreaux has really upset her."

Curry noticed how quickly Jacob Robertson's jaw clamped hard when Bondreaux's name was mentioned, and he knew what his friend was thinking—the same thing he was thinking. What, exactly, had been the relationship between Jesse Bondreaux and Nena Carmack?

Curry then looked at Nena. Her eyes were fixed, staring into space. And there was a savagery in her eyes unlike anything he'd ever seen. And she was very pale.

WHEN THEY FINISHED EATING, Lizzie said she wanted to go home, that she needed to be there in case Jo Ann phoned. A few minutes later, H. C. pulled into the parking lot in front of the apartment building.

"I don't see her car," Lizzie said, quickly scanning the rows of vehicles. "She's not back."

Nena leaned forward from the backseat and placed her hand on Lizzie's shoulder and squeezed. "You want me to come in and stay with you?"

"I'll be okay," she said, opening her door.

"Wait," Curry called out. "I'll walk up with you."

"No. Just come back."

He drove hurriedly to Nena's cottage and waited in the car while Robertson saw her to the door. Then he returned to his own house, where Robertson had left his truck, dropped him off, then sped back to Lizzie's.

"There're no messages on the answering machine," Lizzie said as soon as he walked through the door. "Nothing."

"Did you call her folks again?"

"Her mother just phoned. She has no idea where she could be. She's very upset."

Curry telephoned headquarters. Still no sightings of her car and no word from MHP.

"I can't just sit here," Lizzie said. "Let's ride around."

Curry frowned. "Where to?"

"Let's go," said Lizzie, moving quickly toward the front door.

THEY RODE AROUND TOWN, moving in and out among the thick Saturday-night traffic, driving to the city limits on each main street. After almost forty-five minutes, they returned to the apartment.

Curry stretched out on the sofa in front of the television, resting his head in Lizzie's lap. He flicked the remote control until he found an old James Bond movie. He turned the volume so low that it was hardly audible.

"You know what this does to me?" she said. "It opens up all that horrible stuff about Mama."

Then she told him again as she had a couple of times before about the pain of her mother's murder. "Some people still think Daddy killed her," she said. "I think Sheriff Bramlett does."

"He hasn't said anything about it for a long time. I don't know what he thinks." He was lying. He knew the sheriff suspected Patterson Clouse.

She talked of how she had met Jo Ann Scales when both were first-year teachers at the high school, how they became friends and decided to share an apartment.

"*Who* did she go off to meet?" Lizzie said. Anger sizzled in her voice.

H. C. struggled to keep his eyes open. It had been a long day. A very long day.

SUNDAY MORNING H. C. Curry groaned and opened his eyes only to narrow slits. He could hear Lizzie moving around in the kitchen.

He sat up slowly on the sofa and put his feet on the floor. Lack of sleep squeezed the sides of his head like a vise.

Sometime during the night, he awoke in the darkness for a moment and realized he was stretched out on the sofa with a blanket over him. No doubt Lizzie had covered him up before turning off the lights and going to her bedroom. Then he'd slipped below the surface of sleep again.

The slanting light of the rising sun flowed softly into the room. He stood up, scratched his head and walked toward the kitchen. He was in his sockfeet. Lizzie must have taken off his shoes after he fell asleep.

" 'Morning," he said looking through the doorway. She was plugging in the coffee maker.

She turned to him. Her hair was knappy and her eyes had a wildness to them. "She's dead," she said to him. "I just know it."

Curry hurried to her and took her in his arms. He opened his mouth to tell her she was crazy, but nothing would come out. Nothing at all.

GROVER BRAMLETT TIED MARCELLUS'S NECKTIE and told the boy how much he would enjoy their pastor, referring to Dr. David William. "He was a great pitcher in college. Not a bad preacher, either."

He apologized again to Valeria for not going to church with them. "The colder the trail gets, the more likely he'd get away," he said, stepping out the back door. "Chicken crap dries fast." He kissed her on top of the head. "But I'll come back and pick you up for the funeral."

Valeria felt she ought to go since she and Bondreaux were in the choir together. Bramlett wanted to go just to see who all was there.

She'd also made arrangements for Marcellus to go over to Jimbo Burton's house after lunch. The Burtons lived on a farm and kept horses. "Jimbo said they could ride some," she said.

At headquarters, Bramlett asked about Gilly Bitzer, the Pittsburgh Pirates cap-wearing vagrant who was seen standing next to Jesse Bondreaux's car beside the railroad tracks. No, the dispatcher told him. No one had seen him yet.

Bramlett nodded. Why couldn't things be more simple? Why did everything have to be as tangled as the backlash on a fishing reel? He went into his office and sat down in the swivel chair.

Immediately, H. C. Curry entered and stood in front of the desk. His eyes were puffy.

Bramlett chuckled. "You look like hell," he said.

"Didn't get much sleep. Lizzie's roommate, Jo Ann Scales, is missing."

Bramlett raised an eyebrow. "What do you mean, missing?"

Curry shrugged. "She got a phone call from somebody early yesterday morning, left the house telling Lizzie she'd be back in an hour or so. She was bad upset."

The sheriff sighed. It was getting less and less simple. "What do you make of it?"

"I don't know. Her folks live in Fulton, but she didn't go there. Her mother called Lizzie just a little while ago. Lizzie had called her last night. They're all worried sick. We put out an APB on her vehicle last night. Nothing yet."

"And she was close to some of these girls who hung around Bondreaux's place."

Curry nodded. "I want to stay with this if you don't mind."

Bramlett waved the back of his hand at him. "Do it," he said.

Curry turned and quickly left. Bramlett swiveled around to look out the window. There were few cars parked on the street. All the businesses in downtown Sheffield were closed. Wal-Mart didn't even open until one o'clock on Sunday. And this Scales woman hadn't come in last night.

He shook his head and turned back to his desk. Things were getting more unsimple all the time.

"I SERIOUSLY QUESTION HOW MUCH any of them were really learning from him," Furrell Kohelem said, cupping his hands over a match and lighting a cigarette.

He shook out the match and moved his hand behind his back and exhaled smoke which the cool breeze sucked away directly from the side of his mouth. He had graying hair and was a head taller than Curry, and looked down at him with his eyes half closed. His face, almost pecan-colored, betrayed no emotion, but the deputy could hear the distaste in the voice.

It was the early afternoon, and the two men stood on the browning lawn beside the wide concrete walkway to the front steps of the First Baptist Church. The funeral service had just ended, and oozing from the two double front doors of the church was a thick crowd of people—high school students, parents, teachers, and others—descending the steps and dispersing to the bumper-to-bumper cars that lined both sides of the street.

"Just cake. No solid meat," Kohelem said, drawing on his cigarette. "Clowning around in the classroom, letting the kids do whatever they liked. Of course, he was *popular*. Who wouldn't be with that kind of routine? Give them a few years . . . after they've been in college and all. Then they'll understand the teachers who really helped them were the ones who were strict, who made them put their butts on the seat of a chair and learn something solid. Just wait and see."

Kohelem was Curry's mother's second cousin and taught history at the high school. He had, in fact, taught Curry, Johnny Baillie, and Jacob Robertson when they were at Sheffield High ten years before. Kohelem was the only black man Curry knew who still wore an Afro hairdo.

In many respects, Curry thought, the man remained where he had been happiest—in the troubled sixties. Curry's father once told him that Furrell Kohelem was the only person of color he knew who seemed to enjoy the civil rights movement.

"Any idea who might have had a reason to kill him?" Curry asked.

Kohelem snorted smoke out his nose as he surveyed the crowd still thickly pouring through the doors. "Naw. People don't kill teachers just for being bad teachers . . . or else you'd have a hundred murders on your hands right now." He grinned and his gold-capped tooth glinted in the sunlight. He took a long drag on his cigarette, coughed as he exhaled, then said, "Of course, the man may not have been all he appeared to be. I mean . . ." He paused and nodded at the people coming out of the church. "Many folks saw him as a churchgoing, upright man. On the other hand, sometimes he ran around with the likes of Rabbit Murphey, if you can imagine that." Rabbit was as close to a bonified Hell's Angel that Chakchiuma County had.

Curry nodded. He saw Lizzie and Nena coming down the steps together. Nena was staring straight ahead. In her eyes was a hard, cold look.

Curry asked, "You think there's much of a drug problem at the high school?"

Kohelem pursed his lips and shook his head. "I'm sure we have a bigger problem than our esteemed principal will admit." Curry had heard that Kohelem was still bitter toward Lynwood Wilson because Wilson had been named, first, vice principal and then later, principal. Kohelem felt he himself was much more qualified than Wilson.

"Teachers, too?"

The man's eyes widened. "Teachers? Who could afford drugs on a teacher's salary?"

Curry saw Sheriff Bramlett and Mrs. Bramlett emerge from the doorway. He excused himself.

The sheriff had told Jacob Robertson and Johnny Baillie that they could have the day off, that he and Curry would put in a few hours that afternoon. Curry wondered if this might be a good time for him to speak to the sheriff about the Corvette.

*   *   *

THERE WAS NO SMILE on Howard Skelton's face when he opened the front door to Bramlett and Curry.

" 'Afternoon, Howard," Bramlett said, taking off his hat and smiling pleasantly. "We wondered—"

"We're busy right now," Skelton said, stepping out onto the porch and pulling the door almost to after him. "I told you—"

"Who is it, Howard?" It was Rumi's voice, coming from within the house.

He turned his head and said, "I'm taking care of it." His voice, trying to affect a nothing-to-be-concerned-about tone, betrayed its tension.

The door pulled open wide and Rumi Skelton stepped into the doorway. Rumi was, by anyone's measure, a beautiful woman. She was tall and stately, her hazel eyes sparkled and her perfect teeth gleamed. She looked young enough to pass for her daughter Vicki Ann's older sister. Both wore their blond hair in a swept-back style and were exactly the same height and build. To Bramlett, Rumi Skelton looked the same as she had when she first arrived in Sheffield as a widow with a small daughter many years ago.

She looked surprised to see Bramlett. She smiled and said, "Grover! Not watching football on television?" She spoke with an easy graciousness that was not offensive.

Howard's mouth was slightly parted. He stared at her with confusion in his eyes.

She held the smile, now looking at Curry. "It *is* Sunday afternoon," she added by way of explanation. Then her lips closed over her teeth but the pleasant smile lingered as she looked back at Bramlett, waiting for him to state his business.

"I wanted to talk to Vicki Ann," he said. "I understand she knew Jesse Bondreaux and—"

"She's in bed, Grover," Rumi said, the smile never wavering. "This has been rough on all the kids. You can understand."

Skelton turned to Bramlett. His face was darkening. "I told you yesterday there's nothing she can help you with."

"I don't think I saw y'all at the funeral," Bramlett said. "Of course, there were so many people—"

"We weren't there. Rumi and I didn't even know the man. Vicki

Ann is exhausted. This has been a harried week, with homecoming and all."

Bramlett smiled and tilted his head toward the deputy. "Rumi, do you know Deputy Curry here? His niece was the other queen."

Rumi blinked a couple of times as if she were trying to understand what Bramlett had said. "Other queen?" She, like her husband, not comprehending, even at this late date, that there were two. In a moment, however, the light dawned.

Rumi smiled broadly. "Oh, really? And what was her name?"

Curry grinned. "Veatrice, ma'am. Veatrice Curry." He emphasized the last name.

"Yes . . ." Rumi said, the smile not wilting slightly. She looked back to Bramlett. "Is there anything I can help you with, Grover?"

"I hate to bother y'all on Sunday, but we came by yesterday and—"

"Vicki Ann and I were shopping in Memphis."

"That's what Howard said," Bramlett said, licking his lower lip. His mouth was very dry. He needed a good chew. "The truth is, we need to talk to all the students who used to visit Mr. Bondreaux—"

"Vicki hasn't been by there in months," Rumi said. The smile was gone and there was a chilliness in her voice.

Bramlett sighed. "Now y'all need to know how unpleasant all of this is for me. But I want the two of you to listen to me real good. Like I said, I don't like it any better than you do. But the fact . . . the real straight fact is that we *are* going to talk to Vicki Ann. Now, if we can't do it here at the house, I'll send some deputies out here to pick her up and bring her in." Having finished, he nodded and looked from one to another, then placed his hat on his head. "We'll let her rest this afternoon. But you have her here at three-thirty tomorrow. We'll be back then."

Bramlett turned and walked across the Mexican-tiled porch, stepped down on the brick-paved walkway and strode toward the patrol car. Curry hurried after him.

"What's that all about?" Curry said as he turned the key in the ignition.

"How the hell should I know?" Bramlett said, looking straight ahead. "Unless the Skeltons got some chicken crap on their expensive shoes."

Curry steered the car onto the street and pressed hard on the accelerator. The car lurched forward.

Bramlett turned his head and looked at the side of Curry's inscrutable face. "What's the matter?"

"Nothing," the deputy said. He was boiling inside, boiling at those jerks acting like they didn't know anything about Veatrice being queen.

13

BEFORE GOING BACK TO HEADQUARTERS, Bramlett and Curry made a stop on Butcher Street at a small stuccoed house which was the address for Billy Mosley, the boy who, according to Rozelle Kample, had had an argument with Jesse Bondreaux, presumably about a test grade.

"Billy has gone off with friends," his mother said, standing in the front door. "Is something wrong?" She was tall, thin, and slightly stooped.

"That his car?" the sheriff asked, ignoring her question and nodding toward a dark-blue Honda Prelude parked in the driveway.

"Yes, it is." Her eyes revealed how frightened she was becoming. She tugged at the sleeves of the pink sweater she was wearing.

Bramlett nodded and tried to smile pleasantly. "Have a nice afternoon."

They walked in front of the car, looking down at the bumper. There were several dents and scrapes, not only on the bumper but all around the car. It had not been well cared for.

When they were back in the patrol car, Curry said, "How can a parent have a 'nice afternoon' after two lawmen come around asking after her child?"

"Just being pleasant," Bramlett said. He was smiling but Curry noticed the slight squint of his eyes.

*　　*　　*

"WHY DON'T YOU COME ON TO BED, Grover?" Valeria Bramlett said. She was wearing her bathrobe and standing at the doorway between the den and the kitchen with her arms folded. She was frowning. Marcellus had gone to bed over an hour before and was sleeping soundly.

Bramlett squeezed the watercolor brush he'd just rinsed between his index finger and thumb, letting the water drip into the glass jar half full of dark, blue-black water. "I want to do a few more washes," he said.

"What's wrong with you?"

"Nothing," he said. "Go along. I'll be there directly."

She didn't move, stood studying him for a long time. He definitely wasn't acting like himself. He seemed so irritable, so nervous.

"You want to tell me about it?" she said.

"What's to tell?" He rinsed the brush vigorously in the water jar, clanging the ferule against the glass. He squeezed the water out of the brush again and ran his tongue over his lips. Then he cleared his throat and said, "I've quit tobacco. And I'm struggling to concentrate on anything right now. You wouldn't understand."

She hadn't noticed. Of course, he was all the time sneaking around with it anyway. "When did you quit?"

"Last week." He laid the brush down. "I'm sorry. Go on to bed. I'll be along soon."

The telephone rang. She answered it.

"It's for you," she said to him, handing him the receiver. Then she walked to the sink. She needed a glass of water.

"Yes . . . ?"

She filled a glass with tap water and turned around.

"What?" His voice was loud, startled.

He listened for a moment, then said, "Has the body been ID'd?"

"What is it?" she said, setting the glass onto the countertop and putting her hand to her throat. Her eyes never left his face.

He listened on, at the same time nodding at her that he'd heard her.

"I see," he said. "Okay. I'm on my way."

83

He hung up and stepped back to the table. He looked down at the half-dried watercolor sheet, then suddenly snatched away the masking tape from the four edges. He took the sheet into his hands and crushed it into a ball. He pressed and pressed until it was a very small and tight ball. "Damn! Damn damn damn!"

14

A LIGHT, MISTY RAIN HAD BEGUN TO FALL by the time Sheriff Grover Bramlett reached Lake Coleby. The headlights of oncoming vehicles swarmed across his windshield in bright streaks of light, making him nervous. He didn't see nearly as well at night as he did a few years ago.

The winding two-lane, narrow-shouldered highway had one of the highest fatality rates in the state, and Bramlett's hunched and tensed shoulders were aching by the time he reached the turn-off to the lake. He found the clustered patrol cars on a one-lane graveled road twisting around the northern side of the lake.

He parked behind Johnny Baillie's car and turned off the ignition. He sat with his hands resting on the steering wheel, making no motion to get out. He had no desire to see the body of a young woman who'd been dead probably over twenty-four hours.

Jacob Robertson strolled up to the car. Bramlett rolled down his window. "Evening, Jacob," he said. "H. C. here?"

"Yessir. He's over yonder." Robertson nodded toward the darkness beyond Baillie's car. Bramlett could see flashlights moving around.

"What's it look like?"

"She's been shot in the head. Just like that schoolteacher."

Bramlett gave a low groan and rubbed the bottom of his nose

85

with his knuckle. "This one's a schoolteacher also," he said, more to himself than to the deputy.

"Yessir."

Bramlett opened his door and pulled himself out. "Who reported it? Hunters, was it?"

"Yessir. They're over there." He tilted his head toward the other side of the road. "The tall one is Curt Boice. The other is Max Hemfelt. They're from town."

Bramlett could see two figures standing beyond another patrol car. He walked toward them. Each man had a dog on a leash, Walker hounds, straining a little, wanting to move back to where the car was with the body in it.

" 'Evening," Bramlett said as he stepped up to them. They were only boys, teenagers, one quite tall, taller even than Bramlett. The other didn't stand as high as Bramlett's shoulder.

" 'Evening," they said in unison.

"Y'all found the body, I hear."

"Yessir," the shorter one said. "We was trailing a coon across this here lip of the lake and then Moses—that's this 'un—started jumping up on the side of that car and barking all crazy like. I thought it was just some parkers so I tried to call him off but he wouldn't stop. I went up to drag him back and I didn't see nobody sitting in the car. Then I shined my light on the seat and there she was." He pulled back tighter on Moses's leash. "We went back down to the Texaco station to call y'all."

"Did you see anyone else around here? Any other vehicles?"

"No, sir," they said together.

"We appreciate your help," Bramlett said. He nodded at each boy and then walked toward the knot of flashlights beside the woman's car.

Johnny Baillie met him as he moved toward the vehicle. The car's doors were opened and the dome light shining. Bramlett could see the body was still slumped across the front seat.

"Dr. Thompson is on his way," Baillie said as if reading the sheriff's mind, knowing he would ask if the county's medical examiner-investigator had been notified. "As far as I can tell, there's just one wound—near gunshot right between the eyes about eyebrow level. The flies have already been at work."

86

Bramlett half turned away from the car. He certainly didn't want to see that. "Where's H. C.?" he asked.

"Here." Curry walked toward Bramlett from the darkness behind the car, the circled beam of his flashlight flowing across the ground before his feet. He stopped in front of Bramlett.

"You told Lizzie?" the sheriff asked. He didn't really know the dead woman at all, but he loved Lizzie Clouse, and he knew how worried she'd been.

"No," Curry said. In that one word was a lot of pain. Bramlett could hear it clearly.

"We'll need to ask her some questions as soon as possible," Bramlett said gently.

"I know." The deputy's voice was hardly audible.

Bramlett sucked on the side of his tongue. Suddenly the memory of seeing the woman's body hanging inside an old barn came to his mind. It was awful. And, he remembered with a certain bitterness, he never had a clue as to the killer.

The victim, eyes bulging and tongue protruding out of her mouth, was the mother of Lizzie Clouse. That was several years ago, but he knew for Lizzie it was still a very green wound.

"Why don't you run along and break it to her," Bramlett said. "I'll give you a little time. Then I'll come. Okay?"

Curry nodded and turned away, walking toward his car. His shoulders sagged slightly.

"Those boys said they were hunting squirrels out here yesterday morning," Johnny Baillie said. "They were on the other side of the lake. Said they heard some shooting up this way but mostly it was a shotgun. They did hear one shot, they say, that they thought was a twenty-two rifle."

Bramlett reached into his jacket pocket for a toothpick. Before leaving the house, he'd grabbed a wad of them from the box in the kitchen cabinet. He placed the toothpick in his mouth and chewed on it for a moment, then said, "And that could have been a twenty-five caliber, I suppose?"

Baillie nodded. "Found one cartridge casing. It was just outside the car. Looks like an automatic, just like the other one."

Bramlett turned his head hard to first one side and then the other, trying to loosen the tenseness in his neck. The toothpick was already fragmented and spreading across his tongue. "Okay, Johnny. You're in charge here. I'm going back to town and talk with her roommate. That's Lizzie Clouse, you know."

"I know."

Bramlett wasn't sure, but he thought he detected a bit of feeling, of compassion maybe, in Baillie's tone. Good, he said to himself. Very good. The deputy's cold-heartedness had always bothered the sheriff.

He rolled his shoulders, still trying to loosen the ache, and walked back toward his car. His stomach felt sour. Bubbly. The killing of a sleaze like Jesse Bondreaux was one thing.

The killing of a nice person like Jo Ann Scales was something entirely different. At moments like this, he felt he definitely wanted to retire after this present term. He needed to take a Tagamet right away.

LIZZIE CLOUSE'S HEAD AND SHOULDERS SWAYED back and forth, back and forth. At the same time, she shook her head slowly from side to side. She sat on the sofa, and her eyes were tightly closed. Tears streaked the sides of her face. Every few seconds she struck the tops of her legs with her fists.

H. C. Curry sat beside her, his arm around her shoulders, his body moving in tandem with hers. Bramlett had lowered himself down into one of the armchairs.

Lizzie opened her eyes and stared vacantly across the room. She stopped swaying. "I knew she was dead. I could *feel* it," she said. She started swaying again.

"When exactly was the last time you saw her?" Bramlett asked.

She struck her legs hard. "I can't think straight." Then she wiped her cheeks with both palms and rubbed her palms on the knees of her jeans. "She got a phone call. That was yesterday morning. Early." She paused, took a couple of quick breaths, then continued. "She wouldn't tell me who it was. She said somebody was upset. That she wished she didn't know about it. That she wished none of us knew, or something." She bit her lip hard, then added, "She said . . . she said she'd make us pancakes when she got back . . . that she'd only be gone an hour or so . . ." Lizzie closed her eyes again and leaned her head back on Curry's arm. "Oh, God! I can't believe this is happening. Sweet Jesus!"

"And you have no idea who phoned?" Bramlett said.

"I thought maybe it was a parent."

"Why?"

Her eyes popped open again, stared fixedly, her head still resting on Curry's arm. "That's mostly who she got calls from. She didn't date." She gulped a breath, then said, "I don't know why. She was such a nice person. But it was only parents that phoned. Except, of course, her mother. She called quite a bit. No men. Usually a parent. And Jo Ann was always so patient, so sweet. In fact, she got a call earlier this evening on the answering machine from a parent. Mrs. Topp."

"Katherine Topp?"

Lizzie nodded. "She wanted to talk with Jo Ann about Gail's grades."

Bramlett frowned. "I assumed Gail was a good student."

"Basically. But she is falling off here lately in a few subjects. Too much extracurricular stuff, I suppose." She was silent for a long moment, then continued. "Funny, you know. Mrs. Topp sounded irritated at Jo Ann. She couldn't have known, of course, that Jo Ann was already . . . already . . ." She didn't finish.

"Lizzie, think carefully now," Bramlett said. "Was there anyone— anyone at all—you can think of that Jo Ann had a problem with? Any kind of problem."

She stopped swaying again and looked at Bramlett. She cocked her head slightly and said, "Of course, there's that nut Edwin Charles. She was terrified of him."

Bramlett shot a quick glance at Curry, who gave a half nod in acknowledgement. The sheriff wanted this man checked out right away.

Lizzie continued. "He was a student of hers a couple of years back. He developed a terrific crush on her. Used to phone all the time, all hours of the night. Sometimes he would drop by. A couple of times he walked right into this apartment without even knocking. Sometimes when she went out in the evening, she'd see him standing behind the bushes watching her. He's scary."

"We'll pick him up right away and talk with him," Bramlett said. "Anyone else?"

She shook her head.

Bramlett slipped another toothpick into his mouth and glanced at his watch. "It's late," he said, looking at Lizzie. "We'd better get out of here and let you get some sleep."

She moaned and bowed her face into her hands.

Bramlett stood and looked at Curry.

"I'll be staying a little while," the deputy said, keeping his seat. "Not long. I'll phone headquarters about picking up this Charles fellow right away."

Bramlett nodded and put on his hat and turned toward the door.

15

IN THE MORNING, a cold rain whipped by a strong wind splattered against the windshield as Bramlett backed his car out of the carport. He turned on the wipers, shifted from reverse into drive, and noticed the sky did indeed look like that burnt umber and ultramarine blue wash he'd done on the outhouse. It made a nice sky wash for a watercolor, set a reflective, melancholy type of mood—pleasing in its own way.

At headquarters, Bramlett sat at his desk and scanned the small pink intercom notes Ella Mae had already placed on his blotter that morning, mostly telephone calls to return. Nothing that looked urgent.

He read through the data Baillie and Curry had assembled for him on Bondreaux. When he was through, he rose from the desk, took his hat and stepped out of the office, beckoning Curry to accompany him.

As they went through the outside door to the parking lot, Bramlett said, "I want to check out this guy on the motorcycle—Rabbit Murphey. Then we're going to the high school. I want to talk to the principal again. And this Nena Carmack."

Curry blinked as if startled. "Why Nena?"

Bramlett cocked his head. "Friend of yours?"

He shrugged. "Friend of Lizzie's. Used to date Bondreaux."

"I know," Bramlett said, opening the door on the passenger side and easing himself down onto the seat. He noticed the deputy suppressing a yawn. "How's Lizzie?"

"She stayed home from school today." He started the car, backed around, and drove into the street.

Bramlett watched a piece of newspaper rolling in the wind down the sidewalk in front of the courthouse. "Is she scared?" he asked.

Curry grunted and turned left on Front Street. He didn't bother to reply.

THEY FOUND RABBIT MURPHEY AT WAL-MART. He was working in the sporting goods section. The display aisles were packed with hunting gear: camouflage jump suits, bright orange caps and vests, stacks of boxed ammunition, boots, and heavy woolen socks. They found Rabbit marking prices on dove stools.

He shrugged when Bramlett asked how well he knew Jesse Bondreaux. "We had a few beers together. That's about it. Once he and another guy were out at the Club Hawaii. They seemed okay." Club Hawaii was a honkeytonk near the Grant County line.

"Who was the other guy?" the sheriff asked.

"Noel Hackott."

"You came by Bondreaux's house when Deputy Curry here was there last Saturday." Bramlett paused, waiting for an explanation.

Murphey shrugged again. He held the price stamper by his side and did not raise his eyes from the floor. "I was just cruising. I didn't know the guy was dead."

"You'd been to the house before?"

"Yeah. Just for a few beers. We watched a video." His face suddenly flushed. "Am I being accused of something?" He spoke through his teeth.

"We're just talking," Bramlett said.

"Well, I ain't done nothing, and I ain't saying nothing else."

Bramlett's chest expanded and he drew himself up to his full height. "Would you like to go down to headquarters with us?"

Murphey scowled and put his hands on his hips. "Look, I really didn't know the turkey. We had some beer, we watched the video. That was it."

92

"What about Jo Ann Scales?"

"Never heard of her."

Bramlett held his eyes on the man for a long time, said nothing, then turned abruptly and walked away with Curry hurrying after him.

THE HIGH SCHOOL PRINCIPAL, Lynwood Wilson, offered them seats in two wooden ladder-back chairs in front of his desk. There was a purplish cast under his eyes as if he were losing sleep. Bramlett remembered how nervous Wilson had been when they talked to him on Saturday.

"We've got several pastors here this morning in case any of the students want to talk to them. Everyone is upset." He wiped the corners of his mouth with his thumb and index finger and shook his head. "I mean, two teachers dead . . ." He pressed his lips together.

"I understand Jo Ann Scales had some things to say to you about Jesse Bondreaux," Bramlett said.

The principal shifted around in his chair. "I'm not sure what you mean . . ."

Bramlett glared at the man. "We know she came to talk with you about something she suspected concerning Bondreaux and a couple of girl students."

Wilson took a white handkerchief out of his pocket and dabbed at his forehead and chin. "She . . . she said some things. Of course, you understand these were merely unsubstantiated allegations and . . ." He didn't finish.

"Did you check it out?"

"No," he said, wiping his chin again.

"And you never had any other reason to suspect Bondreaux of unethical conduct as a teacher?" Bramlett was closely watching the man's face—the muscles in his cheeks and neck, the flaring of his nostrils, his movement of his eyes.

Wilson looked down. "No. No. Of course not . . ."

"Didn't Howard Skelton talk to you about the kids hanging around Bondreaux's house?" Bramlett heard his own voice rising.

Wilson forced himself to swallow. "Yes," he said softly. He wouldn't look up.

"You told him you would talk to Bondreaux about it. Did you?"

"No," Wilson said. His voice was very faint.

Bramlett stared at the man for a long moment. "Why not?"

Wilson swallowed again, twice, then said, "I was going to . . . but . . ." He paused and shook his head and closed his eyes for a moment.

Bramlett knew the man could think of no good reason at all for not doing what he knew now he should have done. The sheriff gave a low snort. "Now we'd like to talk with one of your teachers. Nena Carmack."

Wilson cleared his throat, then said, "She's in class."

Bramlett pushed himself to his feet. Curry rose also. The principal didn't move.

"Do you have a conference room?" Bramlett asked.

"I think it would be best if you saw Miss Carmack after school . . . maybe at her home . . ."

"Just show us a place where we can talk privately with her and send for her. Maybe *you* can hold down her class while we talk." Bramlett grinned. He was enjoying this. "Now that would be fun, wouldn't it. I heard you speak at Rotary last spring. What was it you said? How much you missed the classroom?"

THE PRINCIPAL'S SECRETARY was a short, stout woman about thirty or so. She smiled pleasantly and showed them into a workroom with a photocopying machine and shelves of paper. There was a long wooden table in the middle of the room with straight-back chairs, more scuffed and scarred than the ones in Wilson's office. They sat down at the table.

A few minutes later Nena Carmack stepped into the room. Both Bramlett and Curry rose to their feet. There was an anxious look in her eyes. "What is it?" She looked at H. C. "Is Lizzie okay?"

Curry gave a quick shake of his head and averted her gaze.

Bramlett extended his hand toward a chair. He smiled slightly and introduced himself. He had seen her before. Yes, of course. She was the young woman at the ball game with Jacob Robertson.

Nena Carmack sat down slowly at the table. She folded her hands together on the tabletop and gave Curry a curious look, as if wondering what this was all about. Bramlett lowered himself once again into his chair. Curry sat likewise.

"I know this is a terrible time," the sheriff began. "Were you well acquainted with Jo Ann Scales?"

"Yes."

"When was the last time you saw her?"

"Friday. Here at school."

"Do you know of anyone who would have reason to harm her?"

"No. She was a nice person. This is insane."

Bramlett nodded. "All murder is," he said. "I understand you were very well acquainted with Jesse Bondreaux."

She looked sharply at Curry. He was looking at the sheriff, not at her. Bramlett noticed how the color was now draining out of her face.

She looked back at him, meeting his gaze. "I wouldn't say I was a *friend* of his. But I did know him."

Bramlett nodded and tried to broaden his smile. "But you used to date him?"

She stiffened. Again she looked at Curry. He was still focused on the sheriff. "That's been over a long time."

"How long?"

She shrugged. "Six months. Maybe more."

"I know this all may be painful for you—"

"It's not," she said, her eyes becoming very cold and hard. "There was nothing much to it." She tilted her head back and said with a touch of bitterness, "Obviously."

Again Bramlett nodded and cut his eyes at the deputy. Curry, who was still looking at the sheriff, dropped his gaze to the table. Bramlett looked back at Nena. "Then exactly why did you stop seeing him, if I may ask?"

She drew a long breath, released it, and her shoulders seemed to sink slightly. "He was not a very good person."

"Like how?"

"I found out he was also seeing someone else. A married woman in Tupelo."

Bramlett's eyebrows raised. "Oh?"

She was staring at her hands. "He lied to me about it, but I knew the truth. And then . . ." She looked towards the window. Her lips quivered ever so slightly, but Bramlett noticed.

"Go on," he said.

"And then I was given reason to believe he was . . . was having a relationship with a student." She bowed her head.

"By relationship you mean going to bed with this student?"

She nodded without looking up.

"And what is this student's name?"

Her lower lip quivered more, then she said, "I don't have any proof . . ."

"What you tell us is strictly confidential."

"Her name is Cora Hartley."

"And the married woman's name?"

Her cheeks tightened. "Nicole Estis. She's a secretary in Tupelo."

"I see." Bramlett glanced at Curry. The deputy was writing the names in his notebook. "And," continued the sheriff, "how did you find out about the student?"

"Jo Ann Scales told me."

Bramlett nibbled at the corner of his mouth. Then he said, "And how did you find out about Nicole Estis?"

"I received an anonymous letter. I have no idea who it was from."

"Humm," he said, rubbing the back of one hand with his other hand. "You followed up on it, I take it?"

She nodded and held her head up higher. The coldness in her eyes deepened.

Bramlett shifted in his chair. "I'm told Noel Hackott was one of Bondreaux's friends."

Her lip curled slightly in an expression of contempt. "Jesse just used him. He didn't really like him. He didn't really like anyone."

"When was the last time you talked with Bondreaux?"

"I don't know . . . I suppose a couple of months ago."

Bramlett gazed at her for a long moment, then said, "I think that's all we need to ask you for the time being, Miss Carmack. Except . . . perhaps you can tell us where you were last Friday afternoon between four-thirty and five-thirty."

She glowered at him.

He smiled apologetically. "It's just routine. We have to ask everyone we talk to."

Her voice was chilly. "I was at home. Getting ready for a date." She gave Curry a withering look.

"Thank you, Miss Carmack," Bramlett said. "You've been very helpful."

When she had left the room, Deputy Curry said, "You didn't ask Mr. Wilson where *he* was."

"So I forgot. Go ask him, and, while you're at it, tell him we'd like to talk to that girl . . . what's her name?"

Curry glanced at his notepad. "Cora Hartley."

CORA HARTLEY HAD NOT COME to school that morning. Fifteen minutes later, Sheriff Bramlett and Deputy Curry got out of the patrol car on Wesson Street in east Sheffield. It was a one-story board-and-batten house with peeling white paint. In the shallow front yard were two whitewashed truck-tire flower planters in which were dead and browned summer annuals.

Bramlett and Curry were met at the door by a scowling man with a weekend's growth of dark beard. He was of medium height and solidly built.

"What?" he said, almost snarling, looking quickly from Bramlett to Curry.

"Mr. Marshall Hartley?" Bramlett said.

"So?"

Bramlett introduced himself and Curry. "We'd like to talk to your daughter, Cora Hartley." The sheriff was trying to look pleasant. He wondered why this man dressed in a gray T-shirt and faded overalls wasn't at work.

The scowl deepened. He eyed Bramlett with suspicion. "What about?"

"We'd just like to ask her a few questions concerning one of her teachers, Jesse Bondreaux."

The man's eyes snapped open wider and his mouth twisted into an ugly sneer. His teeth were tobacco-stained. "She ain't got nothing to say about him."

"Excuse me?" Bramlett said.

"I don't stutter."

97

Bramlett's neck muscles tensed. "I don't think you understand, Mr. Hartley. This is official law-enforcement business and—"

"I understand this. I'm glad the bastard's dead. If I knew who did it, I'd give him a hundred dollars. I'm just sorry as hell I didn't get to blow his brains out myself."

Bramlett breathed in and out slowly three times, counting each time. Then he said, "Mr. Hartley, we can take you *and* your daughter down to headquarters for questioning . . . or we can have a quiet little talk here and now. You invite us in nicely now and let us talk with her . . . or we gonna throw you in the back of that car out yonder in handcuffs and lock you up for obstructing justice. Do you understand?"

Bramlett drew himself up to his full six-foot-two height and looked down at the man. Hartley glared at the sheriff. Finally, he moved back into the room. Bramlett and Curry followed.

"Cora!" he yelled. "Get in here!"

Bramlett could feel the grit beneath his shoes on the linoleum-covered floor. Sun-yellowed blinds, pulled halfway down, shaded each of the narrow windows. One was torn and patched with duct tape.

A girl wearing a red blouse and tight tan pants walked slowly into the room. Bramlett wouldn't have described her as pretty at all. Her hair was uncombed and her eyes were puffy.

"They wanna ask you some questions," Hartley said to his daughter. His tone was bitter.

"Cora, I'm Sheriff Bramlett and this is Deputy Curry." Then he looked at the father. "Maybe it would be better if we could all sit down."

Cora Hartley sat on a stained bedspread-covered sofa and folded her arms across her chest, not so much in a defiant posture as in a defensive one. Bramlett and Curry each took chairs with threadbare armrests. The father made no motion to sit down. His eyes were fastened on his daughter almost in a threatening manner.

"Are you not feeling well?" Bramlett said to the girl. "We looked for you at school."

She sniffled and slowly shook her head. Her eyes seemed unfocused, staring into space, and Bramlett wondered if she could be on drugs.

"Did you know Miss Scales well?"

"No . . ." she said softly. "I didn't know her at all."

"She wasn't one of your teachers?"

"No, sir."

"But Mr. Bondreaux was."

She nodded and said hardly above a whisper, "Yes . . ."

"I understand you used to go by to visit Mr. Bondreaux after school."

"She ain't been there in months," the father said.

"Is this true?" Bramlett said to the girl, wishing she would look up at his face and see his warm, assuring grandfather's smile.

She sighed. "I . . . I don't remember . . ."

"What?" Marshall Hartley said, his hands now clenched into fists at his side.

The girl flinched. Bramlett and Curry exchanged knowing glances.

"Perhaps, Mr. Hartley," Bramlett said, "it would be better if you let us talk to your daughter alone. Maybe if you'd kindly go into another room."

The man took one step toward the girl, the whites of his knuckles showing, his eyes flashing violence.

"Mr. Hartley," Bramlett said firmly, "if you don't leave this room immediately, I'll take this child down to headquarters and talk to her there." He paused, then continued, his voice soft as if he were speaking more to the girl than to her father. "We came to talk about Jesse Bondreaux, but maybe she has some other things she'd like to tell us."

The man looked back at Bramlett. Their eyes locked. Neither blinked for a long moment. Then the man snorted, glanced around the room and said, "I want a drink." He left then, slamming the door behind him.

The girl immediately dropped her face into her hands and began to tremble.

"It's all right," Bramlett said softly. "It's all right." He sat back in the chair. "Now, Cora. Tell us about Mr. Bondreaux."

She slowly lowered her hands and clasped them together in her lap. She made a quick glance at the door her father had shut, looked at Bramlett for a second, then her eyes fell to her hands.

"He . . . he was the finest, kindest man I've ever known. It's . . .

it's just that a lot of people didn't really understand him . . . not like I did . . ."

Bramlett's eyebrows rose and he glanced at Curry. The deputy's eyes were fixed on the girl. His notepad was on his knee. He hadn't written anything yet.

"Tell me about him," Bramlett said.

Slowly she raised her eyes and looked at him for a second or two, then lowered her eyes again. "He was much more than a teacher. He was a friend."

Bramlett's face hardened. "What do you mean?"

"I mean he was somebody you could talk to . . . *really* talk to."

"Talk? Talk about what?"

She shrugged. "Things. About your parents and friends. You know."

"Tell me."

"I mean, if you'd had a problem with another teacher, you could tell him. He'd understand."

"Did you have problems with other teachers?"

She made a face. "Not really."

"What about with your parents?"

She shook her head.

"You sure?"

"Yes," she said. There was a sharpness to her tone. Bramlett didn't believe her.

"Tell me this, Cora. Did you ever get cocaine or any other kind of drugs from him?"

She looked up at him, confusion in her eyes. "W-what? Oh, no . . . never!"

"Did he use drugs?"

"Of course not." Her eyes narrowed.

Bramlett nodded. "I see. Well, tell me this." He cleared his throat and twisted his hat a quarter turn in his hand, then said, "I understand he was *very* friendly with some of the girls." He watched for the slightest reaction.

Her eyes narrowed and her nostrils flared. "Who told you that?"

Bramlett watched her for a moment, then answered, "Apparently, one of the girls told someone."

Her neck was turning crimson. "She's lying, whoever she is." She

100

pushed the back of her hand across her mouth. Bramlett noticed the diamond ring.

"You engaged?" he said.

"Yes," she said briskly. Suddenly her eyes seemed to soften and she gazed more absently across the room.

"What's his name?" He could see her eyes beginning to tear up.

"Lucian . . ." she said. "Lucian DeBow."

"Does he know about you and Mr. Bondreaux?" Bramlett was pushing hard. He knew she could deny everything, anything—but he sensed an opening, albeit small.

She grew very pale. "What are you talking about?" She looked at him for a moment, but couldn't hold her eyes on his searching gaze. She looked away. "He suspects," she said. She paused and slowly shook her head. "I didn't mean for it to happen. Neither did Mr. Bondreaux. It just . . . well, you know . . ."

Bramlett nodded sympathetically. Beneath the understanding facade on his face, however, was a deepening contempt for this deceased schoolteacher.

"Was this a regular thing? I mean, only once, or what . . .?"

She shrugged. "It lasted a month or so. Then we just stopped. I knew it wasn't fair to Lucian."

Bramlett's eyes widened in surprise. "You were already engaged?"

"No. Not then. But we were going together. We were talking about marriage."

"And Lucian found out about you and Jesse?"

"Not completely. He just suspects." She pushed her hand against her mouth again, then said, "He's confronted me several times. Once I said we just kissed. And then Lucian went into a rage. I certainly ain't telling him more."

Bramlett looked at Curry. The deputy gave a light nod, indicated he had the name and knew they'd be checking this fellow out immediately.

Bramlett looked back at the girl and said softly, "What about anyone who'd had an argument with him or anything like that?"

"Only . . . only Hayes Woodall."

"He's a student, isn't he?"

She nodded. "Jesse found out he'd been stealing things and told him not to come back to the house anymore."

"What kind of things?"

"I don't know."

"And there was no one else Mr. Bondreaux got crossways with?"

Her eyes instantly widened as if remembering something. "There was this man who drove a BMW . . ." She paused, then said, "Jesse called him Noel."

"Noel Hackott?"

She nodded. "Once in the front yard a few weeks ago, he and Jesse were arguing about something. Then Jesse pushed him hard and the man stumbled back. Then he got in his car and left. He went tearing out, I remember."

"What were they arguing about?"

She shook her head. "I couldn't hear. I don't know."

Bramlett was silent for a moment, then suddenly stood up and said, "Thank you, Cora. I hope you feel better."

Curry slipped his notepad into his shirt pocket and stood also. The door across the room jerked open and Marshall Hartley stepped in. His eyes were fierce. "I'd have killed the bastard myself with no more thought than killing a cottonmouth," he said through his teeth.

Bramlett put on his hat and turned toward the front door. He noticed the two mounted buck heads on the front wall with two pairs of mounted deer hooves below them. On one pair of hooves rested a twelve-gauge pump and on the other a lever-action rifle. "You hunt, Mr. Hartley?"

"What of it?"

"Do you have other guns?"

"I got lots of guns."

"A twenty-five caliber automatic?"

"More than one," he said, color rising in his face. "But I ain't killed nobody, if that's what you're asking."

"Maybe you could tell us where you were last Friday afternoon about five o'clock."

The man smiled smugly. "On a job in Booneville. I work for G and T Concrete."

"Rained out today?"

"If you're through asking my daughter questions, I'll thank you to leave."

Bramlett nodded and opened the front door.

As they walked back to the car, Curry said, "That man's got an attitude."

Bramlett sighed. "No, H. C. He's got a daughter."

THE SHERIFF SAID HE WANTED TO GO HOME for lunch. Curry dropped him off at his car in the parking lot at headquarters and then drove to Lizzie's place.

He stood at the door and knocked. A minute passed. No answer. He knocked louder and waited. Still no answer.

He tried the door handle. It was locked. He stepped back and stared at the door.

He certainly hadn't expected her to go anywhere the way she felt. She was too shook up to go to work or do anything. Where in the world could she have gone?

He knocked one more time, much harder than before. "Lizzie!" he shouted.

Another minute passed. Still no answer.

He turned then and hurried to his car.

16

AFTER LUNCH, H. C. Curry followed Bramlett into the sheriff's office. He laid a sheet of paper on the corner of the desk. "I checked out Marshall Hartley," he said. "This is a list of the calls we've had to go to his house. There are three. Each was made by a neighbor. Same thing each time."

"Oh?" Bramlett said, sitting down into his swivel chair.

Curry cleared his throat. "Domestic problems. Each time his wife had been beaten. Once she had to go to the hospital. Each time she refused to press charges."

Bramlett noticed the deputy seemed distracted, was shifting from one foot to another, fidgeting with his hands. "What's wrong with you?" he asked.

Curry shrugged. "I'm worried about Lizzie. You know. This thing with Jo Ann . . ." He paused and shook his head. I went by to check on her a while ago and she's gone out someplace. And . . ." He didn't finish.

Bramlett nodded and said, "I understand." He glanced at the clock on the wall. One-fourteen. "What about Noel Hackott. When is he supposed to get here?"

"He's waiting in the conference room."

*　　*　　*

NOEL HACKOTT LIVED IN SHEFFIELD but owned an interior decorating shop in Tupelo. That morning Curry had telephoned him to schedule an interview. Hackott said he'd rather come to the sheriff's office in Sheffield than have anyone come to his place of business. An appointment was made for one o'clock.

Hackott was seated at the conference table when Bramlett and Curry entered the room. He stood quickly. Today, Hackott was wearing a silk shirt open at the throat, revealing a thick gold chain.

"Please, sit." The sheriff pulled back a chair himself on the opposite side of the table. Curry sat beside the sheriff and placed his notepad on the table.

"Thank you for coming in, Noel," Bramlett said. "I believe the last time we talked you were interested in video tapes of yours which Jesse Bondreaux had."

Hackott squirmed in his chair. "They were my personal tapes and—"

"We haven't recovered any tapes yet," Bramlett said. "When we do, you may be sure we'll consult with you about them." He noticed how the man was perspiring on his forehead. "Now," continued the sheriff, "tell us about your relationship with your friend Bondreaux."

Hackott blinked his eyes rapidly for a moment. Then he said, "He was an acquaintance of mine." He emphasized the word acquaintance. "I wouldn't have called him a friend."

"You told me before he was a friend."

He shrugged. "Not really."

Bramlett raised an eyebrow. "Somehow I had the impression that you were a frequent visitor to his house."

The man blinked again. "I may have dropped by once or twice."

"Humm," Bramlett said. "Someone told us you and Bondreaux once got into a shoving match out in his front yard. You care to tell us about that?"

Hackott's chin jutted slightly. "I don't have any idea what you're talking about."

"Are you denying you and Bondreaux had some kind of argument?" Bramlett's tone reflected incredulity.

"I don't remember anything like that. If we did have a disagreement, it must have been over something minor."

"We were told you and Bondreaux were at the Club Hawaii once together."

Hackott blinked rapidly once again and shook his head hard at the same time. "I don't remember that."

"I see." Bramlett glared at Hackott. The man dropped his gaze at once and seemed to be studying a scuffed spot on the tabletop directly before him. Bramlett gave a low chuckle, as if letting Hackott know he didn't believe him at all. Then he said, "Tell me, Noel. Did you know Jo Ann Scales?"

"No. Not at all."

"Not at all?"

"I didn't even know her name until I heard about her getting killed."

Bramlett watched the man's hands, then his neck and ears. He seemed to be telling the truth about not knowing the woman, at any rate. "Tell me, then," continued Bramlett, "did you know any of the kids who hung around Bondreaux's house?"

"No," he said softly. His neck flushed red.

He's lying, thought Bramlett. "What about any other friends? I know he used to date Nena Carmack."

Hackott gave a wry smile. "She's history. In fact, Jesse had a lot of history."

"Like Nicole Estis?"

Hackott squirmed a bit. He said, "I don't know."

"Who else?"

The man looked up at the sheriff as if considering whether to say anything else or not. Then suddenly, "You know about Katherine Topp? That was one Jesse was quite proud of."

"You're lying," Bramlett said. This man is disgusting, he thought.

Hackott's face went crimson. "No! That's the God's truth. Jesse used to see her."

"Are you telling me they were lovers?" The sheriff's eyes bored into the man.

Hackott squirmed again. "I'm not sure. Not positive."

"Who else is in Bondreaux's history?"

106

Hackott shook his head quickly. "I don't know. I swear I don't know anyone else." His forehead glistened with sweat.

Bramlett leaned back heavily in his chair. "Well, Noel, I'm quite sure we'll be talking to you later. Deputy Curry will want to take a statement from you concerning your whereabouts last Friday afternoon. And Saturday morning as well. After that, you can go." He paused, then added, "For now."

The sheriff stood and left the room.

IT WAS SHORTLY AFTER TWO O'CLOCK. The maid who answered the telephone told Bramlett that Mrs. Topp was out and wouldn't be back till around two-thirty. He told her to tell Katherine that he'd be by about then.

Bramlett and Curry left headquarters and drove to the Billups filling station on Gunner Street. Lucian DeBow, the boyfriend of Cora Hartley, worked at the station.

DeBow glowered when Sheriff Bramlett informed him they wanted to talk with him about Jesse Bondreaux. He was as tall as Bramlett, wiry, with coal-black hair and high cheekbones, and looked to be in his early twenties. His lower lip protruded from the snuff packed behind it.

He wiped his forehead with the back of his arm. "That man was sorry. If I hadn't of thought Cora would have hated me for it, I would have killed him myself." He dampened the snuff with his tongue, then said, "In fact, Mr. Hartley and I talked about it."

Bramlett gave a start. "Y'all talked about killing him?"

"Humph," he said. He turned his head, spat, then looked back at the sheriff, his eyes leveled at Bramlett's eyes. He spoke slowly and deliberately. "We talked about beating the hell out of him. That's what. And if we had, it wouldn't have surprised me none if we didn't end up beating him to death. He was sorry."

Bramlett nodded and looked thoughtfully at the young man for a moment, then said, "But you didn't beat him up, I take it?"

"Naw." Lucian DeBow's look was hard, malicious. There was a tightness to his face as if coiled up within the center of his body was a violent energy, ready to explode.

"Thank you," the sheriff said. He turned and walked back to the patrol car with Curry following.

"YOU SEEMED TO MAKE UP YOUR MIND about him in a hurry," Curry said as he turned the key in the ignition switch. "He sure as hell looked mean enough to kill somebody."

Bramlett chuckled. "Just a good old country boy, H. C. What would you do to someone who was messing around with your girlfriend?"

Curry didn't respond. Bramlett observed a slight twitch near the right side of his forehead as he wheeled the patrol car into the street. The sheriff knew the deputy understood. He said, "Now, I think we need to call on our friend Katherine Topp again."

As the car moved steadily along the city streets, Bramlett gazed at the dark clouds massing in the north. He drew a deep breath.

There was a faint smell of burning leaves in the air. That smell, strangely enough, always took him back to his childhood. He recalled the whole family raking the leaves from the oaks and pecan trees in the front and back yards. Then his father would burn the piles of leaves.

His father was a proud man, and fiercely protective of his family. Just like Bramlett.

Curry turned onto the street on which the Topps and the Skeltons lived. Bramlett thought about the need for more physical evidence and said, "Y'all find anything else at Bondreaux's house?"

The deputy shrugged his shoulders. "No, sir. Still looking. Even went under the house in the crawl space." He gave a sign of exasperation, letting the sheriff know that he had more, much more, assigned to him than he could possibly do.

"What about those telephone tapes? You got to listen to them yet?"

Curry shook his head. "No, sir. Not yet." He sighed. "I'll get to it tonight." Then he turned into the Topps's driveway.

KATHERINE TOPP WAS NOT SMILING as she led the sheriff and deputy into the den once more. As soon as the three of them were seated, she said, "Gail really didn't know this man, Grover. I thought she made that clear." Her tone was impatient.

"It's not Gail I came to talk to," Bramlett said. Looking at her dark hair falling about her shoulders, he now tried to remember her as a blonde.

She raised a questioning eyebrow. "Oh? What's that supposed to mean?"

"We've been told *you* were a good friend of Jesse Bondreaux." He watched her face closely for the slightest reaction.

She looked down at her hands in her lap. Her thumb toyed with her wedding ring. Her lips parted slightly, then closed firmly, before she spoke softly. "I knew him, if that's what you mean."

"Exactly how would you define your relationship with him?"

She shrugged one shoulder, then looked him in the eye. "I knew him, as I said. Of course, I know lots of people."

Bramlett spread his hands as if indicating he meant no harm. "Katherine, we're talking with everyone who did know him, trying to pick up a piece here, a piece there, and soon, we hope, things will start to fit together." He paused. She nodded that she understood, then he continued. "Where did you know him from?"

"He was the tenth-grade class sponsor last year. I helped, along with several other parents on the class dance." Her tone was becoming hard, and Bramlett noticed a slight tightening of her cheeks.

"Did you ever see him outside of working on that project?"

She looked away and was silent for a long moment, then looked back at Bramlett, then to Curry, then away again.

Bramlett knew she could be wondering how much he knew. He gave a teasing smile, trying to indicate somehow without saying anything that he did know something else, something quite concrete.

Finally, she said, "We got together a couple of times. For drinks."
"Where?"

"At his house." There was a slight twitching to her cheek now.
"Over how long a period of time?"

She shrugged again. "A couple of months maybe. That was all."
"Did your husband know?"

She swallowed. Her eyes were now fixed at the floor, and her mouth twisted a bit as if she were trying to decide what or how much to say.

She swallowed again and said, "There was no need for Robert to know anything." She lifted her eyes and met Bramlett's gaze. "There was nothing to it, Grover." She shook her head and held his gaze. "Nothing at all."

"When was the last time you saw him?"

She looked away. "It's been several weeks."

Bramlett's brow furrowed. "Gail is in the eleventh grade now. You said you worked with him on the *tenth*-grade dance."

She closed her eyes and pressed her lips together. "I saw him . . . I don't know . . . at the grocery store or someplace. We just chatted for a moment. The *other* was last year."

Bramlett nodded. "I see. And can you tell me who else may have been a friend of his? Any kind of friend?"

"I really didn't know him that well. He was attractive, funny, someone to be with. For a while. No, I don't know who would kill him or anything like that." She suddenly seemed very tired and not nearly as pretty as Bramlett had always thought her to be.

"Thank you, Katherine," he said. He looked at Curry and nodded. Both men stood up.

ONCE OUTSIDE AGAIN, Bramlett looked in the direction of the Skelton house. "Let's see what little Miss Vicki Ann can tell us now."

A misty rain began just as they drove up into the driveway in front of the Skeltons' house. Curry parked directly behind a red Mercedes convertible close to the front step.

Bramlett rang the doorbell. The wind was now whipping rain across the wide porch. He noticed the wavering reflections of the columns in the rain-mirrored Mexican tile.

A maid dressed in starched white led them into the large sitting room where Rumi, Howard, and Vicki Ann were waiting. Rumi Skelton rose quickly from the couch and crossed the room, extending her hand to Bramlett and smiling.

"Hello, Grover," she said. In her baggy beige sweater embroidered with red and gold flowers and designer blue jeans, she looked to Bramlett as if she'd just stepped out of a fashion magazine. The heavy bracelets on her wrist jingled as she shook his hand. She was smiling warmly but Bramlett noticed a certain apprehensiveness around the corners of her eyes.

"And this," she said, turning toward her daughter, still sitting on the couch with her hands in her lap, her eyes downcast, "is Deputy Curry, Vicki Ann. His sister was the other homecoming queen, I believe."

"Niece," corrected Curry, nodding toward the girl who did not look up at him.

Vicki Ann appeared to Bramlett to be breathing unevenly. Her dark eyelashes were matted as if she'd been crying. She wore no makeup.

Howard Skelton sat stiffly in a leather easy chair glaring at Bramlett, his arms tightly folded across his chest. His lips were pressed together. He had made no motion to rise when the two lawmen entered the room as if to emphasize he was not shaking hands with them nor welcoming them in any way.

"Vicki Ann," Bramlett said after he and Curry were seated, "I know how upset you are, but I have to ask you a few questions."

The girl made no response.

Bramlett continued. "First I want to ask you about Jesse Bondreaux."

Rumi resumed her seat beside Vicki Ann on the couch and placed her hands over her daughter's hands. "Just tell Mr. Bramlett whatever you know, dear," she said, smiling reassuringly at the girl.

Vicki Ann gave no indication that she heard her mother or Bramlett.

Bramlett tried to fix a disarming smile on his face. "I understand you used to visit his house occasionally."

"*Used* to is correct," Howard Skelton said.

Bramlett refrained from telling the man to shut up. "So, you were a friend of Mr. Bondreaux."

She nodded. "Y-yes . . ."

"Could you give us the names of other students who used to go over there?"

"Gail Topp went some, Cora Hartley, Billy Mosley, Lillie Faye Conlee, Duvall Ellis." She paused, then said, "I can't think of anyone else right now."

"We have reason to believe Mr. Bondreaux may have been dealing in drugs," he said. "Do you know anything about that?"

The girl sucked slightly on the corner of her mouth, then gave a quick, short shake of her head, indicating no.

"Do you know any students who are doing drugs?"

A slight shoulder shrug.

"Does that mean yes or no?" Bramlett said.

"No," she said.

Bramlett let himself sink deeper into his chair, breathed a couple of long, slow, relaxing breaths, and noticed Vicki Ann was indeed pretty enough to be in motion pictures. Long blond hair, long legs, high cheekbones, and classical facial features.

How could a kid like this be mixed up with a slug like Jesse Bondreaux? After a long moment, he asked, "When was the last time you were at his house?"

She wet her lips with her tongue, swallowed hard, then said, "I . . . I stopped by Thursday afternoon. Just for a minute or two."

"What?" Howard Skelton said. "But you said—"

His wife, shooting him a warning look, raised one hand to silence him.

"Was anyone else there?" Bramlett said.

She shook her head.

"Do you have any idea who might want him dead?"

Another shake of the head.

"Do you know anyone who drives a small, dark-blue car? Maybe a Honda or a Toyota?"

Her head jerked up and her blue eyes widened as she looked at him. "W-what?"

Bramlett smiled reassuringly. "A dark-blue car. Do you know if any of the kids who used to hang around Bondreaux's house drives one?"

Her lips parted slightly, then her eyes fell to her hands again and she shook her head. She drew a jerky breath, and her mouth quivered.

Rumi slipped an arm around the girl's shoulders. "It's all right, honey. It's all right." Then she turned her face to look at Bramlett and said, "That red convertible outside is Vicki Ann's car, if that's what you're asking."

Bramlett frowned wearily. "That's not really what I was asking." He drew another deep breath, held it a moment, then let it out. "I know this is hard on you all. Obviously, Mr. Bondreaux was well liked and especially close to some of his students—like Vicki Ann. But the man is dead and my job is to find out everything I can that might help us find out who killed him." He looked at the girl. "Don't you want us to catch whoever did this, Vicki Ann?"

She nodded without looking up at him.

"So, is there anything you can tell us about Mr. Bondreaux? Maybe there was someone he had an argument with—or someone who didn't like him . . ."

She shook her head.

Bramlett's eyes narrowed. "Tell me about Jo Ann Scales. How well did you know her?"

Vicki Ann's eyes snapped to look at the sheriff. The eyes were wide, suddenly horror-filled, and her mouth dropped open as if she were going to scream, but she made not a sound and began trembling.

Rumi grabbed her daughter by the shoulders and drew her against herself.

"It's okay. It's okay," she whispered in her ear. Then, in a moment, she half turned her face to Bramlett. "Miss Scales was *very* close to Vicki Ann, Grover. This thing is tearing her apart."

The veins were swelling in Howard Skelton's neck. "She's had enough of this," he said.

Bramlett nodded. "All right," he said, looking at the girl in her mother's arms. "That's enough for now." Then he rose out of the chair.

NENA CARMACK HAD NAMED a secretary in Tupelo as Jesse Bondreaux's latest love. Bramlett and Curry drove the hilly two-lane highway from Sheffield to Tupelo in just over half an hour.

The rain had slacked off leaving the browning leaves of the kudzu which cloaked the roadbanks a dark, heavy brown. The traffic was thicker coming from the town than going into it. They found Adamson's' Insurance Services on Main Street.

Nicole Estis was a short, buxom woman, not yet thirty, with hazel eyes, long dark eyelashes, and dark-brown hair. She asked another secretary to cover her telephone calls and showed the two lawman into a conference room with wine-colored imitation leather chairs and invited them to sit down. Bramlett noticed that she had yet to look him in the eye.

"We've come about Jesse Bondreaux," the sheriff said.

She dabbed at one heavily mascaraed eye with a tissue in her hand, then said, "I still can't believe it . . ."

"We understand you and Bondreaux were seeing each other." He tried to smile and look pleasant.

She said faintly, "Yes," and gave a slight shudder.

"When was the last time you saw him?"

"A week ago." She wadded the tissue tightly with her hand.

"I understand you are married."

She nodded, pressing the hand with the tissue against the side of her mouth. "Actually, we're separated."

"What's your husband's name?"

She raised her head for the first time and looked straight at Bramlett. "Surely you don't think . . ." She didn't finish.

Bramlett shrugged. "Just routine questions, Mrs. Estis."

"Farley couldn't . . ." She paused and shook her head and looked down again. "Farley Estis. Like I said, we're separated. He moved out last summer."

"And you're still married?"

"I'm getting a divorce."

"Were you going to marry Bondreaux once you got a divorce?"

She nodded. "We had talked about going away. Some time soon."

"Where to?"

"San Francisco, Atlanta." She paused, sniffed with the tissue to her nose, then added, "A big city."

"And you hadn't seen him in a week, I believe you said?" Bramlett said. A couple this serious and only thirty miles apart not seeing each other for a week?

She shrugged. "We talked on the phone . . ." Her voice trailed off.

Bramlett cut his eyes at Curry. The deputy was writing on his notepad. Bramlett looked back at the woman. "When precisely were y'all leaving?"

"We hadn't set a definite time."

"We found drugs at his house, Mrs. Estis." He watched her closely for a response.

She cocked her head as if surprised but said nothing.

"How big into drugs was he?" he asked.

She glared at Bramlett. "What are you implying? Jesse wasn't into drugs."

"Could he have been selling?"

"Drugs? You got to be kidding. Who to?"

"A lot of kids hung around his place."

"That's ridiculous," she said. "Jesse would never sell drugs."

"Do you use drugs?" Bramlett's gaze was hard, probing.

She looked away. "I . . . No, of course not."

He rubbed his index finger on the side of his face. There was something strange about this woman. He couldn't figure out at all if she was being truthful or lying through her teeth. "Could you tell us where you were last Friday afternoon around five o'clock?"

"Right here. We didn't leave the office till after five."

Bramlett started to pull himself up out of the chair, then paused and said, "Did you know Jo Ann Scales?"

"No, I did not," she said flatly.

Bramlett rose. "Now, Mrs. Estis, would you mind telling us where your husband lives?"

THE PATROL CAR BOUNCED OVER A WASHBOARD road winding through a pine thicket eight miles south of Tupelo. Bramlett's hat was knocked ajar as he was thrown against the door window. "Dammit. Slow down," he said to Curry.

"I ain't going but ten miles an hour."

"Then go five 'fore you bust up these shocks."

Curry pulled to a stop in front of an avocado-colored house trailer. To the right of the trailer a red-mud splattered Jeep Cherokee was parked in front of a large butane tank.

A tall, angular man pushed open the screen door as Bramlett and Curry got out of the car. His head almost touched the top of the

115

doorway and the straps of his striped overalls dangled unbuttoned. In his hand he held a can of beer. He looked inquisitively at the two lawmen as they approached the trailer.

"Mr. Estis? Farley Estis?" Bramlett said.

He nodded and frowned, stepping down to the cracked concrete stoop. "What you want?"

Bramlett placed his hands on his hips and looked around the bare-earth yard surrounding the trailer. A wheelless, rusting 1952 flathead Ford was to the left of the woodpile.

He looked back at the man. "We've been to talk with your wife." He wished very much right at that moment for a huge chew of Red Man. "About Jesse Bondreaux," he added.

The man's grip tightened on the beer can and his mouth twisted into a jeering smile. "So?"

"You knew he was dead?"

Estis grunted a low laugh. "Yeah. I knew. Saw it in the paper."

Bramlett nodded, studying the man carefully. Then he said, "Did you know him?"

"Naw." His smile faded and he lifted the can and took a long swallow, holding the can from his mouth as its contents drained to a few drops. Then he crushed the can and let it fall to the ground. His eyes were on Bramlett's eyes. "You looking for who did it?"

Bramlett nodded, wondering if jealousy in this man could be strong enough to make him kill . . . or pay somebody else to do it. He said, "You know anyone who might want him dead?"

Estis's eyes widened. "You implying I might've had something to do with it?"

"Did you want him dead, Mr. Estis? He was your wife's lover."

There was a mean, dark look on his face. "What difference would it make? If it wasn't him, it'd just be somebody else."

"Where were you last Friday night about five o'clock?"

"Five o'clock? Right here, dammit. Just like every working day when I come home. Just setting and drinking beer. Y'all want a beer?" His lips curled into a sneer.

"Anybody else can verify you were here?"

"How 'bout twelve empty beer cans?" he said. "Only I dumped them all last Saturday afternoon. Now if you was to go back up this road and cut down that logging trail 'bout an eighth mile or so

116

you'll come to where I slung 'em." He grinned broader. " 'Course, there's so many cans there I don't know how you'll tell—"

" 'Preciate your time, Mr. Estis," Bramlett said, motioning with his head to Curry to follow him to the car.

BACK AT HEADQUARTERS, Johnny Baillie entered the office and took a chair beside Curry's. It was almost six o'clock.

"No luck yet on running down Gilly Bitzer," Baillie said.

Bramlett nodded that he heard and scanned the phone messages on his desk at the same time. The mayor had called again. Also Doc Walhood. Some reporter named Virgil Cooper from the Tupelo paper wanted to talk with him.

Bramlett looked up at the deputy. "Keep at it," he said, referring to Bitzer, "but I think we're looking for someone much younger." Someone the age of his daughter Margaret, Marcellus had said.

Baillie and Curry exchanged puzzled glances. Then Baillie said, "Sir?"

"Nothing." He had to be more careful, he reminded himself. "Anything else?"

Baillie shifted uneasily. "Just one thing. In the canvass all the neighbors around Bondreaux's house were contacted." He took a notepad out of his shirt pocket. "There's a Mrs. Jefferson," he said, reading from the notepad. "She was gone for the weekend when the canvass was done. Drumwright and I went by to see her this afternoon. She lives next door to Bondreaux. She saw him when he came home from school Friday. She said it was about three-thirty."

"Then she may have been the last person to see him alive," Bramlett said, ". . . except for the killer, of course."

Baillie nodded. "She says she saw someone leaving Bondreaux's house Friday afternoon. It was about four o'clock. A woman. And she was in a hurry. Went off screeching down the street in her car, Mrs. Jefferson says."

Bramlett cocked his head. "Oh? And did this Mrs. Jefferson know the woman's name?"

"Yes, sir. She said it was the teacher Bondreaux used to date. Her name is Nena Carmack."

17

H. C. CURRY SAID NOTHING as they drove through the dark streets to the cottage set back from the sidewalk and almost hidden by two huge magnolias. He parked the patrol car against the curb and opened his door.

"Listen . . ." Bramlett said, reaching out and touching the deputy on the arm. "I know she's a friend of yours."

Curry shook his head. "Business is business," he said and got out of the car.

"ARE WE INTERRUPTING YOUR SUPPER?" Bramlett asked when Nena Carmack opened the door. She was wearing black pants and a loose jersey top. Her long-limbed physique reminded Bramlett of women track athletes he'd seen on ESPN.

"Just getting ready to do the dishes," she said. "Come in." There was an edge to her voice, and Bramlett could sense that she was ill at ease or irritated at their visit.

When they were seated in the living room, Bramlett said, "I believe you told us you hadn't seen Jesse Bondreaux outside of school—privately, I mean—in some time . . ."

Nena looked toward Curry. The deputy was looking down at the notepad he'd just taken out of his shirt pocket. His cheeks were taut. She looked back at the sheriff. "So?"

"Someone says they saw you leaving his place Friday afternoon. Says you were in a hurry." Bramlett's voice was low, firm, his eyes steady on her face.

She looked away. Color rose in her cheeks. Then she said softly, "Yes. I was there."

"Did you talk to him?"

She nodded, rubbing her palms against the top of her legs. "He'd called and said he had to see me. I didn't want to go but he sounded so . . . so . . ." She didn't finish.

"And?"

She sighed. "So I went."

"What did he want?"

She swallowed, then said, "He wanted to tell me he was leaving town."

"You mean like moving away?"

She nodded. "Going away and never coming back. Of course, he lied a lot."

"When was he leaving?"

"As soon as he could put together enough money, he said."

"I see. Why was he leaving?"

"He said he'd had enough of Small Town USA—whatever that is supposed to mean."

"Did he ask you for money?"

She nodded again. "Yes."

"How much?"

She glowered. "More than I could give him."

Bramlett gazed at her face several moments. He could see in her eyes the anger and bitterness. Hurt, too. Then he said, "Why should you give him money?"

She sighed impatiently and her eyes darted about the room. "I don't know."

"Schoolteachers don't make much. Where were you supposed to get a lot of money?"

She was grinding her teeth. Then she said, "He wanted me to ask my father for it."

"Had you gotten money for Bondreaux from your father before?"

Again she nodded.

"What does your father do?"

"He owns an automobile dealership."

Bramlett put his hands on his knees and drew a long, deliberate breath, held it a moment, then slowly released it through his nose. He licked his lips, thinking, watching her face closely, then asked, "Was Bondreaux blackmailing you?"

She flinched and shut her eyes tight as if in pain. For a few seconds she didn't move. Then she gave her head a shake and said, "No."

"Then why should you give him money?"

"He just thought he could keep using me like before." She opened her eyes. "That's all."

"Was he getting money from anyone else?"

"I don't know. Probably."

Bramlett rubbed his hand across his chin and mouth. His shoulders hurt. He said, "What time did you go to his place Friday?"

"About four o'clock."

"Why didn't you tell us this before?"

Again she shut her eyes and shook her head. "I was scared . . . I don't know . . ."

"And that was the very last time you saw him?"

She nodded. Her eyes were still shut.

"What did he have on you?" Bramlett's tone was firm.

Her eyes snapped open and she glared at him. Her lip curled in an expression of disgust. "Nothing. I told you that," she said. "Nothing."

Bramlett studied her face again, especially the eyes. *She's lying*, he thought. *Lying sure as hell.* Then he rose to his feet and said, "Thank you, Miss Carmack. I'm sure we'll be talking with you again."

"WELL?" BRAMLETT SAID as soon as they were in the car.

Curry turned the ignition switch. "Sounds like he had something on her," he said, shifting into gear. "Poor Jacob."

Bramlett looked back toward the house. "There's a lot she ain't telling us."

The deputy nodded. "Got time for me to check with Lizzie?" Lizzie's apartment was a short distance from Nena Carmack's cottage.

120

"Sure," the sheriff said as Lizzie's apartment building came into view. "I'll wait in the car."

CURRY TROTTED INTO THE BUILDING and took the stairs three steps at a time as he went to the second floor. He knocked hard on her door, waited a moment, knocked harder, waited again. No response.

The sheriff was leaning against the hood of the car as Curry returned. "Lovely night," Bramlett said, looking up at the sky.

Curry grunted and opened the door to the driver's side. "She's not home," he said. His voice was hoarse.

Bramlett pushed himself off the hood. "I'm sure she's okay," he said. He opened the door and backed down onto the front seat. "Just had a call from headquarters. They picked up that old wino pissing on somebody's front lawn."

"What?" Curry started the car and glanced toward the darkened windows of Lizzie's apartment.

"Gilly Bitzer," the sheriff said. "They got him down at headquarters." He chuckled. "Somebody phoned nine-one-one from a car phone that a man was pissing on his lawn." He chuckled again.

GILLY BITZER LOOKED UP at Bramlett and Curry with reddened eyes and a wan smile as they entered the conference room. His upper teeth were missing and his lip sank back into his mouth. His Pittsburgh Pirates cap was pushed back on his head, revealing his bald forehead. His scalp was mottled with various shades of sun-damaged skin. The hair growing over his ears was long and grizzled, and his stained suit coat was heavily patched.

"Can't stand rich people, Sheriff," he said before Bramlett spoke a word. "You know that. So what if I killed a little grass. I don't give a crap."

Jacob Robertson and Johnny Braille both had half stood when Bramlett entered the room. He motioned them to keep their seats and drew up a chair on the opposite side of the table from Bitzer. He had known the old vagrant for years. Except for public drunkenness, Bitzer had never been a problem.

"Just because you don't like rich people doesn't mean you can take a leak on their lawns, Gilly," Bramlett said.

The old man grinned broader and his upper lip flapped as he spoke. "Hell, Grover. You'd do it if you wasn't a respected citizen. Wouldn't you? Really?" He asked sincerely as if expecting the sheriff to say yes.

"Tell us about the car by the tracks, Gilly," Bramlett said. "The one with the dead man in it."

Gilly Bitzer's grin slowly dropped and his eyes fixed on Bramlett for a moment, then moved deliberately to each of the three deputies in turn. He looked back to Bramlett and grinned again. "So you know I was there. Hell, Grover, you was always a smart kid."

"What were you doing there?"

Bitzer smiled again. "Just resting."

"That your empty bottle we found?"

The man's eyes crinkled as he smiled. "Could be. I've left enough of them aroundabouts."

"Tell us about the car, Gilly. What did you see?"

Bitzer shrugged. "Don't rightly know exactly. I was just resting on the other side of the tracks and all of a sudden like this car comes falling off the bank. I walked over and looked inside and seen him. Then that damn train come by scaring the crap out of me."

Bramlett raised one eyebrow. "You telling us a *dead* man drove that car off the bank?"

He shrugged again. "I reckon somebody pushed it."

"Did you happen to see who that somebody was?"

Bitzer looked toward the ceiling and shook his head. "Naw. I ain't seen nobody."

"You sure?"

The man looked thoughtfully at the back of his age-spotted hand. His fingers began nervously tapping on the top of the table. He said nothing.

"Well, Gilly," Bramlett said softly, "I don't really remember right now what the law says about pissing on people's front lawns. But we gonna have to lock you up until we find out."

Bitzer looked up at Bramlett, one eye squinting. "That so? And how long you reckon it gonna take you to find out?"

Bramlett spread his hands slightly and slowly shook his head. "Can't say. A few days. Maybe a week."

"A *week*?" The man's eyes widened in disbelief.

"Well, it'll give you a little time to think."

"Think? Think about what exactly?"

"About whether or not you saw whoever it was pushed that car over the bank."

Bitzer scowled and blew out his upper lip, his eyes hard on the sheriff.

Bramlett stood. "Let me know if you have any thoughts on the subject, Gilly." Then, looking at Johnny Baillie, he said, "Have somebody take him over to the jail."

"What about supper?" Bitzer asked. "I ain't eat yet."

Bramlett glanced at his watch. "They already served supper at the jail, Gilly. Maybe you'll think better tonight on an empty stomach."

He turned and left the room. Curry followed. Once outside, Bramlett stopped and turned to the deputy. "Have somebody run pick up a hamburger for him. Else he'll make it miserable for everybody over there tonight."

Curry nodded. "You think he knows something?"

Bramlett smiled. "He's lying. I can't imagine *why* . . . but I know he is. A day or so without that rotgut he drinks will probably bring him around." He turned toward his office. "I'm going to supper."

"I WENT AHEAD AND FED MARCELLUS," Valeria said. "Sit down. Yours is in the oven. You want buttermilk?"

"Uh-huh," intoned Bramlett, standing in the kitchen staring at the dried arrangement in the center of the table that Valeria had put together from dying annuals. It struck him that he wasn't hungry. Bramlett could count on the fingers of one hand the times in his life when he hadn't been hungry at mealtime.

"It won't take me but a minute to get it on the table," she said as she filled a glass with buttermilk and set it on the table.

Bramlett pulled back a chair and sat down. He lifted the glass and sipped. Nothing like ice-cold buttermilk. Except cornbread with buttermilk.

She took his plate out of the oven, holding it with a VBS potholder. "Do you really think this killer is still around here? Somebody said it was a whatchamacallit."

Bramlett shook his head. "I don't have any idea what you're talking about." She set the plate in front of him. One of his favorite menus—meatloaf, turnip greens, mashed potatoes.

"Hit man. That's what you call them. Paid to do it. Is that what you think? Is this a gangster?" She stood looking down at him.

He could see the anxiety mounting in her eyes. He shook his head and took another sip of milk. "We don't know yet. But we're moving as fast as we can." He suddenly felt very tired. He knew that she didn't want to mention, did not want to admit, the fact that the killer had probably seen their grandson at the cemetery.

"Any cornbread?" he asked, not knowing why he asked in that he had so little appetite.

"Is food all you think about?" Her voice broke as she spoke.

Marcellus walked into the room.

Valeria turned her back to him. Bramlett knew she didn't want the boy to see her face, was afraid she might lose control any moment now.

Bramlett forced a bite of meatloaf into his mouth and smiled at Marcellus as he chewed. "What you been doing, tiger?" he asked. The meatloaf seemed to grow bigger with each chew.

"Playing basketball at the park with Jimbo."

"Good." Bramlett washed down the meatloaf with a gulp of buttermilk, wiped his mouth with the back of his hand, then said, "You know what's on TV in ten minutes?" Bramlett's eyes twinkled. "Wrestling. And tonight the Undertaker is on. You'll love him."

Bramlett took a mouthful of mashed potatoes, then a mouthful of meatloaf, and then a long swallow of buttermilk. He pushed his chair back. "Go ahead and turn on the TV," he said, motioning for Marcellus to go on into the den. There was a big smile on the grandfather's face.

Marcellus left the room.

Bramlett turned to Valeria. His smile had vanished. Instead, a sober, harried look flattened his face. "I'll watch a little TV with him, but then I have to go back."

She closed her eyes. Bramlett put his arms around her and pulled her to him, burying her face in his chest.

124

18

MRS. LOIS MOSLEY'S SHOULDERS SAGGED more and her nostrils expanded as she drew a sharp breath when Sheriff Bramlett asked if her son Billy was home. She wrung her hands and stared at him with fright-filled eyes.

H. C. Curry, standing beside Bramlett on the door stoop, studied the dark-blue Honda Prelude parked in the driveway and remembered the sheriff's strange interest in dark-blue Hondas and Toyotas. *He's holding back on me*, the deputy thought. *There's something he knows but hasn't told me.*

"Yes . . ." Mrs. Mosley said. "He's in his room. What's wrong?"

"We just want to ask him a few questions, ma'am," Bramlett said.

She retreated from the doorway and the two lawmen stepped into the living room. The room was furnished with an eclectic collection of chairs, sofas, and end tables. The predominate color, even of the badly worn carpet, was hunter green. Curry closed the door as he entered the room.

The woman disappeared down a short hallway, then returned moments later, followed by a short, pudgy teenager whose acne-spotted face seemed drained of color, all the more highlighting the sores.

Bramlett introduced Curry and himself to the boy and said, "We want to talk to you about Jesse Bondreaux."

The boy stood stiffly beside an armchair. His mother, still wring-

125

ing her hands, sank onto the edge of a sofa. She didn't offer them seats.

"You were in one of his classes?" Bramlett said.

The young man nodded. His eyes darted back and forth from the carpet in front of Bramlett's feet to the carpet in front of Curry's feet. But he never looked directly into the face of either man.

"And I understand you used to go over to his place after school a lot."

Again, a quick nod of the head.

"Why?" Bramlett asked. His patience was ebbing. He couldn't muster up a liking for this kid even though he did seem to have a weight problem.

Billy gave a slight shrug of one shoulder. "Everybody else was," he said.

"Who is everybody?"

He named the same teenagers as had been mentioned before and no one new.

"Are any of these kids special friends of yours?" Bramlett couldn't imagine Gail Topp or Vicki Ann Skelton or even Cora Hartley having anything to do with this strange young man.

"Not really," he said.

"Did Mr. Bondreaux ask you to come to his house, or what?"

"Yeah. I guess."

Bramlett thought on this, and decided Billy Mosley probably had invited himself. He said, "What happened when you all were at his house?"

The boy looked up at Bramlett, confusion is his face "Sir?"

"What did y'all do?" Bramlett's back was hurting more.

Billy gave a slight shrug. "Just hanging out. You know. Talking. Mr. Bondreaux was always trying to be so funny, you know."

"Funny? How funny?"

"Telling jokes. Stupid jokes."

"What kind of jokes?"

He made a face. "About pimples, fat people. Stuff like that."

Bramlett nodded. "I understand. And you thought he was directing some of these jokes at you?"

Billy looked toward the ceiling. "I don't know. He was really a very stupid man."

126

"So you quit going over to his place."

"Yeah."

"Why?"

Billy wrapped his arms around himself. "We had a disagreement."

"About what?"

"He gave me a bad grade on a test. It wasn't fair."

"You never told me about that," his mother said.

"What wasn't fair about it?" Bramlett asked.

"It just wasn't. That's all. He shouldn't have done it."

"So, you two had words and he told you to stay away from his house?"

The boy frowned and sneered. "I didn't care. I didn't want to be around there anyway. It was boring."

"Let me ask you this," Bramlett said. "Was Mr. Bondreaux dealing drugs?"

"Drugs?" He looked confused.

"That's what I said. Drugs."

There was a blank expression on his face for a moment, then suddenly his eyes began to glow. "I don't know," he said slowly. "Maybe."

"Was he selling stuff to kids?"

"Yeah," the boy said, his cheeks tightening. "He tried to sell me some. That's how come I quit going around there."

"Oh, my poor baby," his mother said, rising from the sofa and reaching her hands out toward her son. The boy stiffened as she touched him.

"I thought you quit going there because he gave you a bad grade."

"That, too."

"Specifically which kids were buying from him?" Bramlett said.

"I don't remember." He hugged himself tighter.

"Was it Gail Topp?"

"I don't know . . ."

"What about Lillie Faye Conlee?"

"Maybe. She's a creep."

"I think you're lying, Billy," Bramlett said, glaring at the boy. "Why are you lying, Billy?"

Billy Mosley's face because red at once. "I ain't lying. I did see him take a lot of money from one dude. He must have been dealing him drugs."

"What dude?"

The boy frowned slightly. "He drove a BMW. A red BMW."

"Do you know his name?"

Billy shrugged his shoulder. "Jesse called him Noel. That's all I know. Once I saw him give Jesse a chunk of cash. The guy was all upset. It was in the hallway. I was just coming out of the bathroom. Jesse was all pushed out of shape because I saw them and started screaming at me to get out of the house."

"Was that why you didn't go back?"

He curled his lip. "I didn't want to go over there anyway."

Bramlett nodded and looked at Curry. "Okay," he said, turning back to Mrs. Mosley. She stood beside her son, looking at him with anxiety and hurt in her eyes.

"Thank you for your time," Bramlett said and turned toward the door.

"WHAT DO YOU THINK?" Bramlett said as soon as they were in the car.

Curry backed out of the driveway into the street and shifted gears. "Blue Honda," he said.

"I saw it. What did you think about what he said?"

"I think he was lying about something."

Bramlett grunted. "Do you think he was telling the truth about anything?"

Curry shrugged. "Maybe."

"Drugs?"

Curry shrugged again. "I'm not sure.

"What about Hackott and Bondreaux?"

"Maybe."

Bramlett stared at the side of Curry's face. There was a tenseness. He could see it in the young man's eyes, his cheeks, the set of his mouth. The sheriff had caught the reference to the Honda. That was probably the sore. Curry knew he wasn't sharing everything with him.

128

Bramlett looked back at the road in front of them and said, "Just drive, then. Just drive."

JACOB ROBERTSON LEFT HEADQUARTERS for home shortly after eight o'clock. He'd not been able to think about anything except Nena Carmack all day. Everywhere he turned she was in the front of his mind, her image superimposed over everything else he saw. He steered through the dark streets of Sheffield. All was very quiet. He cruised down the street on which she lived.

He only meant to ride by her house. He certainly had no intentions of stopping or even being seen. He slowed to a crawl as he neared the cottage.

The streetlight cast a yellowish glow over the front porch. He thought he saw someone sitting in the swing. He squinted his eyes, and . . . yes, there was someone . . . Nena herself.

Immediately, there was a hard lump in Jacob's throat. His first impulse was to stomp down on the accelerator and get away before she could recognize him. Then, surprising himself completely, he braked, parked against the curb, and got out of the pickup.

"I was just passing by . . ." he began, then stopped. He didn't know what to say. He stood near the bottom of the front steps.

She smiled and hunched her shoulders slightly against the chill. She was wearing jeans and a baggy sweater. "I was just thinking about you," she said.

He tried to swallow down the lump. It seemed to grow bigger. "You were?"

"You remind me a lot of my dad." She paused, then frowned. "He isn't in very good health, though. He's had two heart attacks already. Mother tries to keep him from doing too much. Tries to keep things from him that would upset him." She turned her head and gazed out beyond the street. In a moment she looked back at him. "It's been a hard day." She spoke this as if not wanting to continue talking about her father.

He placed one foot on the bottom step. "Sheriff Bramlett is driving hard on this murder case," he said, and immediately regretted mentioning that because he didn't want to remind her of anything to do with Jesse Bondreaux.

"Yes," she said. "I know." She pushed gently with her feet and the swing moved. "Do you like the sheriff?"

He hesitated for a moment. "He's a good man. Laid back most of the time. Right now for some reason he's all caught up in this case. Seems more short-tempered lately."

"I saw him once with a little boy."

"That was probably Marcellus, his grandson. He thinks the sun rises and sets on that kid."

"Marcellus," she said distantly and looked toward the street again. "Unusual name." She rose from the swing. "I appreciate you coming by."

He understood it was time to leave even though he wanted to stay. He nodded and said, "I'll see you." She reached for the handle to the front door, and he turned and walked back to his truck.

H. C. CURRY TOOK A COLD CAN of Budweiser out of the refrigerator and popped the top. He held up the can and gurgled a fast swallow, wiped his mouth with the back of his hand, and walked slowly into his bedroom.

He set the can on the table beside his bed and slipped a cassette cartridge from Bondreaux's house into the small tape player on the table beside the bed and pressed down the lid.

He eased back onto the bed, propped his back against the headboard, reached for the beer, and pressed down the Play button. There was a static hum, then, "Hi. It's me." It was a female voice. White. Young.

"What's happening?" answered a man's voice, no doubt Bondreaux himself. Funny, thought Curry. He had not expected Bondreaux to sound like the voice on the tape. He wasn't sure what he expected.

"I came by this afternoon but you weren't home," the woman said.

"Faculty meeting after school. Old man Wilson went on and on. He wouldn't be so bad if he knew how to *talk*, for godssake."

"Maybe I could come by now."

A soft chuckle. "I'd like that."

" 'Bye," sweetly intoned the female voice.

130

Curry couldn't match the voice with anyone they'd interviewed.

There was a string of innocuous conversations, each interspersed with the hum—parents concerned about grades their children were making, two rather boring conversations between Bondreaux and the secretary Nicole Estis ("What you doing?" "Talking to you. What are you doing?"), a telephone solicitation from a blind man selling brooms, and a call wanting him to buy ten poor children tickets to a circus sponsored by the Rotary Club in Sheffield.

Then, "Hello?" A woman's voice.

Bondreaux spoke. "Where is it?" he said without even identifying himself. "I told you I wanted it by five o'clock."

"I don't have it. You've got to give me more time."

"Talk to your father. He can give you enough."

"No," she said. "Not now. You know I can't do that. He's sick."

"Shall I talk to him? Better, shall I *send* him a present?"

"You bastard!"

"I'm serious."

"Give me till Friday. I'll get the money."

He was silent for a long moment, then said, "Okay. Till Friday. Or else I'll put it in the mail to your father." Then the line disconnected.

Curry clicked off the recorder. His hand was trembling. He recognized the woman's voice immediately. It was Nena Carmack. He panted several short breaths, then drew a deep one and clicked the recorder on again.

"Listen, scum! This is Marshall Hartley. You stay away from my daughter or I'm gonna tear your guts out! You hear?" A clattering sound and the line hummed dead. Obviously Bondreaux had hung up immediately on Cora Hartley's father, the construction worker with the deer-hoof gun racks who admitted owning a .25-caliber automatic pistol.

Curry reached over and punched the Stop button on the tape player. He drained the last of the beer. They should have picked up that pistol for a ballistics test when they were there. If Hartley was halfway smart, he'd already have dumped it in a river by now.

He leaned over to the telephone on the bedside table, lifted the receiver and punched Lizzie's number. He let it ring ten times. She didn't even have the answering machine turned on. He hung up. Where in the hell was she?

JACOB ROBERTSON FELT RESTLESS. After leaving Nena, he drove past Jesse's Bondreaux's darkened house. There was some unknown factor, some very definite reason why one person should kill another.

In the case of Jesse Bondreaux—not to mention Jo Ann Scales—that reason was unclear. To be sure, Bondreaux was scum. But people didn't usually bother to kill other people just for being scum. Maybe the sheriff was right. Maybe there was still some physical evidence that would reveal that reason.

He turned around, drove back to Bondreaux's house and parked in the driveway. He ducked under the yellow crime scene plastic tape and let himself into the house. He still had the key from the last time he was here.

He walked into the bedroom again. It remained the mess of scattered clothes and jumbled drawers they had left. He returned to the closet. He'd been so excited about finding the false switch box that he hadn't continued his search.

He stepped into the closet and flicked on his flashlight. Beaded board on the walls. Clothes on hangers were pushed away from the rectangular opening in the back where the false switch box had been. He looked at the ceiling.

Plyboard. Unpainted. Something looked odd.

He leaned out of the closet and looked at the ceiling. Beaded board, painted, nine feet high. He looked back at the closet ceiling. Not even seven feet high.

He pressed against the plyboard ceiling. It was nailed in place. But why was the ceiling dropped? Why wasn't it as high as the bedroom ceiling?

He stepped out of the closet and looked at the vent opening above the transom. Vent? Why a vent? The house had window units for air and space heaters for warmth.

He hurriedly moved a straight-back chair to the closet doorway and stood on it. He reached his hands to the vent. It was loose, was not screwed into the wall. He pulled the vent away and looked inside.

132

There, positioned on top of the plyboard and pointed at the bed, was a video camera.

WHEN SHERIFF BRAMLETT ARRIVED HOME, he walked into the bedroom quietly and began undressing in the dark.

"That you?" Valeria said from the bed.

He managed a soft chuckle. "If it ain't, you in bad trouble, lady."

Just as he settled into the bed, the telephone rang. Bramlett fumbled momentarily with the receiver on the night table, then answered. It was Deputy Todd Falkner, the night dispatcher. He switched Bramlett immediately to the jail.

Deputy Andy Crewson, the night jailer, said, "Sheriff, a lawyer is down here raising all kind of hell about Gilly Bitzer."

"What?"

"Wants to know what he's charged with. I told him nothing yet, and he was *demanding* we let him out. I told him I couldn't do nothing without talking to you. He said some not very nice things, and said I'd better call you now."

"A lawyer? What's Gilly Bitzer doing with a lawyer?" Bramlett scratched his chin. "Just who *is* this lawyer?"

"Jason McAbrams."

"*Jason McAbrams!* What is Jacob McAbrams doing representing somebody like Gilly Bitzer?"

"I don't know, sir. But he's awfully upset. What you want me to tell him?"

Jason McAbrams was not a criminal lawyer. He was president of the Rotary Club this year, involved in numerous community activities, and represented many of the wealthiest people in northeast Mississippi. "He's still there?" asked Bramlett.

"Yessir. He's pacing up and down in the hallway."

"Call him to the phone."

Moments later, Jason McAbrams said, "Grover, if you're going to charge my client with something, I suggest you do it right away." His speech was clipped, abrupt.

"Jason, he's an important witness in a case we're working on. I want to question—"

"What are you holding him on? Urinating on somebody's grass?

Then charge him and get the judge to set bail. You can question him all you want later. He's easy enough for you to get a hold of."

"I don't suppose you'd tell me who's paying you?"

"You know better than to ask, Grover. Now, what are you going to do?"

Bramlett groaned. He ought to take another Tagamet. "Okay," he said. "We'll let him out. But I better be able to lay hands on him when I need him, Jason, or . . ." He didn't finish.

"Or what?" The attorney's voice was chilly and smug at the same time.

Bramlett slammed the receiver down into the cradle, then winced and said to Valeria, "Sorry, love. It's just that . . ." He didn't finish.

Valeria said nothing. She was lying on her side with her back to him. As he settled back down into the bed, he knew she was wide awake, anxious. He reached his hand over and patted her rump. He tried to think of something reassuring to say, but was afraid if he spoke she'd hear the fear in his own heart.

19 _____

ABOUT AN HOUR BEFORE DAWN, H. C. Curry got out of bed. He wasn't sure if he'd slept at all. Every hour on the hour, he'd dialed Lizzie's apartment. Never an answer. He instructed headquarters to call at once if there was any word on her.

He shaved, showered, and dressed. Where the hell did she go? Who would she want to see?

He went into the kitchen and flipped the light switch. As he stretched his back, his eye fell on a yellow Post-it note on the table. He picked it up. His mother's handwriting.

It read: "H. C., Lizzie phoned. Said to tell you she was at home."

What? But he'd phoned her place again and again . . .

His mother suddenly appeared in the doorway. Her hands were tightening the sash of her robe.

Chancy Curry, a short, stout woman, with muscular hands. Currently, she was employed at the hospital in housekeeping.

Her nose wrinkled up in confusion. "What you doing up so early?" she said.

He held up the note. "When did Lizzie call?"

"Not late. Around seven last night, I guess."

"Seven?" Curry knew he'd been by her apartment after seven. More like eight or later even.

Home? His face suddenly brightened. *Of course!* Not the apartment. But *home!*

"What's wrong?" his mother said.

He kissed her on the cheek. "Got to run," he said. He hurried back to his bedroom.

"You need to eat something 'fore you leave," Chancy Curry called after him.

"Later," he called back. *Why didn't he think of this before?* he said to himself as he pushed one leg into his trousers.

MINUTES LATER he was bouncing along a graveled road several miles out of town. The darkness of the eastern sky was fading into faint dawn light.

Just beyond a ramshackle pumpkin seller's stand, he stopped in front of a small paintless house. The house sat in the middle of a wide red-dirt yard in which chickens normally roamed. The chickens, however, were still in their coop. The roof over the front porch sagged heavily in the middle.

An aged and battered black Ford pickup truck was parked on one side of the house. Beside the pickup was Lizzie's white Grand AM.

The house was the home where she'd grown up, where her father Patterson still lived. Patterson Clouse had no phone, or Curry would have called as soon as he realized, after reading his mother's note, that Lizzie had gone home.

He walked toward the house. The mud in the yard oozed under his shoes. Then he stood on the porch on one side and scraped his shoes on the ends of the boards. He finished wiping them on the rubber mat before the front door. Then he knocked.

Lizzie answered the door. "H. C.," she said. "What in the world . . .?"

He reached out his arms and pulled her hard against his chest. He said nothing at first, simply held her, and felt the warm relief soaking down through his body. "I didn't know where you was," he said.

She laughed softly and said, "Didn't your mother tell you I called?" She kissed his neck, then added, "I couldn't stay there by myself. I had to be with Daddy, had to talk with him. I was going crazy."

"I was so scared," he said into her hair.

She laughed gently again and said, "You hungry? I'm cooking breakfast for Daddy."

GROVER BRAMLETT GLANCED at the garbage dumpster in the carport as he passed it. Had the garbage truck already come? Of course, fool!

He opened the car door, bent over and pulled back the floor mat. Maybe a string or two of tobacco fell out that he'd missed when he looked before. He reached to his shirt pocket for his reading glasses.

"Grover?" It was Valeria.

He whacked the back of his head on the bottom of the steering wheel.

"What?" he said, backing out of the car, putting his hand to his head.

She was in her slippers and bathrobe, brow wrinkled in puzzlement. "What are you doing?"

He shrugged."Well . . . nothing." He clamped his jaw shut.

She looked at him suspiciously. "Are you chewing tobacco?"

"No. I don't have any tobacco." His tone was harsh.

She frowned. "What's wrong with you? Why are you acting like this?"

He sighed heavily. "Never mind. I got to go to work."

"You haven't had breakfast. Marcellus is still asleep, but I could wake him and—"

"Let him sleep. I'll be home for lunch." He paused, then added, "Maybe."

"He wants to see more of you." Her tone was slightly accusatory.

"I'm sorry," he said. He pressed his lips together. He knew she knew he didn't want it to be like this.

She put her hand on his arm. "You're also upset about Jason McAbrams getting that man out of jail, aren't you?"

Bramlett sank down onto the car seat. He didn't reply.

"Ida McAbrams is a lovely person," she said, referring to the lawyer's wife. Ida McAbrams and Valeria were in the same literary club. "But I don't see how a person like Gilly Bitzer could afford a lawyer, much less a lawyer like Jason."

Bramlett snorted. "Chicken crap on somebody's shoes," he said, rolling down his window and closing the door. And the person wearing those shoes would have to be rich enough to hire Mc-Abrams for Gilly and, at the same time, want Gilly out of jail quick. Lots of chicken crap.

Valeria leaned down and kissed him on the cheek. "Fasten your seat belt," she said. "I love you."

He grunted and turned the key in the ignition. He never wore his seat belt.

AT HEADQUARTERS, Jacob Robertson sat at his desk on the edge of his chair. He ground his teeth and glared up at H. C. Curry. Curry reached his hand to the small, portable cassette player and clicked it off. The audio tape stopped.

Curry would not look at Jacob directly. "I'm sorry," he said, shifting from one foot to the other. "I just thought you ought to hear this."

Jacob said nothing. He felt sick to his stomach. His breathing had become very shallow as soon as he had recognized Nena Carmack's voice on the recorded telephone conversation.

Curry shrugged. "The guy was scum," he said. "She found that out and dumped him. But . . ." He didn't finish. Instead, he shook his head and picked up the tape player.

Curry walked away, and Robertson stared at his clenched hand on the desktop. Deep in his heart, he almost wished Jesse Bondreaux was still alive—so he could kill him himself.

Sheriff Bramlett came through the office suite, hurrying toward his office. Robertson pushed back his chair and stood up.

ROBERTSON FOLLOWED THE SHERIFF into his office. "Why *this* week?" Bramlett said. "Why *now*? This is the week Marcellus and I were supposed to be hunting and even fishing maybe." He shook his head in disgust and sat down heavily in his desk chair.

Robertson told him about finding the hidden video camera in

138

Jesse Bondreaux's bedroom. He told him exactly where it was and that he could not find any video tapes.

"Aimed at the bed, eh?"

"Yes, sir."

"Step to the door, Jacob, if you don't mind, and call Johnny and H. C. to come in here." He then squeezed his forehead between his thumb and fingers. *Dammit to hell! Why this week?*

"So," the sheriff said, after telling the other two deputies about the video camera, "it seems we're dealing with blackmail." He looked from one man to another. "We know Noel Hackott is very interested in video tapes which Bondreaux had. We just didn't pick up on that they were *homemade* tapes. Probably Nena Carmack is interested in tapes also. And whoever else is on them. Where in the hell do you suppose those tapes are?" No one answered.

Bramlett grunted. "Jacob, you're searching for tapes now. Check for any lock boxes at the bank. Check the house again. You know what to do." He looked at Curry. "Did you ever find that fellow who was stalking Jo Ann Scales?"

Curry shook his head. "No, sir. No yet. We've put out an APB on him. He has no listed residence."

The sheriff turned to Baillie. "You check out those other students?"

Baillie nodded. "Drumwright and I interviewed Duvall Ellis and Lillie Faye Conlee. I'm still working up the notes, but I don't see anything special."

Bramlett reached to his mouth and extracted a mangled toothpick and tossed it into the trash can. Then he put his hands behind his head and said, "Gilly Bitzer made one phone call. He didn't know the number. Asked for a phone directory, I'm told. I don't know whether he called McAbrams or somebody else. At any rate, McAbrams was down here in less than half an hour." He loosened his tie. "My suspicion is he called somebody else . . . and whoever that somebody was got McAbrams down here in a hurry."

Johnny Baillie pushed the back of his hand across his chin, then said, "And that somebody didn't want Gilly questioned."

Bramlett looked toward the ceiling. "What address did Gilly give?"

"I've got it right here," Curry said, taking out his notepad. He turned through the pages. "It's in Tupelo."

Bramlett lowered his feet to the floor and stood up. "Let's go see if we can find him," he said to Curry.

Ella Mae Shackleford, Bramlett's secretary, leaned into the office doorway. "Excuse me, Sheriff," she said. "Jason McAbrams's secretary is on the line. She wants to know if Mr. McAbrams is down here."

"Down here? What would he be doing down here?"

"Well, she said he didn't come in this morning and she called the house and Mrs. McAbrams said he left to come down here last night. He hasn't come home yet. She doesn't have any idea where he is now."

BRAMLETT AND CURRY DROVE immediately to the large, two-story Tudor-style house in Chartre Acres where most of Sheffield's wealthiest families resided. On the way, Curry played the telephone tape of Nena and Bondreaux. "That confirms it," the sheriff said. He shook his head in disgust as he thought of the video camera.

Mrs. McAbrams met them at the door. She was fiftyish, blonde with heavy makeup and was wearing a pink housecoat with matching slippers. She stood in the white-and-black checkerboard tiled foyer of the house directly beneath an enormous chandelier.

"I went back to sleep," she said. "When I got up this morning he was gone. I assumed he'd come back last night, then left early this morning. Sometimes he does that."

"His secretary says he missed a nine o'clock appointment," Bramlett said. "She hasn't heard from him."

Mrs. McAbrams frowned. "She would know more of his whereabouts than I would. I'm always the last to know where he's going . . . or been." She closed her mouth tightly.

"Could he have gone on a trip?" Bramlett asked.

She made a face. "He didn't take his toilet bag or briefcase or a fresh dress shirt if he did. And he *never* takes a trip without all that." She looked at the sheriff, waiting for a response. Then she said, "You don't think there's anything wrong, do you?"

140

Bramlett avoided her direct gaze. "Do you have any idea who called him last night?"

"No. We were in bed. He answered the phone. It's on his side of the bed, of course."

"He went down to the jail to see Gilly Bitzer."

"Who?"

"Gilly Bitzer. He's mostly a drunk. Does some yardwork. Thought he might do work for y'all."

She sneered. "Drunk, you say? Why on earth would I have a drunk working for me? My yardboy has been with our family over forty years."

Bramlett cut his eyes at Curry and saw the deputy's cheeks immediately tighten. Then Bramlett looked at the woman and said, "Do you remember what Mr. McAbrams said to whoever phoned him?"

She shook her head. "No. Just something like 'Don't worry. I'll go right away.' Something like that." She placed her hand to her head, then added, "Oh . . . I think he also said 'I'll call you when I know something.' " She shook her head. "I was half asleep, of course." Her eyes became more intent as she looked up at the sheriff. "You . . . you think something may have *happened* to Jason?"

"No," Bramlett said quickly. "I wouldn't say that. We just want to talk to him about his client. That's all."

The look of fear in Ida McAbrams's eyes told Bramlett she didn't believe him. He dropped his eyes and tried to smile as he backed toward the doorway and lifted his hat to his head. He wished he could lie better.

20

AS THEY PULLED ONTO THE STREET, Sheriff Bramlett looked toward the side of the McAbrams's house where a massive, almost leafless water oak's branches spread like arms around the chimney. Beside the trunk of the tree a gaunt, elderly black man in overalls was raking leaves. He moved in slow motion.

Curry saw the man also. He gave a low, almost snarling sound.

Bramlett knew he was thinking about Mrs. McAbrams's term "yardboy," but said nothing. The muscles of the deputy's cheek were still tight.

Curry drove the long block with its stately homes in silence. As he turned the corner, he said, "Where to?"

Bramlett was looking out the window, looking at the huge houses of doctors and lawyers and businessmen. "Did you notice she said McAbrams told the person on the phone 'I'll *go* right away'? Now, if it were Gilly that phoned him from the jail—"

"McAbrams would have said, 'I'll *come* right away.' Yeah, I caught that."

"Which means someone other than Gilly phoned." Bramlett nodded thoughtfully. "I think Gilly saw something. Probably *someone*—someone he recognized—when Bondreaux's car went over that hill. My guess is that Gilly has been in touch with that someone." He paused as if to let this sink in, then added, "And this someone

142

would have to be affluent enough to get an attorney like Jason McAbrams out in the middle of the night."

Curry slowed at an intersection. "Gilly was trying to blackmail somebody?"

"Could be. Can't imagine any other reason why he would lie to us. Someone must be making it worth his while to shut up." They drove another long block. Neither said a word. Then Bramlett said, "Tupelo."

"What?"

"You asked me 'where to.' Tupelo. Let's see if we can find Gilly Bitzer." They were passing a house where a black family—man, woman, and two school-age children—were raking leaves in the front yard. "Call in an APB on McAbrams's car. What did she say it was?"

"A silver Jaguar. Probably the only one in five counties. Probably the whole state."

Bramlett snorted. "And he's representing Gilly Bitzer." Gilly knew somebody important, somebody with money—or somebody who knew how to get it.

IT WAS LATE MORNING when they arrived at Tupelo. "You sure this is the address?" Bramlett asked after Curry stopped the car in front of a brick-and-metal one-story building with a red-and-white sign in front. The sign read THE SALVATION ARMY.

Curry looked back at the address in his notebook. "Yep. This is it."

Bramlett grunted, opened the car door, and pulled himself out.

Captain Steven Caples grinned. "So Gilly gave our address as his home address, did he?" Caples was short, trim, had shiny black hair, and wore The Salvation Army officer's traditional uniform. He spoke with a northern accent. "It *is* his residence one night a month. One night a month is all our regulations will allow him to stay in the sleeping lodge. Of course, he's usually here every day for the noon meal unless he's working someplace. Then the people he's working for feed him. He does a lot of work in Sheffield, I understand. But he hasn't been around in several days. I don't have any idea where you could find him. What's he done now?"

"Just wanted to ask him some questions," Bramlett said. "Do you know where he happens to stay?"

Captain Caples thought for a moment. "Almost anywhere during good weather. Now that it's getting cooler, though, he'll be back at the old fairgrounds, I would imagine, in one of the barns."

"Does he have any friends? You know, fellows he hangs around with?"

"No. Gilly pretty much keeps to himself. He's not like most of the men who come through here. He's not a transient. I'd hire him full-time to do odd jobs around here, but he doesn't want to get that regular, if you know what I mean. Besides, I'm afraid he wouldn't be all that dependable."

"The booze, you mean."

Captain Caples nodded.

"The old fairgrounds are over east of Front Street?" Bramlett said.

Caples nodded. "You can't miss it."

THE FADED BLOCK LETTERING on the white-painted arched wooden sign over the graveled drive announced "Northeast Mississippi State Dairy and Livestock Exhibition." The drive led to a cluster of ramshackle frame buildings and barns bordering a race track. Curry parked near the front of the largest barn.

He and Bramlett got out of the car and stood looking around at the deserted facilities. "Where do we start?" Bramlett said.

All the doors to the large barn were padlocked. They walked to the smaller barn on the right. The side door was hanging by one hinge. They entered and stood in the middle of the building letting their eyes grow accustomed to the semidarkness. The damp smells of rotting hay and mildew hung heavy in the air.

"Maybe you'd better go back to the car for the flashlights," Bramlett said.

Curry left, and Bramlett walked through the powdery dust toward the rear of the barn. Tracked through the dust going in every direction were the footprints of men and dogs. No telling how old some of them were.

He had no idea how many years it had been since the new fairgrounds were built and this one abandoned. The old facility had been left to rats, weather, and vagrants like Gilly Bitzer.

Curry returned and handed the sheriff one flashlight. Bramlett switched it on and played the beam's circle of light along the back wall. "Let's check out that door," he said, focusing the beam on a white plank door with a broken hasp.

The door swung open freely and Bramlett stepped inside, followed by Curry. It was a small concrete-floored room with the musty odor of unwashed humans. Against the wall to the right was an army cot with a bare mattress. The stuffing of the striped mattress bulged out of several rips. A small vegetable crate stood at one end of the bed. On top of the crate was a kerosene lamp.

"This must be the place," Bramlett said, squinching up his nose against the odor. "Home sweet home." The beam of his flashlight was focused on three labelless whiskey bottles beside the mattress.

"Yep," Curry said. "And here he is."

Bramlett turned to look at the back corner where Curry held his light beam. Sprawled on the ground was the body of Gilly Bitzer. About a quarter of an inch below his right eyebrow was a dark red hole.

21

SHERIFF BRAMLETT AND DEPUTY CURRY waited for the arrival of Major Edward Hammermill, chief of detectives with the Tupelo Police Department. Bramlett had known Hammermill for several years. He was in his mid-forties, quite muscular, and very blond. Bramlett had never seen him without a stump of a cigar in his mouth. He was a no-nonsense, get-the-job-done-now type cop, and the sheriff liked him.

Bramlett talked with Hammermill, bringing him up to date on the situation in Chakchiuma County, then he and Curry returned to Sheffield.

"We need a list of people Gilly did yardwork for," Bramlett said to Curry.

He stood for a moment with his hands in his pockets staring at the buzzing activities of the outer office. Deputies, secretaries, clerks. Typewriters, telephones, computer terminals. Yet none of this registered in his brain. What he saw in his brain was a rainy night and a speeding car slashing past his grandson, Marcellus. And the killer of Jesse Bondreaux and probably also of Jo Ann Scales and Gilly Bitzer looking eye to eye with Marcellus.

"Sheriff!" It was H. C. Curry's voice. Bramlett blinked several times, then looked at the deputy. Curry said, "You all right?" There was a concerned look in the young man's eye.

146

"All right?"

"You looked . . . well, spaced out or something."

Bramlett took two toothpicks out of his pocket and put them both into his mouth. His mouth suddenly had a very sour taste. His teeth ground into the toothpicks. "Just thinking," he said. He needed a drink of water.

He walked toward the water fountain. It was when he leaned his mouth to the arched cold water that he remembered the labelless whiskey bottles on the floor beside Gilly's cot. He sipped through his teeth clamped on to the toothpicks, then raised up and turned around.

Curry was staring at him. Bramlett smiled. "Let's go," he said to the deputy, turning toward the door to the parking lot. "I know just the man who can tell us a lot about Gilly Bitzer."

LOW-HANGING BRANCHES slapped at the windshield as the patrol car bounced down the deep-rutted red clay road which cut through the hardwood forest on the eastern edge of the county. The tight canopy of overhead limbs shaded the road from the mid-afternoon sun, and the air was heavy with the scent of ragweed.

"Hot damn!" H. C. Curry said, fighting the steering wheel to maintain control of the vehicle. "I just hope we can get back out of here."

Sheriff Bramlett braced himself by pressing his hands against the dashboard. "Amos Putt figures anybody who wants his stuff is gonna have to pay more than just money for it," he said. "And he, like his daddy before him, ain't ever been wanting for customers."

Curry braked hard after they crested a ridge and looked down at the mucky road before them. Small pools of dark reddish water pockmarked the lowest places. "We'll never get through there."

Bramlett chuckled. "Then this is as far as we go. We'd have to walk to go on. That's probably the way Putt likes it. He can see whoever's coming . . . and he knows anybody with a four-wheel drive ain't us."

"You mean we're going to *walk* through that stuff?"

"No. We are going to just sit here and wait. He's heard us coming. He'll show up directly. If we moved in closer to his cabin he'd just back away into the woods and we'd never find him."

Curry rubbed the back of his hand across his lips, then asked, "How come you don't put him out of business? You don't turn your head from no other bootlegger."

Bramlett took the splintered toothpick remains out of his mouth and tossed them out the window. "The Putts have always been different kind of folks. I doubt we could actually ever find Amos still back in there anyways. And if we were to get too close, we'd have to pay too high a price."

"You mean he'd fight?"

Bramlett chuckled again, put a fresh toothpick into his mouth, then said, "As I understand it, he only makes whiskey in the wintertime. During the spring and summer he's basically in the snake business—catching rattlers mostly, but also copperheads and cottonmouths. There's a good demand for them in a lot of those churches up in Oskula County."

Bramlett paused for a moment, thinking that whereas some of the sweetest-spirited people he'd ever known were religious snake handlers, some of the meanest-spirited people he'd known were non-snake-handling religious people.

He continued. "At any rate, if we were to go after him, it'd have to be in winter. In these swamps and sloughs we'd be all bogged down and fighting the woods more than Putt. And a man like Amos Putt wouldn't hesitate to shoot anyone—law officer or not—who he felt was threatening him. Like I said, I don't really think the price would be worth it." He turned his head and looked at the side of the deputy's disapproving face. "I sure wouldn't want to have to go up to your mama's place and tell her you'd been shot dead by a crazy bootlegger out in some swamp. And I don't think Mrs. Bramlett would care much about hearing the same about me from you. I mean, who'd she have to take out the garbage?" He chuckled.

"Can I help you?" The voice was low, and both Curry and Bramlett looked around both ways wondering where it came from. Then Bramlett saw him, standing about ten yards directly to the right side of the car. The bottom two-thirds of his body was hidden by a mass of huckleberry bushes. He was partially behind the trunk of a huge red oak, positioned, thought Bramlett, for immediate flight into the safety of the heavy woods behind him should the two lawmen appear threatening.

Bramlett made no motion to get out of the car. Instead, he grinned and said, "Hello, Amos. How you been doing? Ain't seen you in a coon's age."

22

AMOS PUTT'S PEOPLE HAD SETTLED in the hills of northeast Chakchi-uma County before there was a Chakchiuma County. They were a Scotch-Irish folk who came from Georgia to Mississippi and staked out homesteads right after the Chickasaw chiefs signed the Treaty of Pontotoc in 1832.

In that rugged hill country, not well suited for cotton, they scratched out their living on small farms, raising sweet potatoes, hogs, corn, chickens, and whatever else was needed for the table and to trade for coffee, sugar, salt, and cloth. They supplemented their diet with a seemingly undiminishable supply of rabbits and squirrels and opossums from the swamps and bottoms which nestled between the heavily forested hillsides.

Now, for at least three generations, the primary cash crop of the Putts had been corn liquor, which three generations of Chakchiuma Countians had considered superior even to the best brands of bonded alcohol.

Amos's father, Jephthah Putt, had been the first to launch into a secondary source of income for the Putt clan. He recognized the potential market for the profusion of poisonous snakes that infested their swamps and bottoms and consequently initiated the family snake-catching business. As long as certain churches felt they could worship God more effectively handling rattlers and

150

cottonmouths, there would continue to be a demand for snake-catching.

"We just want to talk with you a little," Bramlett said. He made no motion to get out of the car. For all he knew, Amos had a pistol in his hand. Maybe pistols in both hands.

Amos didn't answer. Nor did he move, half hidden by the oak tree.

"It's about a friend of ours," Bramlett said. "Gilly Bitzer."

Putt remained motionless for a moment, then turned his head slightly. "What about him?"

"Well," Bramlett said, opening the door and slowly stepping out of the car. "Seems somebody killed him." He placed both hands on top of the doorframe so Putt could see he wasn't holding a weapon. Then he turned his head back toward Curry and whispered, "Get out and put your hands on top of the car."

"What?"

"Just do it," Bramlett said through his teeth.

The deputy got out of his door, stood and rested both hands on the top of the car. There was strong reluctance in his every movement.

Putt eased out of the bushes, moving slowly around the cluster of huckleberry, until he stood not more than five or six yards from the road. He held one hand behind his back. No doubt about it, thought Bramlett. Pistol.

"Who kilt him?" Putt said.

Bramlett shrugged. "That's what we aim to find out. When was the last time you saw him?"

"Not long ago."

"Since last Friday night?"

Putt nodded. "I reckon he come around Saturday."

"We think he saw somebody get killed. And we think that somebody else has now done killed him. Did he say anything about seeing somebody get killed?"

Putt spat a stream of brown tobacco juice toward the ground without taking his eyes off Bramlett. Then he shook his head and said, "Naw."

"Well, did he say anything unusual?"

Putt moved his chew of tobacco to the other side of his jaw with his tongue, then said, "Told me he was gonna be getting a lot of money."

"Money? Who from?"

"Didn't say. I didn't ask."

"And he didn't say anything about seeing a man who had been killed?"

"Nope."

Bramlett nodded his head thoughtfully, then said, "Did he say anything else unusual?"

"Nope."

Bramlett sighed. "Well, we appreciate your time, Amos."

Putt nodded and Bramlett eased back down onto the car seat and closed the door. Curry was quickly inside the car also.

Bramlett looked toward the sky. It was clearing in the northeast. Cerulean blue with a touch of burnt umber. Then he said to Curry, "So, Gilly was expecting to come into a lot of money."

"I wonder what kind of money he already had when he came to buy his bottle," Curry said.

"Oh, Amos . . ." Bramlett called, turning his head and looking back toward the thicket. But the man had vanished.

IN TOWN, BRAMLETT AND CURRY had hamburgers for lunch at the Eagle Café. Then the sheriff directed Curry to Merry Fulton's house. "I remember seeing Gilly Bitzer raking leaves here last week," the sheriff explained.

Merry Fulton was in the backyard working in a flower bed. Bramlett had known Merry since high school. Her husband died of a massive heart attack playing golf several years before. She was a round-faced, matronly-looking woman who never went outside the house without makeup and a pleasant expression on her face.

Merry was planting small azaleas. When she saw the two lawmen approaching, she pushed herself to her feet with a groan, brushed her garden-gloved hands against her smock, and grinned.

"You're just in time, Grover," she said. "I need that urn over there set on the back porch. It's too heavy for me."

Bramlett smiled and nodded at Curry. The deputy stiffened for a long moment, long enough for Bramlett to think maybe he wasn't

152

going to do it. Then with aversion written across his face, he walked toward a mass of sprawling abelia shrubs in front of which sat a concrete urn planted with pansies.

"I like to have them on the porch in the winter," she said. "Nothing like flowers when the days grow cold. When you're alone, you need all the help you can get to keep warm." She winked at Bramlett and he felt himself flushing.

Curry struggled with the urn until he reached the porch and set it down. He then stared down at the front of his uniform jacket as if wondering whether to try to brush off the dirt or not. He bent slightly forward and blew loudly at the dirt, being sure Bramlett noticed what had happened.

"We wanted to ask you about Gilly Bitzer," Bramlett said, paying no attention to the deputy. "I saw him raking leaves here a while back."

"Well, I can tell you this. You can't count on him. He works well enough when he's here. But like this morning, for instance. He was supposed to be here by eight o'clock. Eight o'clock, I told him." She glanced at her wristwatch and shook her head.

"Merry, I'm afraid he's not coming."

She lifted one eyebrow. "Oh?"

Bramlett nodded. "He's dead."

She cocked her head. The impatience still in her face. "Dead? When?"

"Probably last night. Someone shot him."

"Shot him?" Her eyes widened.

Curry was now brushing gingerly at his jacket with the back of his hand. His lower lip pouted.

"When did you see him last?" Bramlett said.

"It's been over a week." She shook her head slowly, thoughtfully, and pulled off one glove. "Who would want to kill Gilly, for mercy's sake?"

"I wonder if you could tell us some of the other people he did yardwork for?"

Curry took his notepad out of his jacket pocket.

*   *   *

153

"LET ME LOOK AT THAT LIST," Bramlett said as Curry backed the patrol car into the street.

Bramlett looked down at the neat, tight handwriting. Robert and Katherine Topp, Ross and Billie Conlee, Howard and Rumi Skelton, and Nena Carmack.

Bramlett looked up at the side of Curry's face. "I see your friend Nena Carmack is on the list. A little unusual, don't you think?"

Curry frowned. "Why?"

"Schoolteacher. Everyone else Sarah mentioned is fairly well-heeled."

"Well-heeled?"

"It's an old expression. You know what it means."

Curry shrugged. "You wouldn't have to be rich to hire a wino, I wouldn't think."

"Humm," Bramlett said, looking at the brilliant red maples lining the street. "I'd like to talk to her again. Would she be home from school yet?"

JACOB ROBERTSON PARKED HIS PATROL CAR on the street in front of Nena Carmack's cottage. So far, he'd made little progress in finding any homemade video tapes. Bondreaux didn't have a lock box at the bank in Sheffield. Jacob had gone to Tupelo and asked at every bank there. Nothing.

He glanced at his watch again and opened the door and stood up beside the car. He heard a vehicle coming.

Nena's Mazda came speeding around the corner and whipped into the driveway. She jumped out carrying a briefcase. She looked surprised to see Jacob.

He sauntered toward her. "You drive like that all the time?" he said, grinning.

She gave him a weak smile. "I know. I drive too fast. I keep telling myself to slow down."

He nodded and studied her face. She looked very tired—tired like she'd not been sleeping well. Her eyes were red-streaked.

"What's wrong?" he said.

She sighed and shook her head. "Nothing." Then she sighed again and said, "Everything."

154

"Can I help?"

She looked up at him. Her face seemed to ease, to relax, and she smiled. "You're a good man, Jacob Robertson. What are you doing here talking to me?"

"You're a good woman."

The smiled faded. "No. No, I'm not."

She turned to walk toward the house. "Jacob, I have to go. Would you excuse me?"

He nodded, opened his mouth to ask again if he could help, then thought better of it, and simply said, "I'll check with you later." He smiled at her, then turned toward his car.

"Jacob . . ." she said.

He looked back at her. She had a curious expression on her face. "Was there something else?"

He shrugged. "Well, I just wondered if you might like to go out tonight. Maybe to get a bite to eat and then see a movie."

She smiled. "What time?"

He brightened. "Six okay?"

She nodded and turned back toward the house. Jacob was whistling as he opened the door of his truck.

ONLY A FEW MINUTES AFTER Jacob Robertson left, Bramlett and Curry arrived at Nena Carmack's cottage. She did not look happy to see the two lawmen at her front door. "May we sit down, Miss Carmack?" Bramlett said after they were inside.

She shrugged, and Bramlett eased himself down onto the couch. Curry sat in an easy chair and busied himself with his notepad, not once, Bramlett noticed, lifting his gaze toward the woman.

Nena Carmack stood stiffly, defiantly, her cheek twitching and her eyes glaring. "I must tell you how unpleasant all this is for me. I don't really think I can tell you anything else about Jesse Bondreaux. Am I suspected of killing him?"

Bramlett tried to smile disarmingly. "Please, Miss Carmack. Won't you sit down?"

She did not respond or move for a long moment. Then she sat on the edge of a straight-back chair, absolutely rigid.

155

"I believe you are acquainted with a man by the name of Gilly Bitzer," the sheriff said.

She nodded. "He used to do yardwork for me."

"Used to?"

She shrugged her shoulder again. "Frankly, I couldn't afford him anymore. Not that he was expensive. He was cheap. I just couldn't even afford cheap anymore."

"And why was that?"

"None of your business."

Bramlett's smile like his patience quickly ebbed. "Please understand, Miss Carmack. Murder *is* my business. Gilly Bitzer is dead—*murdered*—and my job is to talk to everyone who knew him." He paused and observed the sudden paleness of her face. Somehow he was pleased and disappointed at the same time that the news of Bitzer's death surprised her. He continued. "I wonder what you can tell us about him?"

"He . . . he was just an old man . . . Someone told me he did yardwork . . . I don't remember who. I only had him a few times. He raked leaves for me. I hate to rake leaves. Don't really have the time."

Bramlett nodded. Out of the corner of his eye he could see Curry looking down at the notepad on his knee. The deputy held his pencil to the pad but was making no notation. "Tell me," Bramlett said, "did Jesse Bondreaux know Gilly Bitzer?"

She shook her head. "I don't really know. Jesse may have seen him doing work over here for me. I don't know if he knew him, though."

Bramlett arched his back. A small cramp seemed to be developing. Tension, probably. "Miss Carmack, Gilly Bitzer was at the cemetery when Jesse Bondreaux was killed. I think he may have seen something . . . or someone." He paused, studying her face and neck. She made no reaction. "So," he continued, "it's still worth our while to untangle all of Bondreaux's relationships. Yes, to answer your question. You are under suspicion. Everyone who was personally involved with him is under suspicion in one way or another. Can you tell us anyone else who may have had some kind of relationship with him?"

"I told you about Nicole Estis."

156

Bramlett nodded. "And when you found out about her, you said you ended your relationship with him and had nothing else to do with him. But then we found out you visited his house the day he was killed."

"And I told you he wanted me to loan him some money."

"Loan?" Bramlett raised one eyebrow. "I don't recall you saying 'loan.'"

She shrugged. "That's what I meant."

Bramlett stared at her a long moment. A darkness seemed to have folded over her face. "We have a taped telephone conversation of him demanding money from you."

Her eyes opened wide. "You used a wire tap on his phone?"

"No, ma'am. Bondreaux taped his own conversations."

She closed her eyes and shook her head wearily. "He . . . he was very disturbed."

"Do you think there may have been others besides this secretary he was involved with? Students, for instance?"

Without opening her eyes, she slowly shook her head, then paused and nodded once. "Yes, there were students. A few. He was completely amoral."

"And?"

"There was Cora Hartley, of course."

"We know about her."

"And Vicki Ann Skelton. Do you know her? She was crowned homecoming queen last week."

Bramlett's eye twitched when she mentioned Vicki Ann. He didn't say anything.

She opened her eyes and smiled at him. "Does that surprise you, Sheriff?" She seemed to take satisfaction in having shocked him.

"I don't believe it," he said, clamping his teeth together hard.

She smiled in a cynical manner. "It's all a lot uglier than you can possibly imagine, Sheriff. Much uglier."

23

SHERIFF GROVER BRAMLETT ROSE from his desk as his secretary opened the office door and held it open for Vicki Ann Skelton to enter. The door closed, and the young woman stood in the middle of the room, posed almost, thought Bramlett, as if standing in the middle of the football field at half-time with her court before the hundreds of cheering people.

Only the smile, that certain perfect smile of perfect teeth framed by perfect lips that never seemed to waver on such occasions, was absent. Her face was strained, tired, and drawn. Vicki Ann Skelton suddenly looked much older than her seventeen years.

"Please sit down, Vicki Ann," Bramlett said, holding his hand in the direction of one of the chairs in front of his desk.

He'd had his secretary telephone the Skeltons' house as soon as he and Curry returned to the office. Ella Mae simply told Vicki Ann the sheriff needed to talk to her about her *relationship* (Bramlett had told Ella Mae to emphasize that particular word) with Jesse Bondreaux, and the sheriff could either come to the house or she could come down immediately to his office.

The girl told Ella Mae that she'd come right away. Purposefully, he did not ask any of his deputies to join him as he talked with the girl.

Vicki Ann sat down in a chair and crossed her legs. Her jeans had a tear across one knee. Bramlett had never understood why affluent kids would purposely wear raggedy clothes.

He eased himself back down into his chair and smiled at her. "I appreciate you coming so quickly."

She looked at him for a moment, then looked away. Her eyes were bleary.

His mouth was dry. A double chew would make all this much easier. His tongue felt very thick. "Tell me about Jo Ann Scales. How were you involved with her?"

The girl's lower lip quivered, then she said softly, "She was someone I could talk to. She was a very good person."

"And do you have any idea who would want to harm her?"

She shook her head. A shiver rippled across her shoulders.

"Vicki Ann," he said, "we know that Jesse Bondreaux had been romantically involved with several women . . ." He paused, watching her. She made no immediate reaction. He continued. "Were you involved with him?"

Her eyes became slits, and she looked hard at him. "Involved? *Romantically* involved?"

He shrugged, then said, "We have reason to believe he had been intimate with a couple of students."

She flushed and looked at the floor. "That's ridiculous." She shook her head. "Mr. Bondreaux and I were friends. Nothing more. We were *good* friends, but that's all."

"Nothing more?"

"Nothing more."

"We've been told otherwise."

"No," she said. "Whoever told you that is lying. We weren't like that."

She wasn't meeting his eyes, was rubbing her fingers together and gently swinging her foot. Bramlett was searching for signs that she was lying. He wasn't sure. Especially, he wasn't sure whether his keen desire for her to be telling the truth was keeping him for evaluating her body language as he should.

"Did you know he was planning to leave Sheffield?" he said.

She nodded, still without looking at him. "Yes. We'd talked about it several times. He wanted me to go with him."

"Really?" He couldn't mask his surprise.

She lifted her eyes to meet his, and clasped her hands together in her lap. Her knuckles turned white. "We were more than good friends. Not lovers. But more." She paused, looking at Bramlett as if trying to read him, trying to guess what he knew and didn't know. She continued. "We shared with each other a lot. Both of us wanted to get out of this town."

Bramlett fumbled in his coat pocket for a toothpick. There were none left. "So, you were going with him?"

She hesitated for a moment, then said, "I was thinking about it. Of course, my folks didn't know. Jesse's former wife was bothering him."

"Oh?"

She nodded. "They were married years ago for a very short time. Anyway, she'd been bothering him. And he had to get away. He wanted to go to Atlanta and see his daughter."

Bramlett flinched. He wasn't prepared for the mention of a child. The thought of Jesse Bondreaux as a father was impossible to consider. "Daughter?" he said with a gasp.

"Yes. He wanted to be with her. Nothing was more important to him, he said."

Bramlett breathed several deep breaths, then said, "What is his former wife's name?"

She shook her head. "I never asked. I really didn't want to talk about her."

"What do you know about his daughter?"

Vicki Ann wiped at the corner of one eye with the back of her hand. "His daughter didn't even know he was alive—who he was. In fact, he'd just found out about her, he said. And his former wife didn't want him around the girl. She was about my age, he said. But now that he knew she was alive, he had to be with her. So, he wanted me to leave and go with him."

Bramlett swallowed. All of this was very difficult to comprehend. "Why *you*?"

"Because we were friends. He said he thought of me as his daughter even before he knew about his real daughter."

Bramlett gazed at her face. She was indeed a beautiful young woman with fine features, high cheekbones, and it was easy to see why she'd been elected homecoming queen. But it was incompre-

160

hensible to him why she would consider running off with a sleaze like Jesse Bondreaux. Bramlett could not at all see whatever it was women had seen in the man.

He said, "And you were going with him? To Atlanta, I mean?"

She shrugged. "I don't know. He'd talked to me about it for a couple of weeks. I never told him I would go. Then he said he'd get a large apartment for us in Atlanta and I could transfer to one of the high schools there and graduate next spring and he'd pay for me to attend whatever college I wanted to attend. Money was no object, he said."

"Where was he going to get all this money?"

"He already had a lot of money. And more was coming in. It was a business he had. Investments, I think."

"Could it have been drugs?"

She frowned, looking at the sheriff with puzzled eyes. "Drugs? Of course not. He hated drugs. If he told me once, he told me a thousand times, 'Don't *ever* have anything to do with drugs.' "

"Did you know he made secret videos?"

She cocked her head. "What?"

She obviously didn't know. Bramlett could not suppress a sigh of relief. He then said, "And your mother didn't know about any of this?"

Vicki Ann shook her head. "As far as she and Daddy knew, I'd even quit visiting his house." She released her hands and let them fall to her sides. "I really hadn't decided whether I was going or not." She shook her head slowly. "I probably wouldn't have."

"Did he ever mention the name of this daughter?"

She shook her head. "No."

Bramlett wondered if he should ask her if she knew Jesse Bondreaux had also invited Nicole Estis to go someplace with him. He decided against it. Instead, he said, "I appreciate you coming in, Vicki Ann. I may need to talk with you some more, but this will do for now."

"Is it . . . is it necessary to say anything to my parents about all of this? I mean, what does it matter . . . now?"

He shook his head and stood up. "No. It probably won't be necessary. Not right now, at any rate."

"Can I go?" she asked, placing her hand on the arms of the chair.

He nodded and reached toward his back pocket, then tightly clenched his fist. She was quickly on her feet and out the door.

H. C. Curry went home early for supper. As he drove, he listened to another telephone conversation tape. He immediately recognized Cora Hartley's voice talking with Jesse Bondreaux.

"I don't know why that bitch has to come over there all the time," Cora said. The agitation in her voice was obvious. "Why can't you just tell her to stay away."

"Now, now," Bondreaux said in a soothing voice. "She doesn't mean anything to me. You know that."

"I see how you look at her."

"You're imagining things. There's absolutely nothing between us."

Cora's voice became shrill. "Just because her father is president of the bank and she's rich and homecoming queen . . ."

"I don't like it when people yell. I won't talk to you as long as you are yelling." Then there was a buzz. Bondreaux had hung up.

Jacob Robertson found Rabbit Murphey price-marking quarts of Havoline oil in the automotive section of Wal-Mart. He'd noticed in reviewing copies of interview notes that Murphey had mentioned watching a video.

"Tell me about the video you watched at Jesse Bondreaux's house, Rabbit," Robertson said. "Was it homemade?"

Murphey continued stamping the sides of the plastic containers. He shrugged and said, "Yeah. It was all boring, really."

"Did you know the people on the video?"

"Just Jesse. Not the girl."

"Did you happen to notice where he kept the video?"

Murphey held the stamper for a moment as if thinking. In a moment, he nodded slowly and said, "I don't know for sure. It seems he just picked it up off the chesterfield. Or by the chesterfield." He shrugged again. "That's all I can tell you."

The deputy thanked Murphey and left.

162

WITHIN TEN MINUTES, Robertson was inside Jesse Bondreaux's house. He stood in the front room with his hands on his hips surveying the room. He focused on the couch. His grandmother called a couch a chesterfield. He wasn't sure he'd ever heard anybody else say that until Rabbit Murphey did. Weird.

He stepped directly in front of the couch. Then he knelt to the floor and looked under it. It was a sofa bed.

He lifted off the three seat cushions and stacked them on the floor. Then he took the handle at the front of the couch and folded out the bed. Lined up neatly in a row across the bed were five video tape cartridges.

24

A FEW MINUTES LATER, Robertson stood in front of Sheriff Bramlett's desk. He held up the stack of five video tapes for the sheriff to see.

Bramlett smiled. "Now we're getting someplace. Whoever's on those tapes could have been blackmailed by Bondreaux. And one of these may have finally decided he—or she—had paid enough." He reached out his hands and took the tapes. "I'll have Curry look at them. He's been with me for the interviews. He'll recognize anyone we've talked to."

Robertson nodded and left the room.

Bramlett glanced at his watch. Valeria would be phoning in a minute or two to let him know supper was ready. She'd said she wanted to eat early. He reached for his hat on the halltree just as his private line rang.

"I'M GOING OUT BACK AND SHOOT the gun a while," Marcellus said after they finished supper.

"Be careful," Valeria said as he opened the back door.

The Red Ryder BB air rifle was leaning against one of the porch roof posts where he'd left it that afternoon. On the other side of the post was the basketball. The rifle was over fifty years old now, Paw Paw said. He bought it for three dollars when he was a boy.

164

Marcellus lifted the rifle and walked toward the pecan tree. That afternoon he'd shot tin cans set on the back fence and on a low-hanging limb of the tree.

He glanced at the sun. It was a fiery red ball sitting on top of the treeline.

Paw Paw said they could go hunting tomorrow afternoon. He liked hunting. Almost as much as basketball. Maybe.

He leaned over and picked up one of the cans. He weighed it in his hand for a moment, then tossed it back to the trunk of the tree.

He walked quickly back to the porch and leaned the rifle back against the post. Then he snatched up the basketball with both hands. Moments later, he was out the gate and trotting toward Carius Park, dribbling the ball as he went.

BRAMLETT HELPED VALERIA SCRAPE, rinse, and stack the dishes in the dishwasher. When they were done, Bramlett took off his apron and hung it on a yellow plastic hook attached to the side of the refrigerator with a magnet.

"Is it any better?" Valeria said to him. There was a concerned look on her face as she gazed up at him.

"What?"

"You said without the tobacco, you were having a difficult time thinking."

He shook his head wearily. "It's hell," he said. "A living hell."

He left and went out onto the front porch and eased himself down into one of the two rockers. His head ached. He had a tiny fragment of toothpick caught between a tooth and his gum. He'd been worrying with it for hours with his tongue. How long was this stupid withdrawal supposed to last?

Over the years he'd dealt with any number of murder cases. Rarely was anyone killed by someone he or she didn't know. Only in cases of robbery or a few times in a juke joint or a roadhouse when men were drunk would someone kill someone he'd never seen before. Nine out of ten times or better it was not only someone the victim knew but someone he knew very well.

In the case of Jesse Bondreaux there was no reason to think otherwise. Could it be the drug angle? Or something to do with the video tapes? Like blackmail? More than once somebody had finally decided to end blackmail and the threat of exposure by killing the blackmailer.

Vicki Ann Skelton said he was making a lot of money with some business. Either drugs or blackmail could be very profitable.

And what about these people on the tapes, whoever they were. Bramlett had certainly dealt with enough murder cases where jealousy was the basic motive—husbands killing unfaithful wives or their lovers, wives doing the same, though women seldom killed the lover, just the husband. What about Bondreaux's lovers? Could it have been Nena Carmack or that secretary, Nicole Estis? What about Katherine Topp? What if Vicki Ann was lying? What if she was, as Nena Carmack indicated, romantically involved with him?

Or what about Cora Hartley's father? Of all the ones with reason to kill Bondreaux, Marshall Hartley was the one Bramlett could empathize with most. A father protecting his daughter. Or Lucian DeBow, Cora's boyfriend? He certainly seemed crazy enough.

What if Bondreaux was getting his money from blackmail? What if he was holding these video tapes over the heads of his lovers? But how could someone like Nena Carmack afford much blackmail?

Bramlett rocked back and pressed both hands to his head. The pounding seemed to be getting worse.

The screen door pushed open and Valeria stepped onto the porch and stood with her hands behind her back. "I love these cool evenings," she said, looking toward the neighbor's' yard across the street. "I see Bill has already dug up Jan's caladiums."

Bramlett rocked and said nothing. He knew she wasn't really thinking much about caladiums these days. Nevertheless, maybe he could do it this coming weekend.

As if she read his mind, she said, "Saturday wouldn't be a good day. Margaret and John and April will be here. Margaret and John get back from Cancun Thursday, you know."

He nodded. Right now he wished they were back already and Marcellus was with them at home in Memphis.

Valeria continued. "Marcellus is supposed to go on the overnight church youth retreat Friday."

"I don't think that's a good idea."

166

She raised one eyebrow. "Are you close to anything?"

He shrugged. "Maybe," he said. He wished she'd talk more about caladiums.

She said nothing else for a long while, didn't need or want to know more, he knew. All she was concerned about was the safety of her daughter's child.

She stood, looking hard at him. The hum of the evening insects grew louder.

Finally, she stepped closer to his rocker. "I want you to think clearly. That's why I've done this."

She brought her hands from behind her back. In one hand she held a package of Red Man chewing tobacco and in the other hand a plastic cup. Bramlett's eyes widened in amazement.

There was a slight tremor in his hands as he took the package and the cup.

"Now," she said, "maybe you'd best go on back to work."

He stood up quickly and shoved the package into his back pocket and wrapped his arms around her.

THE BASKETBALL SWOOSHED through the net without touching the rim, and Marcellus, standing more than twenty feet away from the goal, threw both arms up above his head and cried, "Three!"

He ran to the ball, caught it on the second bounce and began dribbling back to the three-point circle painted on the outdoor concrete court.

"You stepped on the line," a voice said.

Marcellus flinched in surprise, looked up and held the ball with both hands. Standing in the grass just off the court were two black boys. One was about the same size as Marcellus, the other half a head shorter. Marcellus had been so caught up in playing, he'd not noticed them approaching.

"I said you stepped on the line when you shot," the bigger one said again. "The goal don't count."

Marcellus shrugged, looked away from them in the direction of his grandparents' house, and began bouncing the ball. The two boys walked toward him. He looked up at them again.

Both were wearing red windbreakers, jeans, and Nike tennis shoes.

The smaller one was much darker than the larger. He had a mean scowl on his face and was gazing toward the street where two cars, a smaller blue one and a larger black one, were parked. Someone was sitting in the black car.

"What's your name?" the larger one said. He stared inquisitively at Marcellus, and his face reflected a certain wariness.

Marcellus was now dribbling with his left hand. "Marcellus Collier. My grandfather is the sheriff and I'm staying at his house."

"You don't say?" the boy said, cutting his eyes at the other boy, as if checking for a reaction. The smaller boy's scowl only deepened. The boy continued. "Well, you still stepped on the line."

Marcellus let the challenge go unanswered. Instead he passed the ball beneath his legs to his right hand and cut toward the goal for a lay-up.

"Listen," the boy said. "I'm Jamel Thompson, and this is my brother Romel. You want to play a game of horse?"

Marcellus held the ball on his hip and looked back toward the street. A game would be nice. He'd like that. "Okay," he said without more thought. "Make your shot." He made a bounce pass to Jamel.

Jamel caught the ball and grinned. The look of wariness was gone. "You be after me," he said to Marcellus. "Romel after you."

Jamel executed a jump shot from the free throw line, and Marcellus followed suit, easily making the shot. Romel missed the shot and stomped his foot. He said nothing.

Shot followed shot in the gathering dusk. The older boys put out Romel with five straight baskets. Then the two of them battled on as one by one the streetlights in the park began to glow. Finally, Marcellus missed his final shot, and Jamel whooped in victory.

"I'd better go now," Marcellus said, holding the ball with both hands.

"You had supper?" Jamel said.

"Uh-huh."

"We have, too. Why don't we go to our house and play kick the can or something?"

Marcellus shrugged. "I don't know . . ."

"Just a little while." There was an eagerness in his voice. "We

168

just live over there." He nodded in the direction of someplace beyond the other end of the court.

Marcellus shrugged again and said, "Okay. Maybe for just a little while." He wasn't completely sure whether he wanted to go with them. But Marcellus tended to avoid conflict with people by doing what he was asked. Schoolteachers always praised his cooperativeness, even if they didn't give him high marks.

He followed Jamel and Romel out of the park gong in the opposite direction of his grandparents' house. As they walked along the sidewalk, Jamel asked him if his grandfather had ever shot anyone with his gun. Marcellus said he thought so. He wasn't sure.

Romel didn't say anything. He walked along with his head down, grunting at times as if he didn't think bringing this white boy home was a very good idea.

A large dark automobile drove slowly past them. When it was about a basketball court's length ahead, the brake lights came on suddenly and the car halted in the middle of the street.

Marcellus stopped and stared at the car. He had a strange feeling inside. His breathing became more rapid.

"What's wrong?" Jamel said, turning to look at him.

"I . . . I . . . think I'd better go home."

"Aw, come on," Jamel said. "It won't take long." Romel had also stopped and turned back to look at Marcellus. He had a bewildered expression on his face.

"I'll be back tomorrow," Marcellus said hurriedly. "We'll play another game." He turned around and started walking fast in the opposite direction.

"We'll see you tomorrow then," Jamel yelled after him.

Marcellus looked back over his shoulder. The automobile was turning around in a driveway. He began jogging.

He could hear the car approaching from behind. As it drew abreast of him, he moved off the sidewalk onto the grass away from the vehicle.

The car slowed to match his pace and a window slid down. "Marcellus?" a woman's voice said. "Is that you, Marcellus?"

"W-what?"

"Your grandmother is worried about you. She sent me to find you. Come on. Get in the car. I'll take you home."

Marcellus stopped. He didn't know this person at all. But he also knew he shouldn't have stayed out so late. He didn't mean to worry Maw Maw.

He walked slowly to the side of the car and reached for the door handle.

25

Just as Sheriff Grover Bramlett opened the carport door, the telephone rang. He waited while Valeria answered it. Could be Curry.

"It's Elizabeth," she called to him. "Come speak to her before you go."

Elizabeth was their youngest daughter. She lived in Atlanta, was still single and worked for an advertising agency.

Bramlett took the phone and talked with her briefly, told her he loved her and for her to be careful. He didn't feel very comfortable about her living alone in a big city.

Then he gave the receiver back to Valeria, kissed her on the cheek, and went out the door to the carport.

He chuckled. *They'll be on the phone for half an hour at least,* he thought. It never ceased to amaze him how his wife and daughters could talk on the telephone hour on end.

The evening-shift officers looked questioningly at one another when Bramlett walked into headquarters. It was rare for the sheriff to work in the evening. He told Todd Falkner, the night dispatcher, as he passed his desk, to call in Curry, Baillie, and Robertson.

"Curry's already here," Falkner said.

171

Bramlett gave a grunt and hurried into his office.

No sooner was he seated at his desk than Falkner's voice said over the phone intercom, "Sheriff, there's a Mrs. McAbrams on line four. You want me to take a message or what?"

"I'll speak to her," he said, lifting the telephone receiver.

The woman was sobbing. "I don't know what to do," she said. "Jason has never gone off without telling me where he was going."

"I'm sure he'll turn up, Mrs. McAbrams." Bramlett rubbed his forehead with his thumb and index finger. He wished he could sound more optimistic.

"What about the highway patrol? Are they looking for him?"

"We have put out an all points bulletin, ma'am. Someone will find him shortly. Is there anyone who can stay with you?"

"Stay with me? Why, yes. My daughter can."

"I'd call her, ma'am. And we'll let you know something as soon as we can."

As he let the receiver fall back into the cradle, he looked up. H. C. Curry was standing in the doorway. Bramlett leaned back in his chair. "Got something?" he said.

The deputy entered, laid a sheet of typing paper on the desk blotter and sat down. "I've watched one tape. Those are people I've identified."

Bramlett reached into his back pocket and pulled out the package of Red Man. With his fingers he kneaded the moist, stringy tobacco into a ball and shoved it into his mouth. He still had a small wad in his mouth on the other side of his jaw.

Sometimes when he was especially agitated he found himself putting in a fresh chew before the previous one was completely sucked dry. He knew that getting another chew wasn't just nervousness. It was one of those small, deliberately done actions to delay handling something unpleasant. Having to look at Curry's sheet of paper was something unpleasant.

He picked up the sheet and scanned the names. Cora Hartley, Rozelle Kample, and Noel Hackott. Curry had noted that two women on the tape he didn't recognize.

Bramlett gave a wry smile. "No wonder Hackott was so interested in tapes."

Curry nodded. "With a female."

"I see." Bramlett shook his head slowly, his eyes still fixed on the paper. "He the only man?"

"Yessir. Except for Bondreaux, of course."

"And you can't ID these other two women?"

"No sir. They were both white."

"What?" Bramlett said, looking up at him.

Curry shrugged. "Nothing. Of course, I've just looked at one tape. On fast forward."

Bramlett opened a file folder on his desk and slipped the sheet of names into it. He lifted another file folder and handed it to Curry. "This is a copy of what the principal gave us on Bondreaux. I want you to start checking names and finding out all you can about what he was doing in New York. Talk to his former principal. Find out if he was ever involved in anything. Talk to someone at the police department in this town he lived in. Find out anything—*every-thing*—you can about him."

Curry frowned. "You mean . . . you mean, *tonight*?"

Bramlett's brow wrinkled as he looked at the younger man. "Something wrong with tonight?"

"New York is on Eastern Time and that's an hour ahead of us . . . All these folks will be home and . . ." He didn't finish. Perhaps he finally noticed the seriousness of the sheriff's piercing gaze, the hardness of it. A confused expression came onto Curry's face. He nodded, then said, "Yes, sir," and took the file folder from Bramlett's hand and left the office.

THE SHERIFF LOOKED at a legal pad on which he'd been jotting notes earlier in the day. He saw where he'd written "B's wife." He had drawn a circle around that. He did need to know the name of Bondreaux's former wife, the one in Atlanta. Did she know Bondreaux was planning to come there? Who would know? Didn't Bondreaux's cousin, Gilbert Armstrong, say his mother would probably know?

The intercom buzzed. "Abel Harrington on line six, Sheriff." Harrington was a state narcotics agent who worked out of the Tupelo office.

"Sheriff, we've checked out this guy whose house you found the stash in," he said. "We've got nothing on him."

"Maybe he was just starting out."

"Maybe. But we're still on it. Let you know if anything turns up."

Bramlett replaced the receiver in its cradle. More and more he was convinced drugs had little to do with this case.

Todd Falkner, the dispatcher, buzzed him on the intercom. "Baillie is on the way. I haven't been able to locate Robertson."

"Keep trying," Bramlett said.

In his mind he could still see Valeria standing on the porch holding out the package of Red Man and the plastic cup. She knew this was no time for him to agonize through withdrawal.

Normally she didn't like him working at night or on weekends. But this was different. If he'd stayed at the house, he wouldn't have been able to relax anyway.

The tight knot in the center of his chest hurt more than ever. But if he was going to have a heart attack, it would just have to wait until he'd caught this damn killer.

This whole thing crushed him. Especially now that the videos were involved. He wished the hell it was some out-of-town syndicate-crime type who'd breezed into Sheffield and wasted a dealer. But it was no doubt someone much closer to home. Someone who finally had had enough. And someone, for all Bramlett was aware of, who knew who and precisely where Marcellus was.

Suddenly, Bramlett felt distrustful of everyone and everything. He pressed his lips tightly together as if reminding himself not to breathe a word about Marcellus being at the cemetery, not even to Curry or Baillie or Robertson.

Deputy Johnny Baillie arrived at the office with a disturbed look on his face. He was obviously displeased that his evening at home with the wife and kids was interrupted. He dropped into one of the chairs in front of the sheriff's desk and waited for an explanation.

"Listen," Bramlett said, noticing the thickness of his own voice. "You'll get some time off after all this is done. But we're going to work on this Bondreaux thing until we come up with something. Around the clock if we have to."

"What's so special about this case?"

174

"Never mind." He lifted the Styrofoam cup to his mouth, spat, then set the cup to one side.

He spread out the data sheets in front of him on the desk, glancing over the handwritten notes he'd made and photocopies of notes others had made. Then he looked up.

"Bondreaux has a former wife. She's possibly living in Atlanta, according to what Vicki Ann Skelton told me. I want you to find out this woman's name and whatever you can about her."

Baillie gave a wry smile. "You want me to go to Atlanta?"

"No," Bramlett said. There was an impatient edge to his voice. "I just want you to work on this full-time. Drumwright can take over anything else you are handling." Billy Drumwright was an eager young deputy who assisted at times with investigations.

"Where do I start?"

"How the hell should I know?" Bramlett said. "Here's a copy of the file we got from the high school principal. Call every name given as a reference or whatever." He held up a file folder for the deputy.

Baillie's eyes widened. "You mean *now*?"

Bramlett's cheeks went taut, then he said, "I mean right this very minute."

The deputy took the folder and left. He closed the door a bit harder than usual.

Bramlett ground his teeth. He had a good mind to run out after the deputy, snatch him up by the collar and shake him. He didn't need this smart-aleck attitude. But, no, he didn't even have time to be angry right now.

He began reading the notes again. Jesse Bondreaux was originally from Iskitini, down below Jackson someplace but Bramlett wasn't sure exactly where. He'd never been there, had only seen signs on the highway indicating the turnoff.

Bramlett buzzed the dispatcher on the intercom. "Todd, you get ahold of Robertson?"

"Still trying, Sheriff. He doesn't answer his phone. Must be out somewheres."

Bramlett grumbled and swiveled around in his chair. He needed Robertson now. He needed to ID every single owner of every small, dark-blue car in the county—or in every county of northeast Mississippi.

His private line rang. He snatched up the receiver. It was Valeria. "Marcellus is gone ..." she said. Her voice was trembling. "Gone? How gone?"

"He's not out back. That BB gun is on the porch, but the basketball is gone. I drove down to the park, but no one is there ..."

26

H. C. Curry glanced up from the notepad he was reading when he saw Sheriff Bramlett hurry out of his office, hat already on his head, walking almost at a run toward the rear exit. Mrs. Bramlett must have called, mused the deputy. The sheriff hurried for no one except his wife. He smiled and looked down at the notepad again.

These were the notes he'd scribbled down when watching the first video tape. Besides Bondreaux, only one man. Noel Hackott.

Curry had viewed the entire tape on fast forward, slowing it down to normal speed only when a new scene appeared, and then only long enough to clearly ID the couple being filmed. Out beside the name of Noel Hackott he had written Cora Hartley.

Curry scatched the back of his neck, considering. Cora Hartley was still in high school. Not yet eighteen.

No wonder Hackott was concerned about such a tape if his friend Bondreaux had told him about it. The man could get several years in Parchman for such an indiscretion.

Curry wrote a reminder on a Post-it note to talk to the sheriff about picking up Noel Hackott. No doubt they could lean on him plenty heavy now.

He set the notepad aside and opened the file folder from the high school. Jesse Bondreaux was thirty-eight years old, unmarried, began teaching at Sheffield High School four years ago, was selected

Teacher of the Year his second year, was active in the Little Theater in Tupelo, and sang in his church choir. In New York, he had taught at Adamsdale High School, Albany, New York. The name listed for the school's principal was William Clarington.

According to Directory Assistance, there were three William Claringtons in Albany, New York. Curry dialed the first one. He wasn't home but the woman who answered said her husband had never been a principal.

Curry dialed the second one. A girl—probably in her early teens, Curry guessed—answered the phone on the first ring. Curry asked for Mr. Clarington, then heard her call out, "Dad!"

In a moment, a man answered, and Curry said, "Mr. Clarington, this is Deputy H. C. Curry with the Chakchiuma County, Mississippi, Sheriff's Department. I wanted to ask you a few questions about one of your former teachers, Jesse Bondreaux."

There was a long pause on the other end of the line, then, "Who is this?"

"Deputy H. C. Curry, sir. We're investigating the murder of Jesse Bondreaux."

Again there was a silence, then a choked, "Just a minute. I'll get the phone in my study." Moments later Curry heard the click as the other receiver was picked up and the man's muffled voice called, "Linda! Please hang up the phone in the den." Another click.

"Hello?" the man said. "I'm sorry. I didn't get your name . . ."

Curry identified himself once again.

"Yes. You were saying?"

"I said we're investigating the murder of one of your former teachers, Jesse Bondreaux."

"Murdered? When?"

"Last Friday. According to his employment record he taught at your high school."

"He's been gone for years. I had no idea where he was."

"He's been here in Sheffield four years. Now, could you tell me anything about him? Were there any problems or anything like that?"

"Problems? What kind of problems?"

Clarington's voice was strained, Curry noticed, almost defensive.

"Why did he leave your school?" Curry said.

Silence again. Then, "We have many teachers coming and going. I can't remember the circumstances of every one of them. I would prefer you call me at my office, not here at home."

"Yes, sir," Curry said, feeling the blood rise in his face. "But we're investigating a murder and we feel this is important. Are you telling me you don't remember the circumstances of Bondreaux leaving your employment?"

"This is really not a good time for me to talk." The man's voice now had dropped to a hushed whisper. "Give me your number. I'll call you first thing tomorrow morning. I'll . . . I'll check the files and see exactly why he left. I'm sure no particular reason is given. It isn't required, you know."

Curry had a feeling William Clarington would not phone him in the morning. He was trying to hide something. Curry sensed it in the man's tone.

"Mr. Clarington, Jesse Bondreaux is just one of three people who've been killed since last Friday. We think all three murders are related. Possibly the same person killed them all. We do not know if the killer plans to kill others." He paused, wondering how he could put more pressure on this man who might hang up at any second. Then, "We may need to fly a couple of men up there right away to ask you some questions." This was a bluff, of course. The Chakchiuma Sheriff's Department couldn't afford to fly anyone anywhere.

"No, no. I don't think that's necessary. But I really would prefer to talk to you after I refresh my memory with his file."

Curry sighed. "That would be helpful. But while I've got you on the phone, I'd like you to tell me whatever you can."

"What . . . what do you mean?"

"Let's begin this way, Mr. Clarington. Do you remember a teacher named Jesse Bondreaux?" Curry tried to keep the scarcasm out of his voice.

"Yes. He taught history for us a few years back. I don't remember the exact dates. Are you recording this?"

"I'm taking notes," Curry said. "How did he get along with the students and the other teachers?"

Another long silence. Then, "He was asked to leave."

"Why?"

"There were . . . there were accusations that he was indiscreet with a student."

"A female student?"

"Yes."

"Were any charges officially made?"

"He was asked to leave and he did. There's nothing else that really needs to be said. The parents of the girl wanted it that way."

"I see. Do you know if he was involved with drugs?"

"Drugs? No, I never heard anything about that."

"Could you tell me anything else that might be helpful to us?"

"No. I hope you'll keep this confidential. About the student. It's all past history now, and I don't see why any of this should be dug back up now."

"We're trying to solve a crime that happened last week, Mr. Clarington. Right now I don't know that anything you've told me has anything to do with it. This student thing . . . was this an isolated case or was he involved with other students as well?"

Clarington again was slow in answering. "There were others. I finally told him I was going to the police unless he turned in his immediate resignation."

"And he did?"

"Yes. And we've never heard from him again."

"Did you know his wife?"

"Wife? I never knew he had a wife."

Curry thanked the principal, asked for his office telephone number in case he needed to contact him again and gave him his own number. He had the feeling he should have asked something else, but he wasn't sure what.

He read through the file again. Nothing jumped out at him. He closed the file, drummed his fingers on his desktop, and drew a deep breath. He would take the other videos home and watch them after his mother went to bed.

He opened a lower desk drawer and lifted out a small cassette tape player, inserted one of Bondreaux's self-recorded telephone conversations, and pushed the ear piece into his ear.

There was a hum, then the ringing of a telephone and then a woman's voice answered. "Hello?" The sound quality of the recording wasn't good but was understandable.

180

"It's me," a man's voice said. Curry recognized it as Jesse Bondreaux's.

"I don't want to talk to you," the woman said. She sounded like she was speaking through her teeth, her voice was strained.

"Now, now. Is that any way to treat old friends"

"We're not friends."

"Sure we are. We're more than friends. We're part of each other." Bondreaux gave a low chuckle. "I mean, the way we were. How could you ever forget?"

"What do you want?"

"I'm getting low on cash right now. I need a little more help."

"I've given you all I'm going to give you. You promised me last time you wouldn't bother me anymore."

"Did I? I'm sorry. You know how things kind of get all balled up. Anyway I need ten big ones."

"You're crazy. I don't have that kind of money."

"But we both know where you can get it, don't we?"

"I can't do it again. I've run out of lies."

"Get the money, sweetheart. This is Monday. I'd better have it by Friday or my lips will get awfully slippery . . . just letting words slide out to certain persons who you don't want to hear those words. Am I making myself clear?"

There was a long silence on the other end of the line, then, "I'll think about it. I'll call you back in a couple of days. Don't call me!"

"Don't push, sweetheart."

"Okay. Tomorrow. I'll call you tomorrow."

"By four o'clock. I'll be home by three-thirty. If I haven't heard from you by four, I'll come looking for you, Tidwell."

The line disconnected. Curry listened on but there was nothing else on the tape.

He turned his head and saw Baillie at his desk across the room. "Johnny!" he called. "Come listen to this!"

"IT CAN BE FILTERED," Johnny Baillie said after listening to Bondreaux's conversation with the woman named Tidwell. "Do you think it's someone local?"

"I have no idea," H. C. Curry said.

"I've talked to Gilbert Armstrong, that cousin of Bondreaux's. He asked his mother about Bondreaux's former wife. Her name is Tia Riggs. He has no idea where she is now. I suggested Atlanta, but he said he didn't know. They were divorced several years ago."

"What's that?" Curry asked, nodding at the Polaroid photographs in Baillie's hand.

Baillie smiled with satisfaction. "I went back to Bondreaux's house this afternoon. I found these in a book. A hymnal, in fact." He handed the photos to Curry.

Curry looked at the photographs one by one. Three were taken inside the house. Groups of young people sitting on the floor of Bondreaux's living room and couch. Two were taken outside the house. Four teenagers were standing beside a car. He recognized Gail Topp, Vicki Ann Skelton, Cora Hartley, and— He gasped.

"What is it?" Baillie said.

Curry's eyes were wide with shock. Baillie took the picture from his hand and looked at it. "Say," he said, "isn't this your niece— what's her name—?"

"Veatrice," the deputy said, hardly moving his lips.

THE AUTOMOBILE SPED QUICKLY away from the park and had not turned toward his grandparents' house. "W-wait . . ." Marcellus stammered. His heart was beating faster than when he did the six-mile run with his dad last spring in Germantown, and his breathing was rapid. The car jumped passed two stop signs without even the slightest pause.

He turned his head and looked at the driver for the first time. She was wearing a scarf, and in the darkness he couldn't make out her face. "Where are we—" he began.

"Shut up," she said.

He looked at the houses and small buildings on the sides of the street flashing past. In minutes they were outside the city limits of Sheffield and speeding down a narrow graveled road. Marcellus felt his hand along the side of his door, searching for the handle.

What was going on? Where was she taking him? What was she going to do to him? Could he dare jump out at this speed? Finally,

182

he found what surely had to be the door's release handle and he clamped his hand tightly around it.

The car fishtailed through a curve, almost sideswiping a mailbox and post, then straightened up and rushed on forward. The light from the headlamps began to show dust rising from the road. Another vehicle was just ahead.

In seconds they were plunged into a thick cloud of trailing dust and immediately the glow of two taillights came into view. The woman pumped the brake, slowing the car, and Marcellus clutched the dashboard with his left hand. His right hand still grasped the door handle.

"Damn!" the driver said. She steered to the right, then to the left, trying to find room to pass.

Suddenly the brake lights of the vehicle in front came on and the woman stomped on the pedal. Marcellus was thrown against the dashboard, smashing his left shoulder hard into it, and, almost in one continuous motion, was snapped backward against the seat back.

In the split second the car slowed almost to a stop, Marcellus jerked the door handle and threw his right shoulder into the door. The door sprang open, and he lunged out of the car.

He rolled onto the road, feeling the gravel tear at his clothes and flesh. He sucked dust into his lungs and gagged and shut his eyes tight. He rolled over and over, plunging off the roadbed and into the ditch and thudded against the side of the ditch, jarring his body to a complete stop.

He couldn't breathe. He wondered if he was dying. Then he remembered the car and pushed himself to his feet.

He saw the taillights of the car. The headlights illuminated swirling dust. The other vehicle was gone. The road was too narrow and the ditch on either side too deep for the car to turn around. The rear backup lights suddenly came on.

She had shifted into reverse and was backing up.

Marcellus scrambled out of the ditch and into the field beside the road. He still couldn't breathe.

He ran, stumbling and regaining his balance several times, kept on running away from the road and into the pitch blackness. He didn't look back. He could hear the car engine racing. And on he ran.

27 _____

JACOB ROBERTSON LEANED AGAINST the hood of his pickup looking out at the lake. The moonlight glimmered on the ripples moving across the face of the water. He bent over and picked up a small, flat rock at his feet and skipped it across the surface.

He and Nena were supposed to eat at that new seafood restaurant in Tupelo, then go to a movie. He was wearing a brand-new shirt and jacket that his mother had gotten for him that morning at Reed's in Tupelo.

He was to pick Nena up at her house at six. That would give them plenty of time to drive to Tupelo, eat, and be at the movie theater at the mall at Barnes Crossing by seven-thirty. He'd gotten off work at four-thirty, hurried home, shaved and bathed again, dressed and was standing on her front porch at exactly six o'clock.

His breathing was shallow as he pushed the doorbell. He waited.

No answer. No sounds of movement as if someone were coming to the door. The doorbell was working. He could hear it ringing.

He walked around the side of her house. Her car was gone. Had she gone out or just wasn't home yet? Could she have gotten mixed up on the time.

He returned to the front door and rang the doorbell again. Still no answer.

184

After several minutes he went back to his truck and sat in the cab. Maybe she'd be along any minute now.

He waited another fifteen minutes, then cranked the truck and drove away. He drove aimlessly around town for a few minutes, then made another pass in front of Nena's house. The house was dark and the car was still gone.

Where could she be? Did she simply decide she didn't want to go out with him or what?

Jacob rapped himself with his fist on the side of his head. "Forget her!" he said out loud.

Then he stopped by the Jitney Jr. and bought a six-pack of Budweiser. He didn't drink often himself and was bewildered at first by the array of brands. Then he saw Budweiser and remembered H. C. Curry drank Budweiser.

He drove out to the lake. The first three cans he guzzled as if he were trying to drown the flames in his guts.

He popped the top of the fourth. Was she still in love with this Bondreaux trash? Even though he was dead?

He drank more slowly now, taking shorter swallows, feeling the muscles of his throat contract and pull the bubbling liquid down into his stomach. Forget her!

GROVER BRAMLETT, with Valeria clutching the dashboard and sitting beside him, sped the fourteen miles to the Farrar community with warning lights flashing. The patrol car bounced over the cattle gap at the gate to Rodney Cooper's farm and skidded to a stop near the front porch. The porch was cast in a yellow glow from the bright porch light.

The door of the farmhouse opened at once and a stocky, balding man stepped outside onto the porch. Both Bramlett and Valeria bounded out of the car and up the steps.

"He's all right," the man said. "My wife is cleaning him up."

He led them through the front room and on back to a large bathroom. Marcellus was standing in the middle of the room on a small round bath rug. He was dressed only in his underpants. On his upper left arm and on both knees were ugly abrasions. There was also a scrape on the right side of his forehead.

185

His pants, shirt, shoes, and socks were in a pile in front of the tub. A woman was sitting on a stool beside him with a basin of sudsy water in her lap and a washcloth in her hand. She had a freckled face and smiled warmly when they entered the room.

"He's doing just fine," she said quickly. "I've never seen such a brave young man. Just scratches, looks like. Nothing broken."

The woman took the basin in her left hand and stood. She held out the washcloth to Valeria and said, "Here, Mrs. Bramlett. Maybe he'd like you doing this better than me."

Valeria took the basin and washcloth. "Oh, thank God, thank God," she said softly, as if only now having actually seen him standing there could she accept that he was indeed all right.

"Did you recognize her?" Bramlett said.

Marcellus shook his head. "No, sir. It was dark and she was wearing a scarf or something."

Valeria set the basin on the stool and began examining the abrasions one by one, holding her fingers just above the skin, not touching but as guides for her eyes to be sure she missed nothing.

"You want some coffee?" the woman said to Bramlett, stepping into the hallway.

He shook his head. "No. I don't think so. But I would like to use your phone, if you don't mind, Mrs. Cooper."

"Come this way," she said.

Not a half hour before, Rodney Cooper, cattle farmer in the Farrar community, had telephoned the Bramletts' house. Bramlett himself answered the phone. Cooper told him one of his tenant farmers had come to the house and said a white boy had suddenly appeared at their door. The boy looked all beat up, the tenant said. Cooper went and got him in his truck.

Bramlett stepped out of the bedroom and followed Mrs. Cooper into the den. The telephone was on a small table at one end of the couch.

Bramlett telephoned Johnny Baillie and told him to get an account of where every suspect was today. "What suspects?" the deputy said.

"Just start with a list of every woman we've interviewed," the sheriff said. "*Every*body. I want to know where each one of them was all evening." Then he hung up the phone.

186

*　　*　　*

GLADIS COOPER WRAPPED Marcellus in her husband's bathrobe. Marcellus was almost as tall as Rodney Cooper, and the robe hardly dragged the floor. Bramlett asked the Coopers to please not say anything about the incident for the time being.

"If you do," he said, "you could endanger the boy's life." Both assured him their lips were sealed. Bramlett had no doubt they meant precisely what they said.

On the drive back to the house, Valeria sat in the backseat with Marcellus as Bramlett drove. "I'm taking Marcellus and going someplace," she said.

He nodded. "Sounds good. But where?"

"I don't know. Maybe Sylvia's." Sylvia Mapp was one of Valeria's sisters. Sylvia was a widow who lived on a farm not far away in Grant County.

Bramlett grunted and then said, "I don't like that. Too many folks know where Sylvia's place is."

Valeria gnawed thoughtfully on her lower lip, looking at her grandson with deep concern. She held one of his hands in both of hers. Suddenly, her face brightened. "What about Sissy's? She lives way out from nowhere."

Bramlett nodded in approval and smiled. "Good."

Sissy Green was another sister, also a widow, and almost ten years older than Valeria. She lived alone on her farm seven miles from Cluster, a tiny community north of Greenwood in the Delta.

When they got home, Valeria telephoned Sissy and simply said there'd been some problem and she and Marcellus would be coming right away. She'd explain when she got there.

SHORTLY BEFORE NINE O'CLOCK, H. C. Curry left headquarters and went home. He had tried to reach his niece Veatrice by phone. Austin, her father and H. C.'s oldest brother, answered. She was out, he said. Try again later.

He phoned Lizzie's apartment. She was okay now, she said, and would be staying there tonight. Then he left headquarters, taking the video tapes with him.

His father Witt was already in bed. Witt got up at five each morning. He had to be at his job at the lumberyard by seven.

H. C.'s mother, Chancy, heard her son arrive at the house and came into the front room. "You need anything?" she asked. "A glass of buttermilk?"

"No'm. I got some tapes the sheriff wants me to watch, and I thought I'd do it here at the house. You go on to bed. I'm okay."

She gave him a hug and a kiss on the cheek. "I'm glad you're home safe." Then she returned to her bedroom and closed the door.

His mother worried about him, and at every meal when she said grace, she asked God to protect him. In her mind, she thought of lawmen as involved in gun battles with desperate criminals on a regular basis. Curry reminded her at least once a week that he'd never fired his weapon except at the firing range.

He got a beer from the refrigerator and slid tape number two into the VCR. He leaned back in the recliner and popped the top of the can.

He lifted the remote control and turned down the volume. There had been very little conversation on the first tape. All he wanted, anyway, was a list of people he could identify.

He viewed it as he had the first. On fast forward. He slowed it to normal speed with the beginning of each new episode so he could positively ID those involved, then switched to fast forward again.

Nena Carmack was on the fourth tape and no other. It seemed that during the time Bondreaux was dating her, he was dating no one else. Should he let Jacob Robertson see this tape? His initial feeling was a definite no.

Another new episode was coming on. Curry pushed the Play button. The images slowed to normal speed. It was Bondreaux and Nena again.

"What are you watching?" Chancy Curry said. Her tone was shock and disgust wedded together.

H. C. jumped. He hadn't heard her open her bedroom door and come back into the front room. He fumbled for the Off button. "What?" he said, blinking as he looked at her.

"How dare you bring such trash into my house!"

"Mama, listen. It's not mine," he said. "What I mean is, Sheriff Bramlett asked me to look at these. They're pictures of Jesse Bon-

188

dreaux—you know, the murdered schoolteacher. Anyway, I thought since you and Daddy were gone to bed . . ." He didn't finish.

She placed her arms defiantly across her chest. "You get that . . . that trash out of here right now. And don't you *ever* bring nothing like that into my house. You hear?"

"Yessum," Curry said. He knew there was no sense arguing with his mother. Nobody, not even his father, argued with Chancy Curry. He ejected the tape from the VCR.

"Was you raised to do something like this to your mama?" Her voice was shaking. Her jaw jutted.

"No'm," he said. He stacked all five tapes in his hand. He shook his head in resignation and said, "I reckon I'll take them on back to headquarters."

"I reckon you will. And you better pray the good Lord forgives your ugly self, too."

She stood with her arms still crossed, her feet spread apart, watching to be sure her orders were carried out immediately. Only when her son was out the house with the front door closed behind him did she return to her bedroom.

Curry watched the fifth tape at headquarters. No more of Nena. More of Cora and that Tupelo secretary, Nicole Estis. Three additional women he didn't recognize. Each one unwittingly filmed by the hidden camera.

He jotted down the name of each person as she appeared on tape. He penciled in a question mark when he could not identify someone. There was a blond woman who somehow looked familiar, but he wasn't sure.

He watched to the end, then punched off the machine and leaned back in his chair and breathed a huge sigh of relief. "Thank you, God," he said reverently and meaningfully. "Thank you that my beautiful niece Veatrice was not one of these women."

He sat staring at the monitor for several minutes. It all made the clearest sense. Jesse Bondreaux could have been using the videos to blackmail any one, or possibly even several, of these women. And any one of them, then, would have had good reason to break into his house looking for the tapes.

And, of course, there was Noel Hackott. He was taped with an underage female. He could face statutory rape.

Bondreaux may well have been blackmailing Hackott. Certainly, Hackott appeared to have plenty of money. And he or any one of these women could have come to the point of wanting to kill the man.

And Nena Carmack would have as much if not more reason than most. He remembered the blood on the floor by the front door of Bondreaux's house. And Nena's bandaged hand.

And who was this blonde? She was somebody he knew. She was on the tape several times.

He rewound the last tape to the beginning of the first sequence in which she appeared. He watched. Only occasionally was the blonde's face clearly visible.

A good shot of her face came into view. He pressed the Still button and froze the frame. She was so familiar, yet different . . .

Of course! It was Katherine Topp.

Not the dark-haired Katherine Topp they'd interviewed, but a *blond* Katherine Topp.

He clicked off the VCR, hurried to his desk and snatched up the telephone receiver and punched Bramlett's number.

WHEN BRAMLETT HUNG UP THE PHONE after talking to Curry, he walked out onto the front porch and eased himself down into the swing. The cool night air tingled against his flushed face. Katherine Topp and Jesse Bondreaux? Unbelievable. Could she have killed him? Ridiculous.

The door open and Valeria walked out of the house. "What are you doing sitting out here in the dark?" she said.

"Just thinking," he said. "How's he doing?"

She joined him in the swing. "He's watching TV with milk and cookies," she said. "I've given him some ibuprofen. He's quite uncomfortable."

"He's tough," Bramlett said. "He'll feel a lot better in the morning."

She stared at the side of his face for a long moment, then said, "I just can't understand why someone would want to harm a child."

Bramlett shrugged. "Lots of crazy people in the world. Somebody who's very afraid or trying to protect himself or someone else. Or

190

herself, in this case. Marcellus is a threat to somebody's world." He shook his head sadly and reached to his hip pocket for his Red Man.

"I'm already packed," she said.

"Can't you wait until morning? It's already almost ten o'clock."

She shook her head. "We can be there in two hours. I wish you'd come with us."

He ground his teeth for a moment, then said, "I wish I could."

She gave a faint moan. Bramlett put his arms around her and held her close.

28

DEPUTY H. C. CURRY WAS THE YOUNGEST of seven children. His brother, Austin Curry, was an appliance serviceman for the Sears store in Tupelo, commuting thirty-seven miles each way to work. His vinyl-sided house in the northern section of Sheffield was well maintained, the trim painted white and the foundation shrubs exactly clipped the proper size.

H. C. Curry figured his brother's daughter Veatrice ought to be home by now. He parked on the dark street and carefully made his way up the steep concrete steps from the curb to the shallow front yard. He stepped onto the porch and rang the doorbell.

Austin's wife, Warrentina, opened the door. She was a tall woman, thin to the point of gauntness, whose eyes seemed, to H. C., to reflect perpetual fatigue.

"Austin went out and ain't back yet," she said immediately, before he could open his mouth. Warrentina was like that, always answering questions before they could be asked.

He tried to smile pleasantly. "It's Veatrice I want to see."

Warrentina Curry frowned disapprovingly, standing there with her hand on the doorknob. "It's late," she said, her frown growing deeper.

"I'm sorry, but it's important."

She studied him for a moment as if trying to decide whether to

192

let him in or run him off. Finally, she sighed and motioned for him to come in.

"She in her room studying," she said, closing the door. "I'll call her." She motioned with a tilt of her head toward a chair.

Curry didn't sit. His hands were clammy. He stood looking towards the mantel over the fireplace. On the mantel were at least twenty framed photographs of various sizes: a large one of Austin and Warrentina on the day of their wedding, high school graduation pictures of their three older children, a large color photo of Veatrice from last year's homecoming court when she was the eleventh-grade maid, and lots of baby pictures. Curry turned to look toward the cased opening to the hallway when he heard footsteps.

His niece, wearing a bulky striped sweater and baggy denim pants, smiled at him as she stepped into the room. Veatrice Curry was tall and thin. She smiled at him, showing her beautifully set teeth.

Warrentina, directly behind her, said to her daughter, "You still got lots of studying to do," and disappeared down the hallway. She obviously wasn't interested in whatever her brother-in-law had to say to her daughter.

"Veatrice, I need to ask you some questions," Curry said, then paused and waved the back of his hand at the couch for her to sit. "We found this picture at Jesse Bondreaux's house." He slid the photograph out of his shirt pocket and handed it to her.

The girl looked down at the photograph, holding it in both hands. She nodded, then shook her head. "It's hard to believe someone killed him." She looked back up at her young uncle, waiting.

H. C. licked his lips. "We were wondering . . . well, we knew all those other kids hung around Bondreaux's house, but I didn't know *you* did."

The corners of her mouth lifted into a smile, and she dropped the photograph onto the coffee table and leaned back on the couch. "Naw. That was the only time I was ever there. It was about a month ago. Vicki Ann was giving me a ride home from cheerleader practice, and she said she had to stop by there to get something. I was surprised to see all those other kids. It was almost like a party. Mr. Bondreaux was laughing and carrying on. Then he insisted on all of us standing together like that so he could take a picture."

Curry drew a heavy sigh of relief. Then he pointed toward the photograph. "I see Gail Topp was there that day. Was she riding with Vicki Ann, also?"

"Naw. She was there when we arrived and there when we left." She gave a slight shudder.

"What's the matter?"

She wrinkled up her nose, then said, "I don't know . . . Something was strange about the way Gail and Mr. Bondreaux kept exchanging looks and giggling. Well, it made me uncomfortable. That's all."

Curry made a low moan and shook his head. "I got to be going," he said. Then he smiled at his niece. "I'm glad you're you."

She cocked her head and looked puzzled. "What?"

He laughed. "Never mind," he said, standing up.

JOHNNY BAILLIE WAS STILL AT HIS DESK when Curry returned to headquarters. "It was the only time she was ever there," Curry said. "She really didn't even know the guy. She'd been at cheerleader—"

"I don't know what's eating Jacob," Baillie said, looking up from the paper spread out on his desktop. He obviously wasn't interested in Curry's niece being at Bondreaux's. Curry dropped the photograph Baillie had given him onto the corner of the desk. Baillie continued. "He seems to be in a foul mood. Maybe this dating business ain't for him."

"What?" Curry said.

Baillie looked up at him, scowling. "I'm talking about Jacob. I said he's in a foul mood. I think it's got something to do with that Carmack woman."

Baillie looked across the room where Deputy Jacob Robertson hunched over his desk. Curry followed Baillie's gaze to the tall deputy leaning on his fists at a desk on the other side of the room.

"By the way, Noel Hackott is gone."

Curry looked back at him. "What?"

Baillie shrugged. "You suggested we might pick him up. He didn't show up today at his shop. Hasn't been home. One of the neighbors says he's gone to California for a while."

Curry nodded, then looked back at Robertson. "I dunno," he

said, meaning he really wasn't sure Hackott was worth pursuing. He made his way across the room.

"Nothing," Robertson said in answer to Curry's "What's wrong?"

Curry pulled a gray metal folding chair closer to the front of Robertson's desk. "How's Nena?" he asked.

Robertson brushed at a thick lock of red hair that tumbled over his forehead—a gesture of aggravation Curry had seen his friend do ever since they were playing high school basketball together—and then said, "How should I know?"

"What's that supposed to mean?"

Robertson shook his head. "She stood me up. We made a date for tonight, and I went by to get her and she was gone."

Curry was silent for a moment, thinking, wondering, then he said, "That's tough." He scratched the side of his head. "Gone, you said?" His lips drew tightly together.

Robertson didn't reply for a moment, then he quickly looked up. "What are you saying?" he said.

"When did you last talk to her?"

"Right after school. I stopped by her house. It was about three-thirty."

Curry cleared his throat. "The old man and I were there right after you were—about four o'clock."

Robertson cocked his head and scowled. "Why?"

Curry shrugged. "Just some more questions about Bondreaux." He didn't want to be the one to tell his friend that Nena Carmack had lied about the last time she saw Bondreaux, that she had, in fact, been seen leaving his house not too long before he was killed at the cemetery, or, for that matter, that Bondreaux was blackmailing her.

Curry pulled the telephone on the desk over to him and quickly dialed Lizzie's number. Then, in a moment, "Hey. You seen Nena this evening?"

"No," Lizzie said. "I haven't seen her since school. Not since lunchtime, in fact. Why?"

"Jacob was supposed to have a date with her tonight, and she wasn't there when he went to pick her up."

"What are you talking about?"

"He was just wondering what happened. No big deal."

Curry told her not to worry, then hung up. He looked back at Robertson. Neither man spoke for a long moment. Finally, Curry said, "Call the highway patrol and request an APB on her vehicle."

Robertson nodded.

Curry could see the fear in his eyes. He wished he could say something to ease his friend's mind—but what could he say? He reached out and put his hand on his shoulder. "I'll talk to you later," he said.

He returned to Baillie's desk. Baillie was talking on the telephone. He hung up the receiver just as Curry neared.

"That was Gilbert Armstrong again," Baillie said. "He'd talked with his mother and she said Tia Riggs had been in New York but was now back in Atlanta."

Curry looked blank.

"Bondreaux's former wife," Baillie said.

Curry nodded. "The sheriff said she was in Atlanta."

"I'll run a name check with vehicle registration in both states just to be sure."

"I have a little more to do here and then I'm going out to check on some things," Curry said, stretching his back. He was suddenly very tired.

Baillie looked at him blankly for a moment, then his eyes fell back to the notebook in front of him on the desk.

AFTER CURRY VIEWED all the videos once more on fast forward, he sat back in his chair and reread the names he'd written. Nicole Estis, Nena Carmack, Katherine Topp, Cora Hartley, Rozelle Kample, and Noel Hackott. And five women he'd never seen before.

He locked the tapes in his desk drawer, and left the building. The night air was fresh and nippy. He zipped up his leather jacket and slipped behind the wheel of the patrol car.

He drove slowly through the dark streets of Sheffield. Was Nena

Carmack really in danger? What about Noel Hackott? Where had he gone?

In a few minutes, he stopped in front of the small house where Nena Carmack lived. There were no lights. He drove on down the street to Lizzie's apartment building.

HE RAPPED lightly on Lizzie's door. "It's me," he said in answer to her question.

Lizzie snatched open the door. Her eyes were wide with fright as she looked up at him and backed away from the door at the same time as if expecting the most awful news.

H. C. shook his head quickly. "No. We don't know anything," he said. "We've contacted the highway patrol to watch for her vehicle. I don't know what else to do right now."

She shut her eyes tightly as if in agonizing pain. "H. C.," she said, beginning to cry, "something horrible is going to happen. I can *feel* it."

H. C. reached for her and took her in his arms. Lizzie was trembling. "Just . . . like Jo Ann . . ." she said.

He held her tightly against his body, wanting to protect her, to keep anyone from hurting her in any way. It wasn't really Nena Carmack he was concerned about right at the moment, it was the woman he loved—Lizzie Clouse.

She began sobbing—hard, gasping sobs, and he knew it was not only Jo Ann and Nena that Lizzie was wailing for, but for her murdered mother as well. He pressed her harder against his chest, as hard as his arms could pull.

"Hush now. Hush now," he whispered into her ear. "I'm sure she's okay." He tried to say this with confidence. But his voice broke on the words.

29 ━━━━━━━━━━━━━━━━━━━━━━━━━━━━━

THAT NIGHT, GROVER BRAMLETT SHIFTED from one position to another in bed, trying to relax, trying to lull his body into sleep. He turned his head and looked at the digital clock on the lamp table beside the bed. One-twelve. Valeria and Marcellus should have reached Sissy's by now.

He rolled onto his back and stared at the darkness above him. He drew a deep breath, held it as long as he could, then slowly released it.

Where had that lawyer Jason McAbrams disappeared to? Was he still alive? Or did he have a bullet hole in the head like Jesse Bondreaux and Jo Ann Scales and Gilly Bitzer.

The phone on the lamp table rang. He snatched up the receiver. "Yes?"

"We're here," Valeria said softly. "I'm exhausted. Sissy helped me get Marcellus from the car into the house. He was sleeping so hard. Bless his heart. I'm going right to bed. Did I wake you?"

"I love you," he said.

"Love you, too. 'Night." The line buzzed dead.

He fumbled the receiver back into the cradle. "Thank you, Lord," he mumbled, and closed his eyes. He reached out and patted the empty place on the other side of the bed. He didn't like this. Not at all.

BRAMLETT AROSE AT SIX. Sound sleep had eluded him all night long. Through his mind tumbling like a series of acrobats came every fact he could recall about this case. He pictured every woman he'd interviewed and tried to imagine her speeding away in a car with Marcellus.

He hobbled into the kitchen. His joints always took a little while to loosen up in the morning.

It was Wednesday. Five days since Jesse Bondreaux had been killed. And now two other victims—that he knew for sure. His shoulders ached.

He put on the coffee and wondered if Valeria and the others were awake yet. He wanted to phone but he hated to wake them. Could someone have put a tap on his phone? He tried to dismiss the idea. Maybe Sissy and Valeria had stayed up late last night talking, getting caught up. No doubt Valeria would have told her sister everything.

Maybe they were sleeping in. But surely she'd be up by six-thirty. He couldn't remember his wife ever sleeping beyond six-thirty in all the years of their marriage.

He poured a mug of coffee and eased himself down into his recliner in the den. He pressed the remote control of the TV and watched the weather channel.

The high for the day would be in the mid-seventies. Cloudy. Thirty percent chance for afternoon thunderstorms. And, he thought, a ninety percent chance somebody killed poor Gilly to cover his tracks. Or her tracks.

At exactly six-thirty he phoned.

"Are we up?" his sister-in-law said with a laugh. "What do you think this is? Buckingham Palace? I have a farm to run, Grover. Marcellus has already been out with me gathering eggs and to check on the cows. Are we up indeed!"

Sissy called Valeria to the phone. "What are you doing for breakfast?" Valeria said before even saying hello.

He told her he'd get something at the Eagle Café. "I don't want you phoning anybody," he said.

"Who would I phone except you?"

199

"I don't know. Maybe you wanted to let somebody in your garden club know you'd be missing a meeting or something."

"Grover, you know I hardly ever go to garden club anymore."

"I'll be out of town today," he said. "I'll call you when I get back."

"Where're you going?"

"Iskitini."

"Where in the world is that?"

"Down in south Mississippi. That's Bondreaux's hometown. I want to dig around a little."

"Be careful," she said.

AN HOUR LATER, having filled his stomach with Floyd Clements's sausage, grits, and grease-soaked eggs, Bramlett arrived at headquarters. Curry pulled into the parking lot just as Bramlett got out of his car. Baillie and Robertson were already at their desks.

Bramlett gathered all three deputies into his office. Curry played the telephone tape of Bondreaux talking with Tidwell Dixon. When the tape was done, Bramlett said, "And who is this woman?"

"Gilbert Armstrong mentioned her as an old girlfriend of Bondreaux. And she sure sounds like she has reason to kill him."

"Is there any way to get all that scratchy noise off the tape so we can hear it better?" Bramlett said.

"The lab at Jackson can handle it," Baillie said.

"How you coming on Bondreaux's former wife?"

"Her name is Tia Riggs," Baillie said. "I'm requesting ID checks from the DMVs in New York and Georgia this morning."

"What are you working on?" Bramlett said to Robertson.

The lanky deputy glowered and mumbled something the sheriff couldn't make out. Bramlett blinked a couple of times, looking at Robertson, trying to replay in his mind just what he had said. But nothing clicked. "Say again?" Bramlett said.

"Nena Carmack is missing."

"What? We talked with her just yesterday." Bramlett reached to his back pocket. "Who's taking care of this?"

"I am," Jacob Robertson said. His tone sounded almost like a challenge should anyone else dare to encroach on his turf.

200

Bramlett nodded and wondered how personally involved the deputy was getting with this Carmack woman.

There was a knock. Deputy Drumwright stood in the doorway of the office. He looked at Curry. "We've just picked up Noel Hackott. Where you want him?"

"Conference room," Curry said.

Bramlett looked questioningly at the deputy.

"I'll explain on the way," Curry said, smiling and rising from his chair. "I guess he didn't go to California after all."

"SIT DOWN, NOEL," Bramlett said firmly as he pulled back a chair at the conference table for himself. Curry and Baillie sat down on either side of the sheriff.

Bramlett had told Robertson to get busy on finding Nena Carmack. He knew that's where the young man's mind was. At the same time, he knew whatever Noel Hackott had to say would be about video tapes, and he wanted to spare Robertson any unpleasantness.

Noel Hackott stood on the other side of the table, chewing rapidly on a piece of gum. His face was flushed, and his eyes looked red and watery, as if he'd been drinking. "What's the meaning of this?" He glared at Bramlett.

"Sit, Noel," Bramlett repeated. "Sit down. We want to ask you some questions."

"I need to call my lawyer."

Bramlett cocked his head. "I hope that wouldn't be Jason McAdams."

Hackott gave a start. "What? What do you mean?"

Bramlett shrugged. "Mr. McAbrams is missing."

"Missing . . . ?" Hackott said. His word was hardly audible.

Bramlett, extending his palm, indicated the chair on the opposite side of the table. "Sit, dammit."

Hackott sank into the chair, confusion pulling at his face.

"Now," Bramlett said. "Would you care to tell us about your relationship with Jesse Bondreaux?"

Hackott nervously wiped at his upper lip. "What do you mean?"

Bramlett sighed. He had no patience for this man. "We have a video tape in our possession which was secretly made by your friend Jesse Bondreaux. The woman with you on the tape seems to be quite young."

Hackott gasped. "He said he destroyed . . ." He didn't finish. His head began to tremble.

"Was he blackmailing you?"

Hackott panted several breaths and nodded. "Y-yes . . ."

"Do you have any idea who else he was blackmailing?"

The man was breathing rapidly now. "I . . . I don't know . . ." he said. His eyes were glassy. He put his hand to his chest.

Bramlett pushed himself to his feet. "Lock him up," he said to Baillie. "Suspicion of statutory rape, for now. Maybe murder or conspiracy to commit murder later." His eyes were still on Hackott. The man began gagging.

KATHERINE TOPP SCOWLED when she opened the front door and saw Bramlett and Curry. "Grover, this is getting ridiculous."

"That's exactly how I feel, Katherine," he said, taking off his hat. "May we come inside?"

"I am right in the middle of something. Couldn't we do this later? Who is it about now—me or Gail?"

"Please, Katherine," he said softly.

She heard the pain in his voice, and the expression of irritation on her face gave way to one of worry.

She led them once more to the den and to the couches in front of the fireplace. Bramlett and Curry sat down on one of the couches as soon as Katherine seated herself in the chair.

Bramlett swallowed hard, then said, "Katherine, we found some video tapes Jesse Bondreaux made."

She looked like she'd been slapped in the face. Her eyes popped open wide and the color drained out of her face. Her lips parted as if she were going to speak, but no words came out.

Bramlett waited, but she said not a word. Finally, he said, "Was he blackmailing you?"

She shut her eyes tight and turned her face away. She then put one hand to her forehead and said hoarsely, "Yes . . ."

"How much had you given him?"

202

She shook her head. "Fifteen . . . maybe twenty thousand . . . I lost track . . ." She bit her lower lip, then said, "He threatened to give the tape to Robert." She opened her eyes and looked at Bramlett. "You can't imagine the hell I've been through. It was all just supposed to be one of those quick, fun things. Nobody gets hurt. Then . . . then this crap." Her voice became bitter and her eyes narrowed. "I'm glad he's dead, Grover. I swear to God I am. But I didn't kill him. No way."

He nodded. "Tell me, Katherine, what kind of cars do y'all drive?"

"Cars? I drive that blue Cadillac outside. Robert drives a Bronco."

"What about Gail?"

"A Mazda. A blue Mazda. What is this all about?"

"We need to know where you were last Friday afternoon."

"Here . . . Right here." Her cheeks were taut.

"Can someone verify that?"

"Verify? I was alone. Dammit, Grover. You can't seriously—"

"What about Saturday morning?"

"Saturday? Here. Gail and I were here at home."

Bramlett gave a wry smile. "Was she still asleep?"

"What?"

"Listen, Katherine. You need to tell us whatever you can about this. Do you know anyone else he was blackmailing?"

She shook her head and put her hands to her mouth. "Damn. I think I'm going to throw up," she said. Then she sprang to her feet and ran from the room.

WHEN THEY PULLED into the parking lot at headquarters, Bramlett said to Curry, "Tell Johnny Baillie I want him hard on finding McAbrams. Somebody must have seen a silver Jaguar."

Curry parked the patrol car and looked at the sheriff with a raised eyebrow. "You not coming in?"

"No. I'll be back late tonight."

"Where you going?"

"Bondreaux's hometown. Iskitini."

WITHIN THE HOUR Bramlett had driven to Tupelo and was on the Natchez Trace Parkway heading south toward Jackson. He set his cruise control on sixty and shoved a Clint Black cassette tape into the tape deck. It would take at least four and maybe four and a half hours to get to Gallman County and the town of Iskitini.

The only living soul he knew there—except for the county sheriff—was Jesse Bondreaux's cousin, Gilbert Armstrong. Bramlett knew he could have asked the same questions he planned to ask over the telephone. But he didn't like to conduct telephone interviews. On the telephone you couldn't look into a person's eyes or watch for those subtle twitches in the facial muscles and the slight reddening of the neck that told you someone was lying. Eyeball to eyeball was the only way.

Sometimes it was hardest to see stuff right under your nose. Could Katherine Topp be involved in killing this guy? Or Gail? And what about this Tidwell woman on the audio tape? Obviously Bondreaux was blackmailing her, too. But Curry wasn't sure she was on the videos he'd looked at. Most of those women had been ID'd, but there were several he didn't recognize.

This Tidwell woman was no doubt the high school sweetheart Gilbert Armstrong had told them about. But, after all these years, how did she fit in? He would have to look at those videos himself when he got back. He should have done it already.

Mile after mile, Bramlett resurrected from memory the people he'd talked with over the last couple of days: Gail and Katherine Topp, Rumi, Howard, and Vicki Ann Skelton, the Tupelo secretary, Nicole Estis, and her beer-drinking husband, Farley, the girl Cora Hartley who had slept with Bondreaux and her death-threatening father Marshall, and Gilly Bitzer, who didn't tell the whole truth and now wouldn't have the chance to tell anything else. And this creep Noel Hackott and that woman Jacob was now hounddogging, Nena Carmack. Was she involved in this more than she's saying? Was she, in fact, this "Tidwell" woman? Was that why she'd suddenly disappeared?

The voice on the tape sounded vaguely familiar to him. *Where* had he heard that voice before? And what about those weird students who hung around Bondreaux's place—Lucian DeBow and Billy Mosley? Mosley did have a blue Honda.

Bramlett made good time to Jackson, then headed south on I-55 down past Crystal Springs and began looking for a place to eat. He began to feel hungry by the time he got to Jackson, but the heavy traffic with cars whipping along the interstate in excess of sixty-five or seventy on both sides made him nervous, and he refrained from pulling off the highway until he was at Brookhaven. There he stopped at a MacDonald's and had two Big Macs, a large order of fries, and a chocolate shake.

He ate fast, more because of hunger than hurrying, then walked out to his car. As he reached for the door handle, he noticed the pay phone at the edge of the parking lot.

It had been over four hours since he'd left Sheffield. What if Valeria had been trying to reach him?

He quickly walked to the phone and placed a call to headquarters. The secretary put him through to Curry.

"Where are you?" Curry asked. Then, without giving Bramlett a chance to respond, he hurried on. "We just got a call from Tishomingo County. They found that silver Jaguar at a private cabin up on Lake Pickwick. Your lawyer buddy was inside the cabin. Shot in the head just like the others."

Bramlett caught his breath and didn't speak.

After a moment, Curry said, "Sheriff? You still there?"

"Yeah," Bramlett said softly.

"You coming back now or what?"

"I'll be back this evening sometime. Tell Baillie to go on up there and find out what he can. Who's handling it?"

"It was a highway patrol investigator who called."

"Okay." Bramlett cleared his throat. "Any calls for me?"

"Sir?"

"Did my wife phone?"

"No, sir."

Bramlett hung up the receiver and turned back to his car.

HE DROVE BACK onto the interstate. Who in the hell was McAbrams entertaining? Could he possibly have known the killer more than professionally?

The French fries felt like they were sloshing around in his stomach. Valeria kept warning him to eat more slowly and chew up each bite. He bolted like a dog, she said.

He continued on I-55 until he reached the Iskitini turnoff. The state highway could hardly be called paved. Large sections of asphalt had simply disappeared. And the right-of-way hadn't been cut back last summer. Kudzu smothered hardwood thickets along the road, and Johnson grass was almost three feet high at the shoulder of the pavement.

In less than half an hour he passed a roadside marker that read "Iskitini, pop. 738." He stopped at a Texaco service station and thought he'd better phone Lawrence Kidd, the sheriff of Gallman County, and let him know he was there.

Kidd came on the line. His tone was strained. "What are you working on?" he asked. Bramlett suddenly remembered some things he'd heard about Kidd. Something involving drugs. There'd been an investigation, and Kidd was cleared, but two of his deputies were indicted.

"A murder, Lawrence," Bramlett said. "Three murders in fact. One of the victims was from Iskitini, and I just wanted to ask some of the relatives a few questions."

"Hell, Grover, you sure drove a long way just to ask a few questions." There was still suspicion in Kidd's tone but not as much as before. "How long you gonna be here?"

"I'll be going back tonight."

"Stop by if you can and let's have a cup of coffee. Simpson is not fifteen minutes away."

Bramlett told him he would. Simpson was the county seat and the location of Kidd's headquarters. Bramlett hung up the phone and knew he wouldn't be stopping by to see Sheriff Kidd that evening, or any evening, for that matter.

"It's about a cousin of his," Bramlett told the curious service station attendant in black grease-stained coveralls after he asked the man if he knew where Gilbert Armstrong lived.

"Where's Chakchiuma County?" the man asked, staring at the side of Bramlett's patrol car.

"Up past Tupelo. Did you ever know a man named Jesse Bondreaux?"

The man's eyes squinted. "Jesse Bondreaux? Hell. I don't reckon

206

I've heard that name in twenty years or better." He shook his head. "I knew him in high school. Is he in trouble?"

Bramlett didn't answer directly and waited patiently for the man to tell him how to reach Armstrong's house.

Moments later, Bramlett traveled past the five ramshackle stores that made up downtown Iskitini and continued on the two miles or so farther along the state highway until he rounded a curve and saw the crumbling brick silo the service station man had mentioned.

A narrow, deep-rutted red dirt road left the highway just beyond the silo on the left. Bramlett was glad it hadn't rained for the last few days in this part of the country.

The patrol car bounced along the ruts for an eighth of a mile or so until the road ended at a wide clearing in the pines. At the edge of the forest squatted a paintless frame house with a wringer-style washing machine on the front porch.

Gilbert Armstrong was all smiles when he saw Bramlett. "You caught him?" he said, extending his large hand to the sheriff's even larger hand.

"Not yet."

"I just got in," Armstrong said. "Been out scouting all morning. You hunt deer?"

"Not much," Bramlett replied. "Can we step inside to talk?"

He followed Armstrong into the house and the cluttered front room. A pile of dirty clothes lay in the middle of the floor. "The washing machine don't work," Armstrong said, catching Bramlett's eyes on the clothes. "I just gather them all up once a week and take 'em over to Mama's to be washed."

"I'd like to learn more about Jesse," Bramlett said, leaning back in the tattered upholstered chair, hoping nothing would break.

Armstrong shrugged his shoulders. "Like I told y'all up there at Sheffield, I ain't seen him in years. Neither has Mama. We never knew whether he was alive or dead 'fore I got y'all's call and then had to go up there to arrange that funeral. Say, that was a *big* funeral, wasn't it?"

"It was nice. Now, tell me about Jesse before he left Iskitini."

Armstrong shrugged again. "Ain't much to tell. He lived with his mama. His mama was my mama's sister. Didn't I tell you that? Anyways, his daddy cut pulpwood, same as my daddy, I was told.

Then he ran off. Jesse and I was like brothers growing up. Then he went to Mississippi State. Hardly ever come home after that."

Bramlett tried to look pleasant. "Let's just think about *before* he went off."

"Well . . . let's see. He was an athlete, you know."

"No, I didn't know."

"Sure was," Armstrong said. Family pride was evident in the way he said it. "I used to go to all the games. 'Course I was younger'n him in school. He lettered in three sports—football, basketball, and baseball. I thought he might play in college, but I guess he was too small. He did come home a lot his freshman year. That was because his girlfriend was still in high school. She was a year ahead of me. Then she graduated and went off. He never come home much after that."

"You told us about her. Tidwell Dixon."

"Yep. Pretty little thing. Blonde, good figure. She was a cheerleader in high school. Everybody thought she and Jesse would get married, you know. Then she went off to school. Vanderbilt. She was real smart, you see. Nobody else from around here ever went to Vanderbilt. Claud Smith did go to Tulane. Now that's supposed to be a tough school, too."

"Do any of Tidwell Dixon's relations still live around here?"

Armstrong shook his head. "Not that I know of. That sure was some gal. Hell, I ain't thought about her in years. Man, could she ride a horse. And *shoot*. What you talking about. That girl was a better shot with a pistol than most men I know."

Bramlett started. "Pistol, you say?" His mouth was suddenly becoming very dry.

"Yeah. Her daddy didn't like her driving around at night like she had to sometimes, you know. Like coming home from a 4-H meeting or something. Anyways, he bought her a pistol. Pretty little thing. It was one of those pocket Colts. You know, twenty-five caliber with a six-shot magazine. I saw her once put all six shots in a bull's-eye at twenty-five yards. Can you shoot like that sheriff?"

Bramlett ignored the question. "Where are her parents?"

Armstrong scratched the bottom of his chin. "They moved away not long after she left for college. I don't have any idea where they went."

"Would anybody around here have kept up with them?"

He shook his head and rubbed his chin again. "You want a beer, Sheriff? I was just fixing to get one when you pulled up."

"Go ahead. Now tell me. Think now. This is important. Can you remember anyone at all who was a friend of this Tidwell girl in high school who still lives around here?"

Armstrong pushed against his knees and stood up. He walked through a doorway into the kitchen. Bramlett heard the refrigerator door open, then close, and the pop of the beer can being opened. Armstrong returned, sat down in the chair again, took a long, deliberate swallow, then rested the bottom of the can on his right knee. "Let's see." He was staring into space, thinking.

"Were there any other boyfriends?" Bramlett asked quickly.

Armstrong started to lift the can to his mouth and his hand froze. "Say! Myrtle Nell! Of course! Myrtle Nell Burns."

"That's a *boy*friend?"

Armstrong laughed. "Naw. Myrtle Nell and Tidwell was pretty close at one time. Reason I 'membered just now was what you said about old boyfriends. You see, Myrtle Nell and Jesse was going together—maybe when they was tenth or eleventh graders. Then Jesse dropped her and started dating Tidwell. It was a big thing back then. The fight and all." He guzzled another swallow and then laughed, almost choking at the same time.

"Fight?" Bramlett said.

"Right there in the schoolyard. Myrtle Nell and Tidwell. I don't reckon any of us had ever seen girls fight before."

"It was over Jesse?"

"Yeah. I guess that's what everybody figured. It was cold, man. I mean, Tidwell was supposed to be Myrtle Nell's best friend and her stealing her boyfriend and all."

"And this Myrtle Nell Burns still lives here?" Bramlett wrote the name in his notepad.

"Yeah. She and her husband got a nice house near my mother. You had to pass it when you was driving out here."

GILBERT ARMSTRONG'S DIRECTIONS were accurate and easy to follow. Bramlett found the house with no trouble. He pulled off the county road and onto a long graveled driveway leading up to a ranch-style red-brick house with green shutters. He parked and walked to the front door. An old black iron wash pot, overflowing with pansies, perched on the edge of the porch slab.

A thin boy in cut-off jeans and a black T-shirt answered the door. He said his mother should be home from work any minute now and invited Bramlett inside to wait. The sheriff guessed the boy to be about thirteen or fourteen.

Bramlett had barely sunk himself into one of the easy chairs when he heard a car pulling into the driveway. The woman came in through the side door, stepped quickly into the living room. Bramlett was now standing, hat in hand.

"Mrs. Burns?" he said.

"What's wrong?" she said, her eyes wide and anxious.

"Nothing, ma'am. I'm Sheriff Bramlett from up in Chakchiuma County and I wondered if I could ask you a few questions." Bramlett noticed the boy was standing in the kitchen doorway.

The woman's eyes reflected confusion. Her head gave a jerk and she said, "Questions? What kind of questions?"

"Maybe we could sit down," Bramlett said, waving his hand toward the couch.

She didn't move. The confusion in her eyes gave way at once to suspicion. Bramlett guessed her to be in her mid-thirties, based on the age of Bondreaux. Yet she looked ten, maybe even fifteen, years older. She was a heavyset woman with a fleshy face and frizzled, fraying hair.

She moved slowly to the couch and sat. "You sure you got the right house?" she said.

"You *are* Myrtle Nell Burns, aren't you?" Bramlett said, easing himself back down into the chair.

"Ain't nobody called me that in years. Burns was my maiden name. My name's Harris now."

"I see," Bramlett glanced uneasily at the boy.

The woman caught his look and said over her shoulder, "Scott, go outside."

The boy didn't move.

She turned her head slightly, her eyes still on Bramlett. "Do I have to repeat myself? I said, go outside."

210

The boy then turned and retreated into the kitchen. Bramlett heard the side door open and slam shut.

"Teenagers," she said out of the corner of her mouth. "Now. What is it?"

"Mrs. Harris, I'm investigating the murder of one Jesse Bondreaux."

She blinked several times and her lips parted slightly. She said, "*Murder?*"

"Yes, ma'am. He was shot last Friday night up in Sheffield."

"Shot?" Her eyes widened all the more.

"I understand you knew him."

"Lord, I can't believe it. Jesse?"

"Yes, ma'am. And you were a friend of his I'm told."

She made a low clucking sound of sadness, then said, "That was *ages* ago. We were all still in *high* school."

"When was the last time you saw Bondreaux?"

She closed her eyes for a moment, then opened them and said, "Shot! I can't believe it. Where did this happen?"

"Sheffield," he said again. "That's up north of Tupelo."

She shook her head again. "Never heard of it. What was he doing up there?"

"He was a schoolteacher, ma'am. Now if you could—"

"*School*teacher! God Almighty. Who would have ever thought Jesse would make a schoolteacher?"

"When was the last time you saw him?" Bramlett asked once more.

She looked away toward the kitchen door. When she spoke her voice was much softer. "Not since high school, I guess."

"I understand you and he dated then."

"Murdered!" She turned her head toward Bramlett and looked hard into his eyes. "Why?"

Bramlett set his hat on the floor beside his chair and slipped his notebook out of his pocket. "That's what we're trying to find out. I came down here to learn all I could about him."

She nodded slowly and looked absently toward the floor. "Yes. We dated some. In fact, we were pretty serious, I guess. At least I thought so . . ." Her voice trailed off.

"Then, I understand, he and Tidwell Dixon started going together."

Her eyes, still staring down at the floor slowly narrowed. "Yeah. Tidwell Dixon." She said the name with a certain bitterness, almost as if the pronouncing of it tasted bad.

"When was the last time you saw her?"

She was silent for a while, then, "Years ago."

"Do you happen to have a photograph of her? Maybe in your high school annual?"

She made a wry face. "That was right at integration time. The school stopped doing yearbooks for a few years just like they quit lots of stuff. Things never got back to normal, I guess. No. Even if I'd had a picture of her, I would have torn it up years ago." She shook her head slowly.

"You said it's been years since you saw her. Do you remember how many years?"

"It was that Christmas after we graduated. She was at the post office. Coming out. I was going in. We didn't even speak." She gave a soft laugh. "Funny, ain't it? Here we had been best friends at one time and then that last time we saw each other we didn't even speak. And we never saw each other again." She shook her head. "We did everything together before the deal with Jesse. We roomed together at Girls' State down at Clinton. That was where Tidwell met Ruth Pettis. They decided to room together at Vanderbilt after high school." She sighed. "And we never even saw each again after that day at the post office."

"She was home from school then?" he asked, still thinking about the post office encounter, but at the same jotting down the name Ruth Pettis.

Mrs. Harris nodded. "For the Christmas holidays. Jesse was home, too. I talked with him. On the phone. I reckon I still thought I loved him." She gave another low laugh and shook her head. "I guess he thought he was really in love with Tidwell. He told me they were going to be married."

Bramlett raised an eyebrow. "Married?"

She drew a long breath and slowly released it. "I heard later that Tidwell was pregnant. Susan Murphy told me. She and Tidwell kept

212

up for a while, I guess. Later Susan told me Tidwell had got an abortion."

"Where is Susan Murphy now?"

"She's dead. Died in a car wreck." She shook her head sadly and suddenly looked very, very tired.

"I appreciate your time, Mrs. Harris," he said, reaching down beside his chair for his hat.

30

DUSK HAD FALLEN when Sheriff Grover Bramlett left the Harris house. He drove slowly along Iskitini's main street once again. All the stores were closed, including the service station.

An elderly woman wearing a shawl wrapped snugly about her head shuffled along the sidewalk in front of the post office. She paused and stared hard at him as he drove past. It was full dark by the time he reached I-55.

In a few miles he saw the Simpson exit and remembered Sheriff Kidd's request that he stop by for coffee, but Bramlett had no desire either for a coffee or for Kidd's company. He drove on north, toying with the idea of pulling off at Brookhaven and spending the night.

The trip back to Sheffield would take more than four hours. That would mean he'd be driving way past his bedtime. He didn't see as well as he used to at night, according to Valeria. She now insisted on driving home from church on Sunday and Wednesday nights. He still wasn't comfortable riding shotgun while his wife drove. Something almost unmanly about it.

He took the second Brookhaven exit and parked beside a pay telephone at an Exxon service station. Using his AT&T charge card, he placed a call to Valeria's sister Sissy. The phone rang and rang. He counted. Six rings. Surely they wouldn't have gone anyplace. Ten rings. He replaced the receiver and gnawed at the side of his lower lip.

214

A dark vision sneaked out of the back of his mind somewhere. An intruder was rushing in upon two helpless women and the boy. He shook his head, trying to shake the images loose from the sides of his brain. *Stop it, Grover! Don't think stupid thoughts. She's all right. They're all right. Of course they are.*

Maybe he'd misdialed. He lifted the receiver and tried the number again, being extra sure he dialed correctly. Still no answer. He hung up the receiver, and stepped to the side of his car.

He looked at the various fast food establishments across the road. Burger King, New Orleans Fried Chicken, Captain D's.

He should be hungry but the rumbling in his stomach was more a nausea feeling than a longing for food. He got back into the patrol car and drove onto the interstate heading north.

Pay attention, he instructed himself as he neared Jackson and the heavy traffic. Hundreds of cars whipped along in both directions. Where were all these people going? He didn't like having to pull off the interstate. He'd heard taking off and landing were the most dangerous aspects of flying. It occurred to him that getting off and on a busy interstate was perhaps the most dangerous part of driving on one.

When he was past the main part of Jackson and still heading north, he exited again, parked at a Jitney Jr., and tried Sissy's number once more. Still no answer.

Maybe instead of going back up the Trace northeastward toward Sheffield he should continue on I-55 and turn off on Highway 6 and head for the Delta. He could spend the night at Sissy's, visit a while with Valeria and Marcellus and then return to Sheffield in the morning.

He dialed headquarters. Something new might have turned up, maybe that Carmack woman had been found.

Baillie and Robertson were out. He spoke to Curry.

"Did Johnny find out anything about Bondreaux's former wife?" Bramlett said.

"Yessir. She is living in Atlanta. He got her address and home phone number. He tried to reach her but got no answer. That was some time ago."

"Give me the number." Bramlett held the receiver between his shoulder and cheek while he reached into his shirt pocket for his notepad. He wrote down the address and phone number, then asked, "What's Jacob doing?"

"I think he's mostly trying to locate Nena Carmack."

"I see."

"She's on one of the videos," Curry said matter-of-factly.

Bramlett didn't respond at once. Then he said softly, "Does he know?"

"No sir. Where are you?"

"Jackson. I may not be back till tomorrow morning."

"By the way. Someone's been trying to reach Mrs. Bramlett. Is she out of town or something?"

Bramlett grimaced. "Yeah," he said. He cleared his throat. "Who is it?"

"I don't know. She didn't leave her name."

"Woman?"

"Yessir."

Bramlett didn't respond. He could feel his heart speeding up. He drew two quick breaths, then said, "One more thing. See what you can find out about a Ruth Pettis. She was this Tidwell Dixon's roommate at Vanderbilt. That's her maiden name. Alumni Relations at the college probably knows her whereabouts. You can check when they open in the morning. She was from Starkville maybe. Or Columbus."

As soon as the call to Curry disconnected, Bramlett tried his sister-in-law again. Still no answer.

He looked at the name and number of Bondreaux's former wife, then placed the call. The phone was answered on the first ring. A woman's voice.

"May I speak to Tia Riggs, please?" Bramlett said.

"Whom shall I say is calling?"

"This is Sheriff Bramlett of Chakchiuma County, Mississippi."

There was a long silence, then the same voice said, "This is Tia Riggs."

"Miss Riggs, I understand you were at one time married to a man named Jesse Bondreaux."

There was a long silence, then, "Correct." Her tone was chillish.

"I wonder if I could ask you some questions about him?"

"I haven't seen him since the divorce."

216

"How long ago was that?"

She sighed with impatience. "Seven years."

"How long were you married?"

"Four terrible years. What's he done?"

"He's dead. Murdered."

She gasped. "*Murdered*? Why? How?"

"He was shot," Bramlett said. "We're trying to find out as much about his background as we can. As a matter of fact, I understand he was planning to move there to Atlanta."

"*What*?" The surprise in her voice was obvious.

"We were given to believe he wanted to move there and be closer to his daughter."

"Daughter? What daughter?"

Bramlett frowned. "It was my understanding y'all's child was living with you."

She gave a cynical laugh. "I don't know where you're getting your information, but Jesse Bondreaux and I never had any children. At least that's one blessing."

Bramlett reached his finger to his forehead. He could feel a bad headache coming on. "I see. Did he *have* a child as far as you know?"

"How should I know? Being the philanderer he was, he could have ten children."

"But you don't know of any for sure?"

"No. Well . . ." She paused. "Once he did say something about maybe he had a child out there in the world someplace. That was something he said one night when he was drunk. Of course, he could lie as good drunk as sober. Anyway, he said there was a girl he'd dated a long time ago. She got pregnant and had an abortion, he said. He said he wondered at times if maybe she really didn't have the abortion, that maybe she just told him that."

"Did he ever say what this girl's name was?"

"No."

"Did he ever mention anyone by the name of Tidwell Dixon?"

"Tidwell? No, I don't think I ever heard that name. Who's he?"

"She," Bramlett said. "Did he say anything else about this girl . . . like maybe where she lived?"

"No. In fact, after he sobered up that time, he laughed it off and

217

said I must have read about something like that somewhere, that nothing like that ever happened to him. But, like I said, he was a liar."

"I understand you are originally from New York City."

"New York State," she corrected. "Saratoga. We met when he came to New York to do his master's."

"Was he ever involved with drugs?"

"Drugs? Well, I guess he smoked a little pot. Nothing heavy."

"Would you know of anyone from the time that y'all were married who might have carried a grudge against him? Anything like that?"

"Not that I can remember. If he treated many other people like he treated me, you've got lots of folks out there who could kill him with about as much guilt as you'd have for killing a roach."

Bramlett thanked her and replaced the receiver. For the first time, he noticed a man in a dark suit standing impatiently a few feet from the phone booth. The man was jingling coins in his hand, looking toward Bramlett.

Bramlett lifted the receiver again, saw the increased agitation on the man's face, punched Sissy's number once again, then, when instructed, the number of his credit card. Once again he listened to a long series of rings. No answer. He sighed and hung up and walked toward his car. The man in the suit hurried past him into the phone booth.

Bramlett steered back onto I-55 going north. Where in the world could they be? He'd thought he made it clear that they were to remain at the house. Why didn't anyone ever listen to him?

The National Park Service's brown sign with white letters on the side of the highway announced the Natchez Trace Parkway turnoff was one-half mile away. Sheffield and his own bed lay only four hours to the northeast on the Trace.

He sped past the turnoff. He'd rather go on to the northwest and the Delta and find out nothing was wrong than drive all the way home and find out something had happened.

JACOB ROBERTSON STOOD in Nena's front yard, staring at the dark house and wondering where in the world she was. The woman who lived next door, curious about the patrol car, walked over.

"She went flying out of here late this afternoon," she said. "I

218

was planting bulbs over there . . ." She paused and motioned with her hand at a flower bed that divided the two front yards. "Then she was rushing to her car. I asked if something was wrong. She looked very upset, you see. She said she had to go home. Then she was gone."

"Home?" Robertson said. "Where's that?"

The woman smiled apologetically. "I don't know. What could be the matter?"

Robertson hurried away without answering.

LYNWOOD WILSON, principal of Sheffield High School, hadn't been happy to be told to meet Jacob Robertson at the front door of the administrative building as soon as possible. "I need to see Nena Carmack's personnel file," Robertson said over the phone. "All I want to know is her hometown. You can look it up in the file yourself."

When Wilson protested that the personnel files contained confidential information, Robertson told him he'd get a judge to issue a search warrant and take several other officers to the school and go through *all* the files, including the principal's, if Wilson wasn't at the school door in ten minutes.

Robertson was standing on the front steps of the darkened building when Wilson parked at the curb directly behind the patrol car. It had been eleven minutes, but the deputy didn't bother to complain.

"This is very irregular," the principal said as he led the deputy through the hallway, flipping on light switches along the way.

In the office of the principal's secretary, Wilson pulled open a file drawer, walked his fingers over the top of the tightly packed file folders, then pulled hard to free one. He opened it on the secretary's desk and began looking over the first page. In a moment he read: "Next of kin: Mr. and Mrs. Gerald O. Carmack, 1345 Gaston Street, Columbus, Mississippi."

Robertson jotted down the information in his notebook as the man spoke. He could be there in just over an hour. "Thank you," he said, and turned and hurried out of the building.

He radioed headquarters after he'd turned onto Highway 45

South, tires squealing that he was going to Columbus to follow up on Nena Carmack. "Tell H. C.," he instructed the dispatcher.

Once past Tupelo and Shannon, he opened up, holding the patrol car on eighty, flicking on his warning lights when overtaking other vehicles, and slowing only when slashing through the little no-traffic-light-even towns between Shannon and Aberdeen.

In Columbus he found Gaston Street. It was near the old First Baptist Church. The address Wilson had given him marked a two-story columned antebellum house partially hidden behind massive oaks.

A white-uniformed black woman answered the doorbell. "I'm sorry," she said. "They're all at the hospital."

"Hospital?"

"Yessir. With Mr. Gerald." She paused, noticing the perplexed look on his face. Nena's father. He's had a heart attack."

31

AT THE INFORMATION DESK an older woman with a "Volunteer" patch stitched to her pink tunic told Jacob Robertson that Gerald Carmack was in the medical intensive care Unit. She smiled pleasantly and directed him to the waiting room on the second floor.

A moment later, after he'd bounded up the steps two and three at a time, he stepped into the large room. Couches and armchairs were tightly placed in groupings all over the room. Knots of people were huddled in each grouping.

He walked slowly across the room, looking closely as he passed each family. Then, on the far side of the room right beside a table on which were doughnuts and coffee, he saw Nena sitting on a couch between a woman who looked very much like her and a man about Jacob's own age.

Nena looked up as he walked forward, and her eyes batted in a moment of confusion, the confusion, he knew, of seeing someone out of place. Then she stood immediately. "Jacob! What on earth . . ."

"I . . . I heard . . ."

She introduced him to the older woman, her mother, and the man, her brother Tommy. Tommy was a thin, hard-looking man wearing a plaid woolen shirt and black denim jeans. Mrs. Carmack didn't look old enough to be Nena's mother. All three appeared haggard, drained.

Nena said to Jacob, "Come. Let's get some fresh air."

She led him out of the waiting room into the corridor. "Daddy had a heart attack yesterday. It's bad." She shook her head, closed her eyes, and then wrapped her arms around herself. To Robertson she seemed like a frightened little girl.

"I . . . didn't know . . ." He wanted to take her in his arms but couldn't, was too afraid of how she might react.

"I didn't have time to tell anyone," she said. "I'm sorry." She opened her eyes and looked at him. "You drove all the way down here to see me?" She smiled at him.

"I didn't know where you were."

She shook her head slowly again and looked toward the waiting room for a long moment, then back into his eyes. She smiled. "I really can't believe you came all the way down here to see me."

Robertson's mouth was dry. "Well . . . no one knew where you were . . . and with things being like they are . . ." He didn't finish.

She frowned and cocked her head as if momentarily not following him. Then her eyes widened and she said, "You mean this case y'all are working on?"

He shrugged. "Two schoolteachers. You never know."

"You mean you thought *I* might be a . . . a victim?"

He nodded and shoved his hands into his pockets. "You ever hear of some woman named Tidwell?"

She made a face. "Strange name," she said. "No, I never heard that name."

"It was somebody Jesse Bondreaux knew. Knew right well, in fact." He watched her face as he said the name, watching for whatever reaction she might give.

She drew a quick breath, released it, and looked away. Her forehead knit with aggravation. "What's so important to ask me that you had to drive all the way down here?"

"That's not why I came," he said quickly.

"Sure." She made no effort to hide the sarcasm in her tone.

Jacob felt his breathing becoming more rapid. "Listen to me, Nena," he said hurriedly. "I came because I'm afraid for you. People who have been associated with Bondreaux in one way or another have been killed.

"So?"

He dropped his eyes. This was very awkward for him but he stammered on. "You were . . . at one time . . . a close friend of his."

"That's ancient history."

Jacob's palms were very clammy. A constriction was rising in his chest. "You were identified as the person leaving his house Friday afternoon."

Her eyes were now cold and hard. "Is that what all this is about?"

"No. I told you." He felt he was chasing her away and he wanted to put his arms around her so she couldn't leave. "Nena, please listen to me. The man was killed only an hour or so after someone hurried away from the house. You have been positively ID'd as that someone." He paused, cleared his throat, then continued. "And someone came back later and tore his house apart looking for something. I think I know what they were looking for."

She slowly turned to face him. "Is that so?"

"A video tape," he said. Her eyes, it seemed to him, became even colder. He continued. "In fact, we have all of his tapes."

"Oh?" She glared at him. "And I suppose every damn person in the sheriff's department has looked at them."

He shook his head. He felt like a knife was in his guts, twisting. "Just one person. Not me. Those on the tapes had to be identified. I didn't look at any of them." He hoped against hope that she would deny being on any of the tapes, and that she wouldn't be, that H. C. would tell him when he got back to Sheffield that Nena Carmack was not on a single one of them.

"And who was this one person?"

"H. C."

"Oh great. That's simply great."

"Someone had to. Maybe it was better for a friend . . ." He was hurting more now because she hadn't denied anything. He added, "He watched it all on fast forward." Robertson wasn't sure about this. It was, however, what he himself would have done.

She stared off into space. "Jesse was trying to blackmail me. I'd already given him all the money I had. He gave me a tape. Said it was the original. Then suddenly he had another copy and was threatening to send it to my father. I knew it could bring on another heart attack. I couldn't in any way raise the kind of money he was asking for." She paused and pressed her lips together for a moment, then said, "What is going to happen to the tape?"

"It's locked up in evidence. I don't know what will ultimately happen to it. We don't even know if we've got all the copies."

"Do you think I killed him?" Her voice was flat.

"No, no," he said quickly. "Of course not."

She clutched herself tighter as if chilled. She shuddered. Then she said, "I need to get away from here."

He followed her back into the waiting room. She told her mother she would be gone for a while. They took the elevator to the first floor and walked out through the lobby. "It's a beautiful evening," she said, looking up at the stars.

"My car's over there," he said, nodding toward a nearby no-parking zone.

She smiled and shook her head. "Let's take my car. It attracts a lot less attention."

He followed her across three rows of parked cars to Row D. She stopped at a small dark car and pushed the key into the door lock.

Robertson frowned. "Is this your car?"

She pulled the door open. "It's Daddy's, but he lets me use it a lot."

Robertson stood for a moment staring down at the shiny black Toyota. There was suddenly a bilish taste in his mouth, He opened the door and got in.

BRAMLETT MADE GOOD TIME on I-55 to Winona. He then took US Highway 82 and then sped west into the Delta. He'd considered stopping in Winona and trying to phone again but decided that would take too much time. In another half hour he'd be there.

He almost slid off the graveled county road leading to Sissy's farm, told himself to slow down, everything was all right, had to be, *please, dear God . . . you know I don't ask for much. Let everything be all right.*

As he roared into the yard in front of the farmhouse, he saw Valeria's Buick parked in front. The rear end of Sissy's 1960 Plymouth poked out of the slab-board, crumbling single-vehicle garage.

The porch light came on and the front door opened as Bramlett surged out of the car. His sister-in-law stepped onto the porch.

Sissy Green was short like Valeria, but considerably heavier and

224

wore her white hair cut short. She held a double-barrel shotgun in her hands. "Who's that?" she demanded.

"It's me, Sissy," said Bramlett, striding toward the house.

"Grover? That you? What's wrong?"

"Where y'all been?" he said as he stepped onto the porch. He didn't try to hide the irritation in his voice.

Valeria came to the doorway, looking at him, confusion in her eyes.

"What you doing racing up here like that?" Sissy said. "You could've run over my dog." She stood on the edge of the porch, looking into the darkness. "Sam! Yo, Sam! You there?" she yelled.

Valeria stepped into the house. Bramlett followed her. "Where y'all been? I kept trying to call . . ."

"Church, Grover," Valeria said, still staring at him. "You know this is Wednesday night."

Of course, he thought. *Prayer Meeting!* He should have known.

Sissy came back into the house and closed the door. "You didn't run over my dog, did you?"

"Of course not," Bramlett said. "Where's Marcellus?"

"He's in bed already."

Bramlett sighed and sank into an upholstered armchair. "I really wish y'all wouldn't be leaving the house."

Sissy's eyes got big as she sat down on the couch. "Not leave the house? You serious?"

He nodded. "Please. Just *do* as I say."

Valeria stepped to the side of his chair and put her arm around him. Now, who in the world is going to know we're here? I certainly haven't told anybody. Have you?" She was looking down at him.

"Of course not. But I'd feel a lot better if y'all would just stay *put*."

"Have you eaten?" Valeria asked.

He shook his head, suddenly feeling quite hungry.

Sissy rose from the couch and chuckled. "Chicken all right? We've got some left over from supper."

She left the room, still chuckling softly to herself. Valeria kissed him on top of the head. "It was sweet of you to worry, Grover," she said.

"I just don't see any reason for y'all—" The first ring of the telephone interrupted him.

"I'll get it, Sissy," Valeria called, moving toward the small doily-covered table across the room.

She lifted the receiver. "Hello?" She turned her head slightly, then said again, "Hello?" She waited a moment, then replaced the receiver. "I just hate it when folks do that. I mean, if they got a wrong number, at least they could say 'Excuse me' or something."

She gave Bramlett a wan smile and walked to the couch and sat down. Bramlett was still staring at the now silent telephone.

H. C. CURRY GOT LUCKY. The second Pettis family in Starkville he phoned said, yes, Ruth Pettis was their daughter, was something wrong?

No, Curry explained. The sheriff's department was trying to locate an old friend of hers named Tidwell Dixon.

"Tidwell Dixon?" Mrs. Pettis said. "Gracious, that was years ago. I doubt Ruth has seen her since college." She did give Curry her daughter's telephone number. "She's lived in Memphis ten years now," the mother continued. "And she is Mrs. Chester McNeal."

The deputy thanked her and assured her again nothing was wrong. Just routine, he said.

He wished there were some way he could reach the sheriff. He'd gone to Iskitini, he said. But from there to where?

When the sheriff had phoned, he said he'd be back by mid-morning tomorrow. It would have to wait till then.

He lifted the file folder from his desk and leaned back in the chair. He began reading again—as he had done at least ten times, he knew—the file notes. Jesse Bondreaux's resume, interviews with all the people who had been questioned, dossiers on Jo Ann Scales and Jason McAbrams. His eye lingered on the name Nicole Estis.

He remembered the dark-haired, buxom secretary he and the sheriff had talked with in Tupelo. She and Bondreaux were planning to run away someplace. Maybe.

Maybe Bondreaux shelved those plans after deciding he'd take the white queen instead. Possible. And Curry remembered the woman's estranged husband standing on the stoop of his trailer home with a beer can in his hand.

He looked at the brochure he'd picked up when they were leaving

226

the office where she worked. He hadn't bothered to read it before. Adamson's Insurance Company. Office Hours: 8:00 to 4:00.

He started to put the brochure back on the desk, then quickly pulled his hand back and read the office hours again. Four o'clock?

He sat in the chair upright and leaned over the desk to reread the interview with Nicole Estis. When asked where she was around five o'clock Friday afternoon, she had said, "Right here. We didn't leave till after five."

What if she left at closing time? Four o'clock? She would have had plenty of time to leave Tupelo and be in Sheffield by four-thirty. Maybe she would bear talking to again.

Her home number was listed at the top of the interview page. He dialed the number. Perhaps at least he could ask if she worked late that afternoon—past the four o'clock closing time.

The telephone was answered on the second ring. "Mrs. Estis?" he said.

"She's not here. Who is this?" a gruff female voice said.

"This is Deputy Curry, ma'am, with the Chakchiuma County Sheriff's Department. May I ask who you are?"

"This is Fran Engel. I own this apartment and my tenant has disappeared."

"Disappeared?"

"That's right. Is she wanted for something?"

"What do you mean *disappeared*?"

"I mean she owes me a month's rent and is a week behind in paying and has *left*. I came in just now to check out the apartment and all her clothes are gone. It's a furnished apartment."

"I see . . ."

"I want my money," the woman said. "If you find her, I want to know. Did you get my name? Fran Engel." She then gave Curry her telephone number.

Curry stood up. He needed to contact the sheriff. Where the hell was he?

Curry sighed and slumped down into his chair again.

AT ELEVEN O'CLOCK Bramlett was still awake. Everyone else was in bed by ten.

227

"I won't stay up too late," he'd told Valeria. Sissy had made a bed for him on the couch in the living room. Valeria was sleeping with Marcellus in a double bed in the other room.

He walked out onto the front porch. The night sky was clear and the stars bright. He smelled the cooling air. Crickets hummed from the tall grass of the field bordering in the front side yard.

He poked a large chew into his cheek, tasted the sweet juice flow through his mouth and the nicotine calming his nerves. He hadn't forgotten about the negative influence on his grandson. He would quit, he promised himself, just as soon as this case was over. He turned and carefully sat down in the swing.

A half hour before, he'd phoned headquarters again. Curry and Baillie had both gone for the night, the dispatcher said. He phoned Curry at home for an update.

Now, he asked himself—why would Nicole Estis disappear? None of this made any sense. As far as he'd thus far figured, the killer had murdered Bondreaux, and then killed the vagrant Gilly Bitzer and the schoolteacher Jo Ann Scales to cover his, or, more probably, her tracks. But what did Nicole Estis have to do with the murder?

Did she really work till five o'clock or did she lie. Why did she give them a false alibi . . . unless . . . But no, he still couldn't see Nicole Estis as the killer.

At first, after he'd been told Nena Carmack had vanished, he tried to fit her back into the equation. But Curry just now said Robertson had called in and said she was with a sick father in Columbus.

He heard the distant cry of a screech owl—a cry that sounded like a baby. And he thought of Marcellus and wondered if there was any way possible that the killer—the person speeding out of the cemetery in that small, dark automobile—could find out Valeria and Marcellus were in Sissy's house—or even that Valeria had a sister in the Delta . . . and he knew it was not only possible but likely, given enough time. Given enough time anyone could find out anything.

He looked toward the darkened single-lane road leading up to the house from the county highway and the black woods beyond. Could the killer have already found out? He shuddered, stood up and went back into the house.

32

EARLY THURSDAY MORNING Sheriff Grover Bramlett groaned. He'd been lying awake for hours, it seemed. Sissy's couch was too short by a foot at least for his body. He couldn't stretch out in full. He switched from side to side with his legs bent at times, his torso bent at other times.

He moved every few minutes, trying to relax, trying to lull his body into slumber, trying to get comfortable, trying to stop the images of people he'd talked with the last few days flashing in the back of his mind, as well as the yet blurry image of Tidwell Dixon. And a phrase Miss Mabel Applewhite, his high school Latin teacher, had forced him to memorize kept reverberating in his mind: *Tempus fugit*. Time flees.

The grandfather clock which stood in the hallway bonged four times. Bramlett threw back the blankets Sissy had spread on the couch for him and sat up. He was still dressed except for his shoes.

These he pulled on quickly, rose to his feet, and stood looking toward the hallway and the closed door behind which was the bed where Valeria was sleeping with Marcellus and wondered if he could slip in and kiss her good-bye without awakening her. He knew he couldn't, knew that she would get up and fuss at him about the fact that he needed more sleep and at least should wait to leave until she could fix him some breakfast.

Instead, he blew a kiss toward the room and opened the front door and stepped out onto the porch, closing the door quietly behind him. Sam, a bluetick hound, was sleeping on the porch. He raised his head in curiosity but gave no sound as Bramlett moved down the steps and walked toward his car.

THREE HOURS LATER Bramlett pulled into the parking lot of the Eagle Café on Front Street in Sheffield, had a full breakfast, then went to headquarters. At his desk, he looked over the notes left him by Curry and Baillie.

At eight o'clock, Colonel Whitehead was conducting another television interview with reporters on the sidewalk in front of the building, and Curry, Baillie, and Robertson were sitting in the captain's chairs in front of Bramlett's desk. Bramlett held a one-page report Baillie had written up about the crime scene at Lake Pickwick.

"The highway patrol is handling it," Johnny Baillie said. "A neighbor in the cabin next door said she only knew McAbrams to speak to. Said that sometimes there was a woman with him. A much younger woman."

Bramlett's eyebrows lifted. "And?"

Baillie shook his head. "She couldn't give us much of a description. She never really got a close-up look at her."

Bramlett looked at Robertson. "You talk with Mrs. McAbrams. See if she suspected anyone her husband was seeing."

"We could have her look at video tapes," Curry said. Bramlett set his jaw and looked at the deputy. "We will if we have to. Right now, I want you two to follow up on Nicole Estis." He looked from Curry to Baillie, then said, "I'm going to Memphis to talk with the McNeal woman," he said, referring to the former roommate of Tidwell Dixon.

Jacob Robertson sat stiffly in his chair. Twice he mentioned visiting Nena Carmack at the hospital and couldn't see any way that she could possibly be involved with these killings other than that she dated Jesse Bondreaux a long time ago and had nothing else to do with him after they broke up.

Bramlett grunted. Right now the main thing, as far as he was concerned, was to track down this Tidwell woman. She would be

230

someone in her mid-thirties. He wondered if she was one of the women on the videos Curry couldn't identify.

H. C. Curry and Johnny Baillie drove to Tupelo. First they visited the office where Nicole Estis worked. No, her boss told them, Nicole didn't come to work this morning. In fact, she'd stayed only an hour or so the day before, then suddenly left. That was around ten. Was something wrong? Baillie said they just wanted to ask her some questions.

They drove to Nicole Estis's apartment building. The landlady let them into her rooms. "She didn't leave nothing," the woman said, a cigarette dangling from her lips. "Not a damn thing. And she owes me. She in some kind of trouble or something?"

"Not that we know of," Curry said, his eyes surveying the plain studio apartment with vinyl-upholstered furniture. "We just wanted to ask her some questions. You know any friends of hers?"

The woman shook her head. "A man came once in a while."

"Did you know his name?"

She shook her again. "A schoolteacher from Sheffield, I understand."

"Did he look like this?" Baillie showed her a photograph of a smiling Jesse Bondreaux.

She brightened. "Yeah. That's the one."

In less than fifteen minutes the two deputies, under the watchful eye of the landlady, had covered every square inch of the apartment. They found nothing which could tell them anything about Nicole Estis. Nor did they find anything that hinted at where or why she had gone. There was absolutely nothing in the room to indicate that she had ever been there.

Bramlett reached Memphis by noon. He was amazed at how calm and comfortably he drove through the heavy traffic in the city, just as if he'd grown up in Memphis.

As many times as he'd been to Memphis to visit Margaret and the kids, he had never been able to get used to the hundreds and

231

hundreds of vehicles racing back and forth on every street. But now his mind was focused on greater dangers than mere traffic.

He'd stopped in front of a liquor store and spread out a Memphis street map across the steering wheel. He located the street he was looking for, refolded the map as best he could, and found the street with little difficulty.

There was no traffic on the curving oak-lined street as he cruised slowly past the stately homes with wide, immaculately kept lawns and planting beds.

"Big-city doctors and lawyers," he mumbled out loud. "Probably even a big-time preacher or two." Then, noticing the numerals in wrought-iron anchored beside a brick-paved front walk, he said, "This is it."

The woman who answered the door was dressed in a pink jogging suit with light-blue running shoes. Her hair was blond and swept back and her eyes were as blue as her shoes.

"I'm Grover Bramlett," he began, twisting his hat in his hands. "Are you Mrs. McNeal? Ruth Pettis McNeal?"

She looked no more than Margaret's age to Bramlett but had to be five or six years older. She frowned and nodded without speaking.

"I'm with the sheriff's department in Chakchiuma County, Mississippi," Bramlet continued, "investigating a murder of one Jesse Bondreaux."

Mrs. McNeal looked to the right and to the left as if she were trying to see behind him, trying to see if any of her neighbors could be standing nearby and hear what the sheriff was saying.

"Come in," she said, moving back into a foyer floored with wide, gleaming hardwood planks.

She led him into the living room and offered him a seat. Bramlett sat on the couch while the woman perched in an adjacent side chair. "What did you say the name was?" she asked.

"I'm Sheriff Grover Bramlett, ma'am."

"No. I mean, the name of the person you said?"

"Jesse Bondreaux."

She nodded, still frowning. "Do I know him?"

"Actually, we're trying to locate an old friend of his, Tidwell Dixon."

232

Her eyes widened and her face first registered recognition or remembrance or both, and then anxiety. "What's wrong?"

"With Tidwell Dixon? Nothing, as far as we know. We're just trying to locate her."

She slid back further in her chair and smiled. "Tidwell Dixon. Yes. When you first said Jesse, I knew I'd heard the name but . . . God, that's been so long ago. Actually, I never knew the man."

"Do you know where Tidwell Dixon is now?"

She shook her head. "We lost touch. I don't have any idea where she is." She shrugged. "You know how it is."

Bramlett nodded and felt maybe he shouldn't have wasted the time coming all the way up to Memphis. Yet he had wanted to interview her face-to-face. That was always best.

"I see," he said. "How long has it been since you've seen her?"

She tilted her head slightly backward, half closed her eyes as if in thought, and looked toward the large windows that faced the street. Then she shook her head. "I really can't remember seeing or hearing from her since she left school."

"When was that?"

"In the middle of our freshman year. Well, the middle of second semester, actually." She looked back at Bramlett and frowned. "Is she in some kind of trouble?"

"Not that we know of," Bramlett said, not believing what he was saying, but, at the same time, not knowing anything different. "Why did she leave school?"

"She was pregnant. And this Jesse you mentioned was the father."

Bramlett nodded. He remembered his interview with Myrtle Nell Harris. "I understand she had an abortion."

Mrs. McNeal raised one eyebrow. "Abortion? Well, that's news to me. She seemed very determined to have the child. In fact, there was a home for unwed mothers right here in Memphis where she was planning to go. She showed me all the paperwork. I remember she was having a hard time finding a place where she could stay and have the baby and still keep it afterward. Of course, things are different now. But that's the way it was then. And she really did want to keep that baby."

Bramlett rubbed his hand across his mouth. He couldn't see how any of this fit anything else. Then he said, "Do you know the name of the home?"

She shook her head. "No. I doubt they're still in business anyway. Most of those places folded up, you know, after abortions became legal."

"You're sure she had the baby?"

Mrs. McNeal shrugged. "I don't know why not. The home was Catholic, I remember. They agreed to take her because her parents were going to pay the costs. That way she could keep the child. Of course, I was still at school in Nashville so I didn't see her while she was here. But I do know she wanted that baby." She paused and her face registered an expression of remembrance again. "Yes, of course. Now I remember. She definitely didn't want to marry the child's father. This Jesse. She said she'd told him she was having an abortion. She didn't want any further problems."

Bramlett looked across the room, thinking on this, then looked back at her and said, "I wouldn't think there'd have been many Catholic homes like that . . . what? Twenty years ago?"

"Eighteen," Mrs. McNeal said with a smile. "I wish I could remember the name of that home." She pursed her lips and her brow knit. Suddenly, her eyes widened and she grinned. "Say! I may have something." She rose to her feet and gave a low laugh. "My husband says I'm the world's worst pack rat. I never throw anything away." She began walking out of the room. "Excuse me. I may have just what you're looking for." Then she was gone.

Bramlett leaned forward in his chair and glanced at his watch. Would a home like that give him any information at all? He doubted it. He sighed. This Memphis trip was probably not a good idea. Waste of time. He glanced at his watch again. Maybe he should drive down to see Valeria before going back to Sheffield.

Mrs. McNeal appeared once more, carrying a shoe box. She resumed her seat, placed the box on her lap, and said, "These are letters I received in college. Can you believe I still have them?" She began thumbing through the box. "Let's see. That was my freshman year . . . Ah! This is it." She whipped an envelope out of the box. "This is from Tidwell while she was here in Memphis. And that was the only time I heard from her."

She slid the letter out of the envelope and read it. "Humm. I'm

234

sorry. She doesn't mention the name of the home. There's no return address, either." She read some more, shaking her head. "She just says she's going to be okay, tells me not to tell anyone where she is . . . and . . . she has a nice roommate. Her name is Sarah Timmons, and she's from Mississippi also. Someplace called Shuqualak." She pronounced the name very slowly.

"What?"

"Here." She handed him the letter.

He read it entirely, then said, looking up at her, "May I hold on to this for a while?"

She smiled. "Sure. I haven't looked at it in years. Probably not since I got it."

"What about a picture? Do you still have your college yearbook?"

"Now that is a sore subject around here. My husband gave a box of old books to the goodwill store a while back, and I'm sure all my yearbooks were in it. He says no, but last year I was going to my reunion at Vandy and I couldn't find a one." She shrugged. "Maybe they'll turn up one day."

"May I use your phone?"

She led him to the telephone in her husband's study. Bramlett stood at the claw-footed mahogany desk and placed the collect call to headquarters in Sheffield. The secretary put him through to H. C. Curry.

"I want you to check out the name Sarah Timmons. She was from Shuqualak about twenty years ago."

"Where?"

"Shuqualak. It's down toward Meridian."

"You coming back now?"

"No. Not yet," he said. Then he hung up the phone without saying good-bye.

33 ─────────────────────────────

Sheriff Grover Bramlett leaned on the desk for a moment, his eyes fixed on a sliver-framed photograph of Ruth McNeal with a man he assumed must be her husband. The photo was several years old.

"Are you okay?" Mrs. McNeal asked.

"I need to make another call," he said.

"Sure. I'll wait outside." Then she left the room.

Bramlett phoned his sister-in-law. Sissy said, "They're not here right now, Grover. You want Valeria to call you when she gets back?"

"What do mean, not there? I told y'all to stay put. Not to leave the house."

"Really now, Grover. Aren't you taking all this a little too far? No one can possibly know they're here."

"Listen to me, Sissy." His voice was choked. "Someone has already killed four people. I think that someone is determined to try to kill Marcellus next. Do you understand that?"

There was a long silence on the other end of the line. Then, "I understand."

"Where did they go?"

"Into town. They had cabin fever. Marcellus just needed to get out, so Valeria took him into town. They should be back any minute now. They were just going to the grocery store to get a few things for me. You know, bread and milk."

"Listen to me now," he said. "When Valeria gets back, you tell her to stay put, dammit."

"No need to swear, Grover."

"Just do it, Sissy," he said through his teeth.

"Calm down. I'm sure they're all right."

He gave a big sigh, then said, "Have y'all had any more of the wrong-number calls?"

"Wrong number? Well . . . let's see. No-o-o . . . Wait a second. There was a strange call this morning."

"Tell me. Hurry."

"I answered the phone. Someone asked to speak to Valeria. I said 'Just a minute' and called her to the phone. I thought it must be your secretary with a message from you or something."

"Who was it?"

"I don't know. Before Valeria got to the phone, they hung up."

Bramlett gripped the receiver, and straining as if he were trying to choke the receiver. "Do you know what store they went to?"

"Of course. There's only one in town. Sunflower."

"Go to town and find them."

"Okay, Okay. Don't worry. I'll take care of it."

BRAMLETT LEFT THE MCNEAL HOUSE, tires spinning. He pulled into the street, and in minutes was on I-55. He heard the blare of horns as he cut in front of two other cars before he swung into the fast land.

Suddenly he wasn't frightened by the swift-moving big-city traffic. In fact, it didn't seem to be moving fast enough at all.

Just south of Memphis he pulled off the interstate and used the telephone at an Amoco station. He first phoned headquarters in Sheffield. No, the secretary told him after she'd checked. Curry had gone out. He didn't leave any message about finding someone. "And Colonel Whitehead says to tell you the Corvette will be delivered tomorrow morning and you still haven't assigned anyone to it."

He hung up the receiver and squeezed his temples with his thumb and forefinger. He didn't have time to fool with his administrator's drug dealer-seized vehicle right now. He phoned Sissy's number. No answer. And all he could think about was Valeria answering the telephone at Sissy's and no one speaking on the other end.

In moments he was back on the interstate and didn't realize how quickly the speedometer climbed to eighty.

34

As SHE WAS DRIVING the straight-as-a-plumb-line county highway into town, Sissy fully expected to see Valeria's car coming toward her. Cotton fields flanked both sides of the road as far as the eye could see, and green cotton pickers crawled over the long white rows.

She didn't meet Valeria's car returning from town. Neither did she see it at the grocery store parking lot. She parked in a handicap space, mumbling as she opened her door, "At sixty-five I'm as handicapped as most," and went inside.

"Yes, they were here," Betty McCaleb said, a heavyset checker, the only one on duty at the moment. "Your sister don't look much like you, though." She was smiling, pleasant, ready to pass some time.

"Where did they go?" Sissy asked with rising agitation.

Betty McCaleb shrugged. "I don't know. Didn't say."

Sissy stood outside the store for a moment looking up the half-deserted street. Where in the world would they go if not back to the house. What was there to see around here anyway?

VALERIA PARKED IN FRONT of Sissy's house. "You can take one of the bags and I'll take the other one," she said to Marcellus. There were only two bags, both small.

239

"Sissy's car's gone," Valeria said as she walked up toward the house. "She didn't say anything about going anyplace, did she?" Marcellus shook his head and intoned a negative and got out of the car with one of the bags.

Valeria lifted the other bag off the front seat and closed the car door. "She must have run an errand," she said. "We'll just go inside and wait for her."

"I'm tired of being in the house, Maw Maw," Marcellus said. "I want to shoot some basketball."

There was an old netless hoop fastened to a rough plank back-board behind the barn. On that hoop with its bare earth floor Sissy's two sons refined the skills which earned them outstanding high school careers and eventually college basketball scholarships.

She smiled at him and said, "Go ahead. Just don't go up in the loft of the barn, remember. Aunt Sissy says those boards are rotten."

She took the bag from him as she stepped up onto the porch, and smiled as she watched him run off. It was good to be here. She felt safe.

THE SKY OVERHEAD WAS PERFECTLY BLUE and the sun bright. Marcellus took off his denim jacket and laid it across the tittering fence that angled out from the barn. He picked up the basketball.

He'd found the ball that morning in the room he and Maw Maw were sleeping in. Aunt Sissy said it used to belong to her boys. It was flat. She located a bicycle-tire pump and a ball needle. He was surprised that she knew to lick the needle so she could insert it into the ball before she pumped it up.

Aunt Sissy also showed him pictures and newspaper clippings after breakfast in a thick scrapbook of her sons Jim and Jerry when they were playing high school basketball and then college basketball at Delta State. She told him about the goal out behind the barn.

"They learned to dribble on the ground," she'd said. "After that, dribbling on a hardwood court was a snap. Everybody should learn to dribble on dirt."

He began to dribble. He'd never played basketball on dirt, only on concrete or hardwood. The ball felt funny as it came back up to

240

his hand. Sometimes it hit a small rock or an uneven place and veered as it rose. He had to play it much lower to the ground.

He shot at the goal. The backboard was weathered, and wobbled when the ball struck it, making a thunking sound. He at once was into an imaginary game. An important game, and he was the star forward. It was the state championship for the high school he'd attend in three years.

He was so intensely involved with his game—of *games*, in that he won several with last-second goals—that he didn't hear the woman walk up. Then he saw her.

She was smiling and wearing a heavy blue jacket. "Hi," she said. "You're Marcellus, aren't you?"

He held the ball and looked at her. Did he know her? He wasn't sure. Somehow she did look familiar. "Yes, ma'am," he said.

She was still smiling. "You're Valeria's grandson, right?"

"Yes, ma'am." He'd heard that voice before.

"She's my friend." She glanced at the ball under his arm. "I've been watching. You're good."

"Thank you," he said softly, self-consciously, looking down at the ground. Was it in Sheffield? Or Memphis?

She looked in the direction of the house for a long moment. The view of the house was blocked by the barn. Then she looked back at him. "I just walked up from the gully back down there," she said, nodding her head in the direction from which she'd come. "It looks like a good place to target practice. Do you shoot?"

He shrugged. "Not much. My grandfather took me squirrel hunting last Saturday . . ." His voice trailed off. There was something so familiar about this woman. Then, in a flash, he knew she was the woman in the car.

She glanced toward the house again. There was the sound of a car arriving. Then she looked back at him, still smiling. She took her hand out of her pocket. In her hand was a gleaming black pistol. She pointed it at his head and said, "Come with me. We need to talk."

35

GROVER BRAMLETT SLID TO A STOP in front of Sissy's house, kicking dust and gravel into the air. Sissy turned her head and shut her eyes. She was just getting out of her own car in front of the garage.

Through a haze of dust she looked at him, fists on hips. "Grover Bramlett! You gonna kill somebody driving like that!"

Bramlett saw Valeria's car parked near the front porch and felt his neck muscles begin to relax. All the way from Memphis over the last two hours he'd felt nauseous but kept stuffing chewing tobacco into his mouth, throwing out old chews before they were sucked dry and shoving in new. As he climbed out of the car, he noticed the driver's side of the vehicle from the window to the rear panel was stained with streaks of wind-dried, brown tobacco spittle.

"Where's Valeria?" he said.

"I been out looking for them and just got back. I haven't been inside yet, but the car's here. Settle down, Grover. You'll live longer."

He followed her into the house. Valeria was sitting at the kitchen table drinking coffee.

She smiled and stood. "Grover! We didn't expect you." She walked to him and held out her arms.

He gave her a hug, then said, "I need to get back to Sheffield. I hope we're getting close to locating this Tidwell Dixon woman. I think she's a key, somehow."

242

"You want coffee?" Valeria asked, taking a clean cup from the dish drainer.

He nodded. "I think she may be on one of those videos. I don't know. The man was blackmailing several people."

Valeria filled the cup and set it on the table. "It's so good to be away from all that."

"We found Jason McAbrams," he said. "Dead."

She flinched. "No!"

Bramlett turned to Sissy. "I need to use the phone," he said.

She pointed at the yellow telephone on the kitchen counter.

MARCELLUS SET THE BASKETBALL on the bare ground near the edge of a boundary of knee-high weeds. His eyes were fastened to the barrel of the pistol pointed at him. He felt like he was going to wet his pants.

She motioned with the gun. "Come. Let's walk down to the canyon. I just want to talk with you."

He hesitated and cut his eyes toward the house. Could he run? No. She'd kill him on the spot.

She frowned and motioned harder with the gun. "Let's go," she said.

He turned and walked on ahead of her down the trail.

It was a cow trail, the dark delta earth chewed ragged by countless hooves going and coming. He carefully stepped over the piles of cow dung, dried as well as fresh.

He could feel the sweat running down his sides from under his arms. He could hear her following right behind him.

In a few minutes the trail curved to the right along a ridge. "Step down there," the woman said. She gave him a push on the shoulder.

To the side of a waxmyrtle bush was an old washed-out road. The road descended quickly and ended at the edge of a bluff. Marcellus did as she instructed.

He walked to the edge of the bluff and looked down. Below was an abandoned sand quarry. Bulldozers in years past had carved out tons of sand, leaving a flat floor forty yards or so across with bluffs ten to twelve feet high on three sides.

The woman stepped beside him. A narrow, twisting trail led down to the quarry floor.

"We'll go down there," she said, again motioning with the pistol.

She took one step down and turned and looked at him. For the first time, his eyes met her eyes. There was a frightened look to those eyes. And suddenly he pictured her, saw her eyes, not standing as she was on the edge of the bluff but looking up at him through the rain-splattered windshield as the car whipped past him in the cemetery.

BRAMLETT TELEPHONED HEADQUARTERS and asked for Curry.

"Got lucky," H. C. Curry said after he answered the call. "Shuqualak has only one Timmons family. Sarah Timmons is their daughter. She now lives in Guerneville, California."

"You got a phone number?"

"Got two. Home and work."

Bramlett jotted down both numbers.

"When you coming back?" Curry said.

"Soon. What are you working on now?"

"When you called, I was listing everybody we've interviewed and written the car they drive beside their name. Especially, I'm noting small, dark cars."

"And?"

"And . . ." Curry paused, then said, "Hey, I saw a photograph of several of those kids and there was a car . . . Let me check this out. You be back today?"

Bramlett gave no definite time, and hung up.

"SARAH'S FLOWERS," a voice answered the phone.

"Sarah Timmons, please," Bramlett said.

"Speaking." There was no trace of a southern accent in her voice.

"From Shuqualak?"

"Who is this?" she asked, her voice rising.

Bramlett quickly introduced himself and told her the nature of his call.

244

"That was all a very long time ago. A lot of unpleasantness back there. I really don't care to discuss that period of my life."

"Have you kept up with her at all?"

"No." She was silent for a moment, then said, "That was eighteen years ago. We were quite close. We were a lot alike. But, of course, different in one big thing."

"How's that?"

"I didn't want to keep my child. She did. That's all she talked about. Her baby. She used to ask me what I thought about certain names. I remember she said if it was a boy she wanted to call him Stephen. And she finally decided if it was a girl to call her Victoria Ann.

Bramlett blinked his eyes, then said, "Victoria Ann?" There was a hoarseness in his voice.

"She thought Victoria was such a pretty name. Not like *Tidwell*. She hated the name Tidwell. It was some old family name, of course. That's why she didn't like me calling her that. And I didn't. She said she hated going home because everyone called her that. I can't remember where she was from."

Bramlett said softly, "Iskitini."

"Yes. That was it."

Bramlett was having difficulty breathing. "And what did you call her?" Somehow he knew the answer to the question even as he asked it.

She chuckled. "Well, at first I just called her *Roommate*. Then I gradually shortened it to *Roomie*. Then, after a little while, she started going by that name herself." She paused, then added, "She spelled it R-u-m-i. Odd, don't you think?"

36 ⎯⎯⎯⎯⎯⎯⎯⎯⎯⎯⎯⎯⎯⎯⎯⎯

IN THE KITCHEN, the telephone receiver fell from Grover Bramlett's hand and clattered onto the cradle and bounced askew. With trembling fingers, he righted it, then snatched away his hand. His breaths came in short jerks.

Valeria stared wide-eyed at him. "What?" she said. She held up both hands as if to protect herself from an expected blow.

Bramlett gripped the countertop tightly. "It's Rumi Skelton," he said.

"Rumi . . . ?" Valeria's mouth pursed in confusion. "What's Rumi?"

"The killer."

"No." She spread her fingers and held her hands to her ears. "No!"

"Yes . . ." he said, almost gasping as he spoke. "Jesse Bondreaux was Vicki Ann's real father."

Valeria shook her head hard.

He continued. "I think sometime after he arrived in Sheffield, he figured it out . . . and Rumi didn't want the girl to know. That's why he was blackmailing her. I don't know. Maybe she found out he was planning to take her away with him."

She looked at him, eyes pleading for this whole thing to be some horrible mistake. "Why?" she asked with her lips only, the air not coming out to make the sound.

246

Bramlett closed his eyes and shook his head.

"But . . . why that teacher?"

"She was Vicki Ann's confidante in a way. I think she thought Bondreaux was intimate with the girl. I don't know if she was or not."

Valeria clutched the edge of the table and shut her eyes.

"Rumi had to silence her," Bramlett continued. "And Gilly. And Jason McAbrams." He sighed heavily and opened his eyes. "The old tangled web thing. It never ends."

He lifted the telephone receiver and punched the number of headquarters in Sheffield. When he had H. C. Curry on the line again, Bramlett said, "I talked with Sarah Timmons—"

"Listen," the deputy said, talking rapidly, "I need to tell you. My niece says the blue Honda in that photo was Vicki Ann Skelton's—"

"It's Rumi Skelton."

There was immediate silence on the other end of the line, then, "What?"

"Find her and lock her up. And, dammit, you don't let her out no matter how many lawyers run in there."

"Rumi Skelton?"

"Yes. Now find her."

There was a pause, then Curry said, "She traded that Honda for the red Mercedes last Saturday in Memphis. That's what they went shopping for."

"Go!" Bramlett said through his teeth.

He slammed down the receiver and leaned back against the counter. His shoulders slumped.

Valeria looked up at him and said, "Is it over then . . . ?"

"Not until we lock her up."

"No," she said, trying to contradict what she knew he meant.

"Yes," he said. "She knows someone else saw her at the cemetery."

"But . . . but Rumi *knows* Marcellus!"

Bramlett nodded. "That's why y'all are staying here until we find her."

"Surely you don't think . . ." She paused and put both hands to her mouth.

"I don't want to say what I think." He pressed his lips together.

Then he looked in the direction of the hallway. "Where is Marcellus, anyway?"

"He's out back shooting basketball."

Bramlett frowned. "He needs to be in the house. I'd feel better if he wasn't outside right now."

She stood up. "I'll go get him," she said, moving toward the back door.

Bramlett walked slowly into the living room. He stepped to one of the front windows, parted the sheers with one hand, and looked out over the flat fields flanking the drive leading up to the house.

Then with his right hand he felt his hip and the hard weight of his Smith & Wesson. He unsnapped the holding strap and withdrew the revolver. He rotated the cylinder with his fingers, looking down at the dark-gray noses of the bullets, then replaced the weapon.

He heard the shout even before she snatched open the back door. "Grover! Grover!"

He dashed through the kitchen and was at the back door just as Valeria stepped inside.

Her chest was heaving as she sucked in gasps of air. "He's gone!" she screamed up at him. Her eyes were wide with panic.

Bramlett pushed past her and stepped down into the yard. "Where . . . ?"

"Behind the barn," she said after him, following him as he ran through scattering chickens and past the pecan tree.

Moments later he stood under the basketball goal. The worn basketball lay at the edge of the clearing on the grassless earth against the massed wall of weeds.

Valeria ran up beside him, crying, mumbling, praying. She looked around wildly. "Marcellus!" she screamed into the air.

"*What?*" Sissy yelled. Neither of them had seen her running from the house. She was carrying her dead husband's shotgun.

Bramlett frowned, staring at the gun in the woman's hands.

"I know how to use this thing," she said, jutting her jaw.

Bramlett looked around helplessly.

Then they all heard it. Sharp and distinct. A single bark of gunfire.

37 ⸻

THE THUNDEROUS CLAP SMASHED into his ears and he sprawled into the waist-high grasses and, for a moment, lay perfectly still. The woman had ordered him to step down onto a trail descending to the canyon floor. "Move," she'd said.

His eye had fallen to her shoulders as they stood together at the edge of the bluff, and he felt the blood rushing into his face. He took half a step to the edge and suddenly thrust up his hands and shoved against her right shoulder.

She tottered for a second trying to regain her balance, and he broke into the thicket of brambles on the side of the road. Then came the first shot.

He lay still and immediately realized he was not hit. If he lay there much longer she would find him. He began scurrying away.

"You come here, dammit!" she screamed, and fired again.

"KEEP BACK!" Bramlett yelled at Valeria. "You'll only be in the way."

He ran down the road and could hear her footsteps crunching on the road behind him. He glanced back. Sissy was scurrying after him, holding the shotgun with both hands in front of her.

"No!" he said over his shoulder. "Stay back!"

"This goes to the old quarry," she said.

There was another shot. Bramlett ran harder, pushing his legs.

He reached the end of the road and stood with his revolver held high, looking over the floor of the quarry. In moments Sissy was at his side.

Bramlett ran his eyes quickly around the edge of the bluff bordering the floor of the canyon. He saw nothing.

He looked along the rim where the pine forest on the other side was flush with the canyon rim. Then he saw something, he thought. A slight movement.

He was aware of Sissy's labored breathing at his side and for a second wondered if she was going to have a heart attack.

He leaned his head down so that his mouth was right beside her ear. "You stay here," he whispered. "I'm going to work my way around—"

He stopped in mid-sentence. Between two trees on the far rim of the canyon stood Rumi. She was picking her way through the undercover thickets around the pine trees.

"She's . . . she's looking for him," he whispered. "Maybe she hasn't seen us . . ."

He stopped again. He saw a slight movement on the other side of the thicket from Rumi. Marcellus. It had to be Marcellus.

His eyes strained to focus more clearly. Yes. The boy was crouching beside a large huckleberry bush. Stationary now. And Rumi was moving toward him. She was not fifteen feet away.

Bramlett put his hand on Sissy's shoulder. "Stay back," he said, at the same time taking one tentative step downward onto the twisting path that led to the quarry floor.

Rumi was walking on the rim of the cliff, now in full sunlight, working her way around the thick bush. Marcellus still crouched motionless on the other side. Another step or two and she would be able to see around the bush, be able to see the boy clearly, would not be more than five feet from him.

Bramlett jumped down to a narrow ridge, almost lost his balance, then steadied himself, and lifted his revolver, gripping the weapon with both hands as he'd seen cops on TV do, trying to hold it steady on the woman.

"Rumi!" he shouted.

She turned and looked at him. A distance of thirty or forty yards separated them across the canyon floor.

She immediately raised her arm and fired. The dust not more than two feet to Bramlett's right erupted into the air.

He tried to hold her in the sights of the revolver but couldn't and, although his grandson was maybe seven or so feet from her, he couldn't fire and risk hitting him.

"Drop your gun!" he yelled, stumbling down the trail.

She fired again, and Bramlett heard the bullet smash in the steep slope of the canyon only a few feet to his left.

He reached the floor of the canyon and began running—his lungs pumping like a bellows—crouching and running and he heard another explosion from the pistol quickly followed by another, and instantly Bramlett felt the pain sear through him and his body collapsed.

He rolled over. His face pressed into the earth and he tasted sand in his mouth and felt his heart racing. The pain came from his left arm. A boiling, flaming ache. He wasn't sure whether he'd been hit once or twice.

Then he heard a woman's voice. "Hold it right there!" It was Sissy's voice.

He arched his head, pushing against the ground, looking for her.

Sissy was standing on the rim of the canyon about twenty yards to the left of Marcellus. She'd run along the rim while Bramlett tried to charge across the canyon floor.

Rumi was already around the bush and had her pistol pointed directly at Marcellus. She was standing right over him.

She suddenly put the muzzle of the weapon right against the side of his head. Slowly Marcellus rose from the ground.

Rumi grabbed the collar of his shirt and held the pistol against the side of his head.

"Throw that gun into there!" she yelled at Sissy, at the same time indicating the floor of the canyon with a shake of her head.

Bramlett was trying to count—one, two . . . no, no. *Two shots before we got here. Two shots when I was standing. Then . . .* of course! *Two more shots while I was running!*

"*Throw it!*" Rumi screamed, jerking Marcellus's head back.

Sissy looked confused.

"Stop . . ." Bramlett said with a gasp, pushing himself to a sitting position.

Sissy looked toward him.

"No . . ." he said hoarsely. "That's six shots!"

Sissy still looked confused.

Bramlett stood and shuffled forward. "Six shots! Her weapon only holds six cartridges . . ."

Suddenly Marcellus spun around, breaking loose, and at the same time pushed both hands against Rumi's chest.

She tottered for a moment on the edge of the cliff, then with a startled cry fell.

38

LATE THAT AFTERNOON, Valeria Bramlett telephoned H. C. Curry and asked him to meet Margaret, John, and April when they arrived at the house there in Sheffield. She asked him to tell them to come on at once to Sissy's.

They arrived shortly before nine o'clock that evening. "I'm never coming home again," Margaret had said after she heard the whole story.

They left at once for Memphis, taking Marcellus with them. Bramlett assured Valeria their daughter would soon settle down. She and the kids would be back to visit them in Sheffield real soon.

The following morning, Friday, Valeria drove her husband back to Sheffield. Sheriff Aubry Sistrunk of Leflore County had one of his deputies transport Rumi Skelton back to Sheffield to be incarcerated in the Chakchiuma County jail, and had another deputy drive Bramlett's car back to Sheffield.

Rumi suffered a possible concussion in her ten-foot fall, was scratched and bruised but, miraculously, broke no bones. She was treated at the Greenwood hospital and released into Sheriff Sistrunk's custody.

Bramlett had been treated at the same hospital. He'd been shot once. The steel-jacketed .25-caliber slug had neatly pierced his forearm, missed all arteries and bones, and the attending physician at

253

the emergency room didn't think he even needed to be hospitalized. Bramlett left with his arm in a sling.

Valeria stopped at the pharmacy to have the doctor's pain medicine prescription filled. The doctor said it would help Bramlett sleep the next couple of nights.

At the checkout counter Valeria opened her purse and took out her billfold. Bramlett stepped beside her and placed four new packages of Red Man on the counter.

Valeria's eyes widened as she stared at the chewing tobacco. "What is that?" she asked, turning up her nose.

"Sustenance," he said, jutting out his jaw a bit.

"I only got you that nasty stuff so you could think to solve this one case. You were the one who was going to quit."

He nodded. "I am. But not right now. Maybe when this arm heals up." He winced. "I have a hard time getting easy."

"Humph. Then you pay for it yourself." She opened the billfold. "And don't think you're going to chew that nasty stuff in the house."

"Yes, ma'am," he said with a grin. It had been a long week—a very long week. And suddenly he realized that for the first time since last Friday evening, he felt no knot in his chest.

MONDAY MORNING H. C. Curry looked up from his desk. Jacob Robertson was standing over him. The tall deputy had a scowl across his face.

"I was just by the evidence room," Robertson said. "There seems to be a problem."

"Oh?"

"We logged in five of Bondreaux's video tapes. There're only four in the evidence room."

Curry looked surprised. "That so? You sure there were five?"

"Positive." Robertson glared at Curry. "You were the last person to have them."

Curry shook his head. "I had them at the house again this weekend. I can't believe I could have mislaid a tape." He puckered his lips as if in deep thought for a moment, then suddenly exclaimed, "Oh, no! It couldn't be."

254

"What?"

"The smell of burning plastic! Of course, that must have been what was burning."

Robertson looked all the more confused.

"Last night I had some rubbish to burn for Mama. I carried it all out back and burned it in the fire pit. I must have accidentally let that tape get in with the rubbish. Dammit to hell!"

Robertson could tell Curry was pulling his leg. But why? What was he trying to say? "You think you might have burned a tape? Destroyed evidence?" he asked.

Curry scoffed. "I didn't destroy any evidence. There was nothing on that particular tape that had anything to do with the case. If I had my way, the rest of those tapes would be burned right away also."

Robertson blinked and looked at him. "You mean . . . you mean, that Nena—"

"Nena isn't on any of the tapes in the evidence room. I've been through the whole set twice."

Robertson blinked faster several times, then mumbled his thanks. He didn't know what else to say.

Curry jumped up. "Sheriff coming in," he said.

COLONEL WHITEHEAD, the administrator, stopped Bramlett before he could enter his office. Bramlett looked at the administrator, who stood almost as if he were at attention yet had a strange, wry smile on his face, as he waited to hear whatever seemed so important.

"The car is here," Whitehead said.

"Car?" Bramlett said.

"The drug dealer's vehicle. It's ready for your assignment."

"Let's see this thing," he said with a chuckle.

He followed Whitehead through the rear door to the parking lot. Curry hurried after them.

In the parking lot, the Corvette was surrounded by several deputies and office personnel. The car, now painted white and gleaming in the morning sun, was streaked with sheriff's department markings, including a large law-enforcement shield on each of its two doors and lettered in red paint on both sides and across the back: "Seized from a Dope Pusher."

"It's fully equipped," Whitehead said, beaming. He held up the set of keys for Bramlett to see.

Bramlett walked around the vehicle. In spite of all the official decorations, it still looked like what it was—a sleek sports car.

Without even looking at them, he knew half of the deputies staring gape-mouthed at the car were lusting for it, each one hoping against hope that Bramlett would speak his name as the new possessor of such power, beauty, and grace. Only Baillie and Curry had been so bold as to actually make a request for it, but Bramlett knew every man in the department—with the possible exception of Jacob Robertson who would rather wait for a truck—longed for the sports car.

Bramlett smiled and held out his hand palm up to the administrator. Whitehead gently laid the set of keys on the sheriff's palm.

Bramlett's hand closed tightly on the keys. Then he opened the driver's-side door and squeezed himself down into the seat. The dashboard, with all the gauges and dials, brought to mind what an airplane's cockpit must look like.

He inserted the key into the ignition and turned the switch. The engine roared to life. He let it idle for a moment, then reached across his bandaged left arm to touch the window button. The window slid down noiselessly.

Bramlett smiled as he looked up at Whitehead. "I like it," he said. "You can give my old car to whoever you like."

Then he shifted into gear and drove through the corridor of deputies onto the street.